THE EXILE

Also by William Kotzwinkle

WILLIAM KOTZWINKLE
THE EXILE

E. P. DUTTON · SEYMOUR LAWRENCE · NEW YORK

*Published in the United States by E. P. Dutton/Seymour Lawrence
a division of NAL Penguin Inc.,
2 Park Avenue, New York, N.Y. 10016.*

*Published simultaneously in Canada by
Fitzhenry & Whiteside Limited, Toronto.*

*Library of Congress Cataloging-in-Publication Data
Kotzwinkle, William.
The exile.
I. Title.*

PS3561.085E9   1987   813'.54   86-24380
ISBN 0-525-24526-X

Designed by Steven N. Stathakis

10 9 8 7 6 5 4 3 2 1

First Edition

THE EXILE

"There was a time, and I was there."

Wisps of steam rose from the hot tub, where two perspiring movie producers were discussing world history.

"It's Pebble Beach, and Cliff is in the cabana getting a knob-job from this girl from the Bay area. . . ."

"That's not the way I heard it."

"Sure, we busted right into the cabana waving champagne bottles and shouting, 'Surprise!' . . ."

The hot tub was sunk in a redwood patio, connected to a large, Moorish-style house; the house was bordered by flowers, palms, a pair of old oaks, and a little stream that ran through the sloping canyon. Other guests wandered there, and the stream slipped quietly by, human forms reflected on its tranquil face; on the far bank a large Doberman stalked the edge of a high wire fence, to insure that the mood of tranquility remain unbroken. Anything that came over the fence was his.

The party's host, David Caspian, walked up a stone path through the cactus garden; like his attack dog, Caspian had a lean, muscular physique and shared as well the animal's suspicious air, for his agent walked beside him, speaking about a deal. The agent, a penguin-shaped individual, was dressed in an expensive jogging suit in which he'd never run five steps. "Did you read the script I sent over?"

"It's in the compost bin, Myron." Caspian pointed toward his vegetable garden. "Bad scripts make good mulch but it takes two years."

"You didn't like the character?"

"Sentimental."

"Sentimentality is the wave of the future, David." Myron Fish dogged along beside his client. Caspian placed his hand gently on top of Fish's head. "Myron, it stinks."

"We'll change the script. We'll have you meet the abused child after she's had counseling."

Caspian continued walking; his last picture had been a sweet one, in which children had upstaged him, and drawn out of him the gooiest performance of his career, for which he'd received an Oscar nomination. Myron Fish now sought every opportunity to recreate the formula.

"Children are an endangered species, David. You could do a lot for them."

"Agents are an endangered species, Myron."

"They can't kill us off, we breed too fast."

Caspian and Fish walked toward the house; red roof tile gleamed, and walls of yellow adobe reflected the sun's brilliant glare. Sliding doors framed a sunken living room, where other guests were enjoying a slice of Caspian's life. He slid the screen open for Fish, and they stepped into the crisscrossed conversations:

"He's been existing from development deal to development deal but all he's developed so far is an ulcer."

"It's a living."

"Well, now he's going to Disney, with an office on Goofy Lane."

A massive stone fireplace graced one side of the room; on the other side, a wall had been swung open and a bartender was inside the niche, mixing drinks, a spotlight shining down on his gleaming black hair and white jacket. Waiters carried drinks and food around the room, keeping the fuel flowing smoothly as the guests refreshed themselves and continued to talk. There were big stars, little stars, would-be stars, hangers-on, and an assortment of suits from the studios.

". . . a wonderful new position at Universal, in three years I'll be having a triple bypass."

". . . we've received very glittering comments."

"He doesn't want glittering comments, he wants numbers."

"And roses floating in his toilet. He's unrealistic."

In each corner of the room electric eyes were clicking, resetting themselves, watching over things.

"David, they're offering you big points, you're crazy not to take it. I'm talking real percentages, not producer's net."

"Over here I think we have some toadstools," said Caspian, pointing to the buffet table.

"Ok, I'm through pressing you. Hope and heartwarming human material don't interest you, I can't understand why, but I'm not going to push any longer. Someone else will make America laugh and cry healthy tears. Someone else will collect the Oscar." Fish walked off clutching a peanut dish and Caspian circulated, out of the living room and into the high ceilinged entrance hall, where other guests were talking.

". . . on location in a very uptight Polish city and a teamster backed a Rolls Royce into the sacred statue of Maria Theresa."

". . . have you ever noticed her hands? The cracks are filled with guacamole dip."

Caspian opened the front door and stepped outside. Parking attendants had lined the road with automobiles and now stood idle in the drive, wearing sultry looks and waiting to be discovered by agent, producer, or crazy lady. He walked around the side of the house to the herb garden. His cat was resting in the aromatics, slitted eyes raised to the sky, where a hawk was circling, its wide wings barely moving as it floated on the warm currents. Caspian gazed upward, his own eyes slitted against the sun. He knew the habits of hawks; he'd found a mountain top that was in their migratory route, and on one particular day every year he was able to watch hundreds of them at a time, riding the mountain winds.

The hawk made a long slow loop out over the hills of the canyon, and Caspian followed with his eyes, toward peaks that he knew intimately. Hardly a day went by that he did not go up into the hills and wander; the terrain was stark and unsparing, the fierce power of the sun in every rock, plant, snake, bird, or animal that resided there. He was an experienced amateur naturalist, but all his knowledge of the life of the hills was accidental, for he went there not to identify and classify, but to meet the unidentifiable, a nameless, always changing feeling in himself which the land created. He enjoyed his hours in the hills, and was jealous of them should he be forced to surrender them for dubious activities such as this garden party he was throwing today. The hills were looking down on him as he hosted the Hollywood gathering, and he felt embarrassed about it, as if he were betraying a trust—but then, the hills had seen countless generations of jackasses come and go.

The hawk was gliding back from its circle above the hills, and he watched its return over the trees of his property, and saw its beak open in a call—but the sound of his party drowned out that haunting, rasping cry. Suddenly, the hawk dropped into a dive, Caspian saw its spindly legs extend, talons outstretched, and they seemed to point directly at him.

He leaned away, and a vague dream flashed, but it was gone before he could grasp it. The hawk's claws vanished and the bird caught an upward current. He watched it spiraling away over the hills, and the feeling returned, of a predator met in a dream.

He walked through the garden, and then to poolside, where dreams of rapacious beings were replaced by the sight of Julius DeBrusca; the producer was seated in a deck chair, expounding on the arcana of filmmaking. "Guilt in this town is a wonderful, wonderful tool. Paramount just fired Sy Bullit, and out of guilt about it they're going to make three pictures he's had hidden away for just such an emergency." DeBrusca gazed at his circle of listeners. "When the finger of God points from the clouds and says, 'You're next,' you'd better have a property or two stuffed in your shoe."

He gestured with a half-eaten burrito toward Caspian and Caspian walked on, to the garden buffet table, where a screenwriter was loading his plate with food. He peered up at Caspian. "May I talk to you privately?"

Caspian looked around the empty table. "There's no one here but us, Ed."

"You owe me four thousand dollars." Ed Cresswell was a thin, spectral man with a face too pale for California, as if he shunned the light of day. "I'm sure it was an unconscious error, but by sending me a check four grand short, it probably means you think I'm not worth what you're paying me."

Myron Fish appeared at the end of the table. "Do I hear business being discussed?"

"Myron," said Cresswell, "you're looking very trim in your jogging suit."

The roly-poly agent nibbled a cracker. "Monkey glands, Mr. Cresswell, have you tried them?"

"Where are they?" Cresswell looked around the buffet table, fork hovering.

"We've discovered an error in bookkeeping," said Caspian. "I owe Ed four thousand dollars."

Fish took another cracker. "Never pay writers. I hope you

haven't?" He looked at Cresswell's plate. "How do you stay so thin?"

"Through constant worry. About agents."

"Perhaps I'll open a reducing salon," said Fish.

Cresswell shuffled off with his plate, a look of permanent defeat in his demeanor. Fish turned to Caspian. "What kind of neurotic trash are you having him write for you? Are there any children in it?"

"No."

"We won't be able to raise a nickel. People want to see you in family entertainment." Fish's voice lost its bantering edge. "There's very little margin for error in this town, my friend." He turned and crossed back through the garden.

Caspian remained at the table, trying to calm the wave of fear that Fish had so expertly set in motion—Fish, master of manipulation, who knew just what shot would plunge his client into the waters of uncertainty. Caspian chewed compulsively on a series of weird, dainty sandwiches to deflect his attention from the image that held him, the recurrent nightmare image, an image based in hideous truth—of the thousands of aspiring young actors who arrived by the busload every day in L.A. Down the steps of the bus they came—wonderfully handsome, viciously aggressive, and all of them perfectly capable of playing the parts he himself played.

While he—he had a few grays hairs now. He could no longer eat as much as he wanted because it all went into the love handles of his midsection.

He put the plate of weird sandwiches down, grabbed a cognac on ice from the tray of a passing waiter—except he couldn't drink as much as he used to.

But the image remained in his brain—the busloads of new faces that the fickle studios and the media salivate for. What is untried is better, for anything can be projected onto it—new faces with new expressions; new young actors who were naturally plugged into the new style of moving, speaking, breathing. Young guys with bodies like iron, who'd had the benefit of the very latest in exercise equipment.

Calm down, you don't need a Nautilus machine. You've got ten major films behind you. That should be good enough to get through the afternoon with.

Except you're forty-five, said the voice of Myron Fish, in a posthypnotic suggestion programmed into him time and time again by the little agent, who had never lost an opportunity to keep his client on the defensive, for agents must always keep everyone on the defensive.

And the agents, of course, were right. They were always right.

Caspian picked up another sandwich, and had swallowed it before he'd even had a chance to chew it.

Because at age forty-five, there was the little matter of sex appeal on camera. His sexual energies had ceased to be straightforward. He no longer knew how he was coming across on screen to the major movie audience in America, people ten and twenty and thirty years younger than himself. Did they think he was cold soup? Quaint? Corny? Old-fashioned? A joke?

The raw vitality of young actors on a set depressed him immeasurably, because he couldn't play the physical combat scenes the way he used to. Once he'd been able to punch with the best of them, but now the stuntmen had to take it easy with him. Did it show on camera? Three bad films and an actor's career was over. That was the formula. Three flops and you go make films in godforsaken places where you can still get your price—like Guam. And then you sign a ten-year contract to advertise antacid tablets. And then you hire a ghost to write a lying biography about you.

And then you die.

He turned his back on the buffet table, sucked his gut in, and walked on, to where a studio vice-president in charge of advertising and publicity was drinking himself into a stupor. The executive began speaking as if he and Caspian were in the

---

7

middle of a conversation. "None of the directors look at the ad. Their eyes go directly to the bottom to see their name in the credits. Is it spelled right, is it big enough. Actors are no different. Let me tell you about the most bizarre presentation I ever made." He put the glass to his lips, drank, lowered his voice. "Guy Lockwood was in intensive care at Cedars of Sinai, preparing to die. But he had a likeness approval in his contract for any image we ran of him in our ads. So I had to take the entire campaign to the hospital. The family had gathered, waiting for the final curtain call. At the appropriate moment, when he opened his eyes for three seconds, we ran in with the ad and showed it to him. He approved it with what had to be one of his last gasps." The vice-president swayed in front of Caspian, eyes glazing over, and Caspian reflected on poor Guy, concerned *to his dying breath,* to his last goddamn gasp, with how he looked. So that he shouldn't lose popularity. So that some young punk didn't try to muscle in on his reign. So that his next role was assured. In actor heaven. Or somewhere.

Caspian turned, and saw his wife across the lawn, making her rounds of the party, a number of the afternoon's guests coming from her corporate advertising world. He caught her eye and she made her way toward him. "If I can go wrong, I do."

"What happened?"

"I made a crack about somebody manufacturing pants for oversize women. And standing in the group over there is a man who manufactures pants for oversize women."

Carol Caspian was barely five feet tall, with curly black hair streaked blonde. She wore a cream chemise with flame cuts along the hem, revealing her shapely legs; she lowered herself onto a lawn chair, wrapping her arms around her knees. "What the hell, I'll just go take a bath in my wok."

Caspian pointed at the buffet table. "Have you tried the dip?"

"That's why I'm so tired, it set off a string of orgasms." She put a hand to her hair, fluffing out her short curls. "Isn't

that the guy from the *Hollywood Reporter*? The one who looks
like a retired French satyr?"

"Go over and be nice."

"I'd prefer the hypocrisy of a lovely note." She pivoted in
her chair, her gaze sweeping the circle of guests in the yard.
"Don't turn conspicuously, but there's a young woman here from
the agency, very bright, very chic, the art director brought her,
and she wants my job."

"Is she good at what she does?"

"*Don't* look over your shoulder, please, I'd rather she thought
we were totally ignoring her, which we are."

"I'm sure you've got nothing to worry about. Nobody could
do what you do."

"I'm not worried. I just tell everyone she wears Jockey
shorts."

Carol remained curled in her chair, and Caspian continued
along the garden path, reflecting now on his wife's insecurities,
which dovetailed so perfectly with his own, and intensified them.
Their marriage was a perfect match—a pair of nervy egotists
running scared at the top. Why am I talking to myself this
way? Because of this goddamn party, which Myron made me
throw so that *he* could talk to Julius DeBrusca. A party to which
I am obliged to invite certain young actors, so it doesn't look
like a geriatric convention. I have a houseful of them at the
moment, not to mention a pool and yardful, and it's gotten me
crazy. Which is also what Myron wanted. So that I'd sign to do
a film I didn't want to do.

He ducked in under a bower of grapes that formed the
entranceway to a door nearly concealed by leaves. He opened
the door and entered, into the shadows of his office. He switched
on a stained glass lamp; rainbow light shone on his massive oak
desk. He opened it and took out his corporate record, where he
found that he had in fact underpaid Cresswell. Why? Because,
just as Cresswell suspected, something in him didn't want to
pay. Because Cresswell was writing a thoughtful script, of the

kind the studios never want to see. Because, in this town, a good script is a bad one. Because, as Myron says, we won't be able to raise a nickel. So I'll plow my own money into it, it'll fail, and I'll be selling antacid tablets ten years before my time.

As he corrected the error in the record book, his shadow fell on the office wall, onto a European cabaret poster—1930— a red and white female figure in top hat leaning against a marble pillar, beside her a male shadow importuning, suggesting the dangers of the dance. Caspian put his record book away, turned to the poster. When he was young, he'd gone to Rome and acted in spaghetti westerns, then drifted to Germany and ended up in an ensemble company doing Brecht revivals. The poster always brought it back to him—the seedy clubs of Berlin, the melancholy music, the dancers.

Outside on the path, he heard Julius DeBrusca and Myron Fish walking past. ". . . when we came back to the set for the banquet scene the teamsters had eaten all the steaks."

"Next time you'll use painted plastic."

They continued on, conversation growing fainter. ". . . David's trying to change his image, but will the public buy it?"

"I have a space spectacular coming up," said DeBrusca. "We'll talk, we'll get rowdy."

The footsteps crunched down the path. Caspian opened his liquor cabinet, took out his best cognac. He swirled the amber spirit around in its glass, inhaled the pungent aroma. The pleasant warmth spread through him as he sipped, and a golden haze followed. He finished the glass and poured another, sitting quietly for awhile, enjoying the cool, dark atmosphere of the office. Opening his desk drawer, he took out his checkbook and wrote the check to Cresswell. As he pressed it to the desk blotter, he heard a sharp, snapping sound from behind his ear and then a voice, whispering feebly, *"You've nailed the lid too tight, I'm suffocating."*

He hurried to the window. But the garden path was empty. He turned around, facing back into the office, as the inner door opened and Ed Cresswell stepped through from the adjoining billiard room. Cresswell paused inside the doorway. "You look like somebody just walked on your grave." He glanced down at the check on the desk. "If the four grand means that much to you, forget it."

"I didn't hate him as he deserved to be hated." The party was over, and Carol lay in bed beside him, discussing her previous husband, a man who occasionally haunted the last hours of her day. "He was a real lounge lizard, a sheik, lying in wait for the vulnerable." She settled a pink satin bolster behind her, and Caspian sipped a brandy nightcap, a green melon concoction he'd found lying around at the party's end. "I wonder what they call this thing."

"I was young, I didn't know that if you don't want to do something, you don't have to." Carol slipped down along her satin backrest and pulled up the sheet. "He said he'd get me high sniffing a burning comb. I fell for it." She rolled over, took a Valium, and tucked the sheet around her shoulder. Her breathing slowed, and she twitched off to what passed for her sleep.

He turned out the nightlight and slid down beside her. Faces from the party came to him, and floated away like painted balloons. Something was troubling him. The young actors? No, he was over his fit about them now. But what was it then? Something to do with—Ed Cresswell—yes, and the check. No, not the check.

The coyotes had begun their nightly round of the canyon, one of the pack howling from the hilltop. Neighborhood dogs woke, growling nervously, and he felt their tension filling the air. His cat skittered up a tree outside the bedroom window, and his Doberman was pacing back and forth in the yard. Carol woke and looked around sleepily. "I thought your producers went home."

"Coyotes."

"They're after the hamsters down the road. People shouldn't be allowed to keep them."

"What have you got against hamsters?"

"I used to date a guy who raised them in his bathtub." Carol punched the pillow lightly and laid her head into it. "He also wore a burgundy polyester sports jacket. Where are you going?"

"To check on the dog." Caspian crawled from bed and stepped into the hall. He must have fallen asleep, for he remembered a dream now—something opaque, disturbing. He walked down the hall to his office; he opened the desk drawer and took out his pistol, a German Walther. It was loaded; the children of stars were kidnappers' targets. He tucked the gun in his belt, put on a jacket and left the office.

The hall was lit by the lamps of an indoor greenhouse, their soft glow playing on the tiled floor, the black orchids seeming to watch those who came and went. He slipped quietly out of the house, closing the door gently behind him.

The darkness greeted him, its cloak filled with things that night alone could teach. Night was a character, sometimes the lover, more often the villain in the piece. One courted it, and he'd been doing so for years—a connoisseur of moonlight and the soft edge it laid upon the world. To prowl the hills, to be the shadow of himself, a silent inquirer—from this he'd learned to underplay emotion, to use each appearance in a scene as if he'd come suddenly out of hiding.

His dog ran toward him, eyes bright with hunting lust. Caspian walked across the garden, drew the latch on the gate, and he and the dog stepped outside together, onto the road.

The nervous yapping of the coyotes suddenly ceased, followed by a low muttering growl as the pack ran off, with a neighborhood pet in its teeth. He saw them crossing the road ahead of him, and their yapping began again as they started to climb through the underbrush of the hillside. His dog leapt after the pack, chips of volcanic rock sliding down as he scampered upward. Caspian followed, past sharply pointed leaves, and cactus clinging to the dry, sloping land. Above him, he could feel the will of the pack.

Breathing heavily, he reached a bridle path that cut across the first plateau. The coyotes were already beyond him, and the bridle path was soft beneath his step; it was traveled regularly by the equestrian set, who rode like fabled nobility by day but did not venture out at night, owing to that other fabled presence of the canyons, the Manson gang, whose spirit still haunted all these hills, for miles around. When people lived in houses with living rooms ninety feet long, other people got ideas.

On either side of the path the spines of cactus plants were tipped by moonlight, their limbs like the gesturing arms of alien creatures, their roots tenaciously fastened to the arid soil. His step between them on the soft path was soundless, and no one but an animal would know that he was traveling there; but the animals always knew, except for the single occasion when he'd taken a coyote unaware, come upon it from behind, so close he could have grabbed its tail; the animal had whirled about, and something had flashed in its eyes—acknowledgment that a man had counted coup on it.

He'd stored that moment, had used it in films, recreating the hills around himself, their danger and their rules—he was a convincing adventurer, his movements on camera suffused with the air of the stalker.

Now, the lights in the canyon were lost from view as he continued along, into the more desolate reaches of the hills. The bridle path turned and sloped downward to a dried river bed. He crossed over the smooth stones of the bed and climbed the far bank, pushing through the underbrush. He stepped out onto a flat, arid plain. To his right a shadow moved, and then a rifle and bayonet were glistening in front of him.

"*Your papers,*" barked the soldier.

He jumped back, pulled out the Walther, and fired. The bullet whined into the empty darkness and from the top of the volcanic spire came the long howl of a lone coyote.

*　　*　　*

"Why were you shnorking around out there?" Carol was sitting in the kitchen in her robe when he returned.

"Did Alicia wake up?" Caspian looked down the hall toward their daughter's room.

"Sleeping like a lamb, she's probably taking my Valium again." Carol opened the refrigerator. "I'm so hungry I could eat an inner tube."

"I've been having weird dreams lately."

"You know what I tell my staff about such things—" Carol brought a tray of hors d'oeuvres out of the refrigerator and placed them on the counter.

"What do you tell them?"

"Closing ratio and dollar volume, that's what counts, not how did you sleep, darling."

"There's something in the canyon."

"That we know. But don't encourage it, please?"

He opened his jacket and Carol's eyes widened. "You're running around outside with a gun? Who are you, Mister Rhythm? We have a prehistoric dog to take care of security." Carol picked up the pistol with two hands and held it at arm's length. "I'm going to put this in the refrigerator. You go to bed. Dream you're a retired person from Michigan."

He watched as she opened and closed the refrigerator door, her petite form bristling with nervous energy. She would be staring at the ceiling until morning. "Sorry," he said, "I didn't mean to upset you."

"It's all right, you've gotta suffer if you want to play the trombone." She put her arm through his, and led him down the hallway toward their bedroom.

*　　*　　*

He swung off the boulevard and down the steep slope to the parking lot behind Butterfield's. The attendant came forward and took charge of the Mercedes, exhibiting the usual indifference to its fine nature; the tires burnt rubber and Caspian shut his eyes as his beautiful machine shot into a dangerously narrow space. If I say anything I'm the asshole, he thought to himself, thus avoiding another of those confrontations one cannot win, when parking attendants take courses in the perfect rejoinder.

He crossed the lot toward the restaurant, reminding himself that the eatery he was about to enter was once the house of John Barrymore, and that fame and riches fade to Endive and Goat Cheese Salad, $5.95. The entrance was up a stone staircase lined with ivy, growing since Barrymore's day and outliving him. Caspian climbed the steps to the rainbow-lit patio where he was guided to Myron Fish's table. The diminutive agent sat surrounded by tropic vegetation, drink in hand, a plate of sashimi in front of him. "David, you're looking thirsty. An Irish Creme for Mr. Caspian and another Russian Mule for me." Fish waited for the waiter to depart, then leaned confidentially toward Caspian. "I've read the script of DeBrusca's film. It's a sophisticated space epic. Herman Armas is directing, it's megabucks, and DeBrusca understands you're like a son to me."

"I'm not interested in floating around in a sci-fi flick."

"David, would I put my own son into outer space if I thought he'd be unhappy there?"

"I'm not going to do it," said Caspian, suspecting he might, because Armas's last three films were Oscar nominees.

"It's what you're looking for. There are absolutely no children in it, although to be frank there will be some midgets playing heartwarming Martian animals."

"I'm interested in reality."

"The thing that eats the spaceship is real, David. But realest of all is the money."

"I've got enough money."

"You can never have enough money. This table is money, those potted trees are money, the meal I'm paying for tonight is money." He raised his Russian Mule. "Here's to your good health, which is also money. Do you know how much real estate the medical profession owns in Los Angeles county?"

The other tables on the patio were gradually filled, conversations blending beneath the hanging branches; Caspian panned his gaze slowly over the garden to the distant wall, where vines crept down through the soft lantern light. The yellow was that peculiar California shade of gold that L.A. nights lent to every café, every garden; he lingered in its sensations, which seemed to say that the evening was always a movie, wherever you went, lit by specialists in the trade.

A starlet made her entry onto the patio, her eyebrows two crescent moons, her makeup and hair like the vamps of the thirties, her breasts softly moving beneath red and white satin.

"You're distracted, David." Fish leaned across the table. "Is something troubling you? Confide in me, that's what I'm here for. Are you having a little hassle in your marriage? If you are, you can talk to me about it and save a psychiatrist's fee. A man who's been married five times, as I have, can be counted on for good advice."

"What's your advice?"

"Get absolutely the best lawyer you can find. Don't spare

any of the initial expense, it only hurts more deeply later." Fish put the rim of his glass against his chest. "This is from the heart, David. I've been there, I know what a woman can do to a man in court."

Caspian took a piece of bread from the basket and buttered it slowly. "You're a sensitive guy, Myron."

"I've lived, my friend. I've suffered." Fish put his pudgy little hand in the basket. "I know what terrible mental anguish is. My first wife has been on the dole for twenty years. She shops, she skis, she shops some more."

"My marriage is ok, Myron."

"Are you sure? It can sneak up on you in little ways when you're not looking. She buys a new Ferrari, she wants her own ball club. Have you noticed? Or am I prying?"

"You'd never do a thing like that." Caspian drained his glass. "But you can order me another of these splendid drinks."

"That's the attitude. No brooding on personal problems. You're a talented man." Fish extracted another piece of bread from the basket. "To feel right, you have to be working all the time, at the controls of a spaceship." Fish mimed a steering wheel, then slid his chair around and gazed at the starlet, whose table was across the aisle. She glanced back discreetly, with the question every starlet has in her eyes, to which Fish made unspoken answer, *but of course, my dear, I'm an agent.*

". . . and you know the kind of director Armas is, David, you know the sort of touch he has." Fish was picking bread crumbs out of the folds in his shirt. "He transforms everything into . . . into . . ."

"Shit is the word you're looking for."

Fish gazed back at Caspian, the reflection of a thousand deals in his eyes, past, present, and to come. "Everything's shit, David. We just rearrange the scenery. Didn't Plato say that?"

Caspian looked into the leaves behind Fish's shoulder, where something had moved, small and green. " 'There are more things between heaven and earth, Horatio . . .' "

"If you're going to start talking about Cresswell's script,

you will pay for this dinner." Fish poked the air with a pudgy finger.

Caspian watched a tiny lizard come out of the leaves, just behind Fish's elbow. The lizard stared at Caspian, its tongue flicking in and out, and then it was gone, back along its secret passage in the vines.

"There's not a star in the business with the charm you've got," said Fish. "Well, maybe one or two others . . ."

"Myron, can we eat in peace?"

"Only if I'm assured that you're not shmoozing around with some European producer."

"I go for long walks in the hills. You ought to come along some time."

"Are there refreshment stands?"

"Every hundred yards."

"David, I understand—you're a serious actor, you like to take chances. If it flops you can call it a defensible failure, you attempted a unique mission. But the financiers don't listen, not for one fleeting sensitive moment, to the speeches losers make. You can crawl into their office quoting your rave reviews, but they have a switch behind each ear, and when a film bombs they turn it off and leave it off. They acknowledge your lips moving, but their minds are elsewhere. Do you know where? On gigantic human space epics with enormous special effects. They are thinking about all the money they can make on the other planets. You're reading them a rave you got on public TV, but they're seeing lines of American children clutching tickets for the next showing of Dingbats from Outer Space. They're seeing plastic toys shaped like geeks from East Venus. They are not seeing your critically acclaimed movie thirty-five people enjoyed on a wet night at the UCLA film school."

"One thing about you, Myron, you're always in the trenches."

"I'm trying to save you from art, David, it's as simple as that."

"I appreciate it, Myron."

"You want a life of continuing comfort as technology improves? You want everything money can buy?"

"You know that's all I dream about."

"Then listen to your Uncle Myron. You're at a brilliant crossroad in your career. An actor gets there once every five thousand years." Fish paused, as the waiter brought a dish of deep-fried parsley. Fish picked up one of the crisp sprigs and waved it at Caspian. "You're about to become a Major Idol. Don't you see that yet? This film with DeBrusca will do it for you."

"Play it, Myron."

"I am playing it, my friend. A Fish never fatigues. If you do *Star Rover,* you'll have palaces, yachts, *and* quality. De-Brusca's lining up some monster talents."

Caspian nodded. He'd been here before, riding on the rails of Myron's promises. Some of them were kept, some were swept under the rug and life went on its way. And he found it curious, that after all these years, he still swallowed Myron's line about the crossroads of a career. His mind always lit up on that one, his own fantasy machine clicking on: in *this* film everything he was as an actor would surface, and dreams would come true. And tomorrow Myron would say the same thing to one of his other clients.

The starlet at the next table was placing a cigarette into a slender holder, and as she did so, she crossed her legs in Fish's direction. Caspian glanced toward her. ". . . *all identity erased,"* said a feminine whisper at his ear.

Startled, Caspian stared at the girl, but she had already turned back toward her escort, and the whisper was blown away with the summer wind through the leaves.

Carol Caspian entered the drive in her BMW, parked it crookedly and stepped out, a new pair of spiked heels in her hand. Caspian looked up from his cactus garden. "Another failed attempt at a towering image?"

She winced with each step as she came toward him, and sat on the garden bench, rubbing her toes. "Tomorrow I'll have to wear a pair of hot dog buns." Her briefcase strap slipped from her shoulder. "And we didn't get the account. A pitch, no sale. It was completely my fault."

"I know what the next ten sentences will be."

"Violent incompetence, that's all I've displayed this week. I feel like a three-hundred-pound basket case. I have the personality of a potato pancake."

"Seven more to go."

"When we gave the presentation to them, I could see it in their eyes. They were fixing on the potential for failure;

they could see themselves being rammed up the ass with a tax shelter."

Caspian put an arm around her shoulder. "You're home, it's a nice day, relax."

"I hate advertising."

"There's some pesto in the house, I made it myself. Fresh basil from the garden. Shall we?"

"Did you sign with DeBrusca?"

They walked toward the front entrance. "I'll be weightless in space for the next three months."

"Not if we eat all the pesto." Carol grabbed the heavy iron latch and swung the door open. They stepped together into the long hall, and she hung her briefcase on a Victorian halltree. "If I'm fired the only thing that'll be hurt is my pride of gender. All those stupid male faces at the meeting."

"They didn't want a humorous commercial after all?"

"They started looking like parakeets who breathe underwater."

"Not even a smile?"

"These are guys who stick it into the cornflake box every morning." Carol padded on down the hallway and stopped off in her daughter's room. He listened to them talking, Carol's tone changing, lightening up, but when she came back along the hallway he saw she was wearing her fluffy bunny slippers, a sign of dark depression, for she only wore them when her spirit had been reduced to a shuffle. She descended the stairs into the living room and draped herself on her fainting couch, feet up, the foreshortened couch accommodating her small form. "I'm so tired of pandering to Middle America."

Caspian nodded, as was expected of him; they'd eat themselves into a mild stupor, watch a movie on video, and by midevening the crisis would have passed. An inexpensive solution to the working woman's angst. Once he would have thought it too mundane a solution; experience had taught him differently.

He climbed the few steps out of the living room, toward the kitchen. The indoor greenhouse was glowing, its tangle of vines climbing a stone wall as in a jungle cave. A fly was buzzing down in the petals of an African violet, the delicate sound of its rapture filling the little glass room. He entered the chamber, its warm moist air heavy with scent and the dark dreams of plants; there was magic in them, a secret you could breathe into yourself.

"Hey, what's going on?" Carol called from the living room. "If I don't get pesto soon I won't be able to walk."

He stepped from the greenhouse, into the hall. Carol lowered her voice, talking to herself. "Should I take up belly dancing? Would it relax me?"

Caspian walked around the kitchen counter. The maid had left it spotless as always; occasionally she lifted a piece of Carol's jewelry, pawned it to buy cocaine, sold the coke, and returned the jewelry. The gardener had told him how the scam worked, and Caspian noticed that whenever something temporarily vanished, the maid was even more conscientious—pressing his pants, straightening his wardrobe, polishing his shoes. It all seemed part of successfully functioning capitalism.

He went to the wine rack, took down a bottle of Burgundy. As he reached for the corkscrew, a wave of melancholy struck him, and he felt his simple evening sliding out of place; the atmosphere of the house had thickened as before a storm, and he heard the low murmur of thunder. But the day was dry, cloudless; the storm was only here, inside, pressing on his eardrums. Within the thunder he heard the sharp crack of a rifle. And then a voice in his ear. *"We hit the bastard. Look at him drop."*

Insane, high-pitched laughter echoed from his daughter's room. He raced down the hall and stopped at her door. Alicia Caspian looked up at him, startled. On the floor in front of her was a toy clown, whose arms and legs moved by battery power, and whose voice was a weird, computerized laugh. "What is it, Daddy?" asked the little girl, as the toy clown walked toward him, arms outstretched.

"Nothing, honey. I thought . . . I heard you call me."

"It's just the Electronic Clown," said Alicia. "I put in new batteries and it makes him hairy."

She pressed a button on the hand control set and turned the clown around. Caspian watched it walk across his daughter's room, the electronic creature laughing again. Caspian backed out of the doorway and returned to the kitchen, the open wine bottle still in his hand.

"David, I'm dying of hunger." Carol had left the couch and was climbing the couple of stairs toward the kitchen. A frown creased her brow. "Why are you emitting the alpha waves of a carrot?"

"I was lost in thought."

"*I'm* the one who blew an account today. You can't have your nervous breakdown until I get over mine." She opened the refrigerator door. "Let's eat that pesto."

She dragged out the bowl and dug straight into it with a fork. Watching her, he reflected on the many advantages there were to having a wife who did not offer you a penny for your thoughts every five minutes. At times, of course, he might as well be married to a telephone answering machine, which said, in the most delightful and amusing way, "I'm busy now. Leave a message and I'll get back to you later."

*   *   *

Victor Quatrelle drove, his paunch cradled up against the steering wheel, a paunch made famous in motion pictures and TV, for he was, in his own words, "the best fat actor in the business." Caspian sat beside him in the front seat of the Olds, as Quatrelle told him what he knew about working with Julius DeBrusca. "I did *Love Affair* with him, Janet Lingstrom's first picture. He got her an incredible suite in Cannes when they promoted the film." Quatrelle's face contorted to an approximation of DeBrusca's gnomelike visage, and his voice dropped into a replica of the producer's rasp. ". . . you'll have a suite like this, Janet, wherever you go. Like this, if not bigger, and everything in white. And you'll have white dogs, Victor, what are those skinny dogs, afghans, two of them. And the perfumes and the flowers, and a white Rolls Royce." Quatrelle flicked his turn signal and came off the freeway onto Lincoln Boulevard, his imitation of DeBrusca dropping away as he continued: "And when we left Janet salivating in her suite and walked down the hall to the elevator, Julius turned to me and said, 'You know something? I got bigger tits than she does.' "

The Oldsmobile moved smoothly down the thoroughfare, and Caspian watched Venice float by, ugly, baking in the sun. He and Quatrelle had been friends for years, and Caspian valued him as one of those actors with enough technique to plunge into mediocre material and give it life. It was a point with him, and with Caspian as well, that they could join themselves to a simple adventure film and still give the audience something to make them think. It was risky, of course, as on the regrettable occasion they'd come out looking like they were in a different movie from the one the rest of the cast was in, and the critics did not fail to notice it.

Quatrelle turned off into one of the side lanes that intersected the canals of the neighborhood; the automobile climbed up a little bridge over a channel of tidal water in which rowboats floated lazily on their moorings. "Nice little bit of typhus breeding in there," said Quatrelle, and turned again, onto another back street in Marina Del Rey. The street was narrow, went one way; Quatrelle flicked his signal again and turned into the open garage beneath his building, parking between a silver Rolls and a Cadillac Seville.

The door to the apartment house was protected by a pair of formidable locks. They rode the elevator to the second floor, and stepped out, onto a balcony constructed above an inner courtyard, in which a lone palm tree grew, its branches reaching up and dangling over the balcony railing. "It's costing me a hundred grand a year, but I get the occasional coconut." He opened the door to his apartment and they entered.

The apartment faced the ocean, and a telescope stood trained upon the beach below. Quatrelle went to it and made a quick survey of the sands. "Always something interesting—yes, right there, she's wearing nothing but two beanbags and a shoelace." He carried the scope out onto the terrace and Caspian joined him at the rail. The beach made a long slow curve toward Santa Monica. In the other direction was Los Angeles Airport, a steady stream of jets leaving it and climbing out over the water. Caspian sat down on a canvas chair, hand going into a spider web. An empty beer can was under the chair, beside an ashtray loaded with butts. "No lovely lady in residence?"

"A disturbing fungus appeared on the tip of my lily," said Quatrelle from behind his scope. "The Beverly Hills cock doctor removed the foreskin as a precautionary measure and now I can't have any serious erections for a month."

"That's not like you, Victor."

"It's almost a sex change, isn't it." He capped the telescope, and turned toward Caspian. "Is there a part in *Star Rover* for me?" He twisted his face into a leer. "A Plutonian pervert who oozes over young girls?"

"How do you get along with Herman Armas?"

"I was in the first film Armas directed. On day one of shooting he was so terrified he forgot how to start the picture. Couldn't think of the word *action.* He finally blurted out *begin.* But it took everything out of him. Now he thinks he's Bergman, and he'll give you as much personal contact as a water fountain." Quatrelle led Caspian back inside, to the little bar off the kitchen, where he concocted a drink he called a Boiled Owl.

"Let me show you something I've been working on." He brought out a small wooden box which he'd constructed in the shape of an old vaudeville stage. "It'll have a spring in it, and some little puppets." He opened an envelope and took out two old photographs, carefully cut and backed with cardboard, of a baggy-pants comic and a young girl, their costumes from a bygone era.

Caspian picked up the male figure. "Your old man?"

"My grandfather and grandmother. This was one of their routines. The Jew and the Soubrette." Quatrelle chuckled. "A little early anti-Semitic comedy." The knee and elbow joints of the figures had been hinged, and strings attached. Quatrelle hung the Jew and the Soubrette in the little theater, then turned a crank that set them dancing, arms and legs swinging.

"I'll put a music box inside it, maybe rig a little curtain for the front." Quatrelle hummed an old music hall tune, compressing his lips to make tiny trumpet sounds. His brow creased, and he punctuated the sound of the trumpet with that of a sputtering little drum.

Caspian watched as Quatrelle made the Soubrette shriek, and the Jew dance after her across the miniature vaudeville stage.

"What a wonderfully naïve time," said Quatrelle, looking over the top of the little stage, "to be able to do something so infinitely tasteless."

Caspian reached for his glass, but as he brought it toward him, his wrist suddenly went loose, and the drink landed on the floor.

"Eighty-six that drunk, he's had enough."

"Sorry," said Caspian, putting the empty glass on the bar. "For a moment, it felt like—" He looked at the dancing Jew and the Soubrette. "—somebody pulled one of my strings." He took a bar napkin and wiped up the spilled booze, the sensation still in his arm, as if it had not quite been his own.

"All right, Grandma," said Quatrelle, bringing the Soubrette up out of the little theater, "that's enough for today." He brought his grandfather out after her, and tucked them both back under the bar. "At the age of seventy, Grandpop dressed up in a gown and wig and drove down Hollywood Boulevard in a convertible. When he got to a stoplight he looked up at the driver in the truck next to him and said, in his best old lady's voice, *'How'd you like a nice blowjob, sonny.'* " Quatrelle put the little vaudeville stage under the bar. "So what do they expect from me?"

He guided a rented car through memories. Up ahead were the familiar smokestacks of Pittsburgh, dead now, their fires no longer leaping into the sky, and the buildings of the old steel industry empty shells. When he'd been a child, the skyline had been a magic inferno, great towers belching flames of red and gold.

He'd grown up in the shadow of these giant black towers, and even at night, in his bed, he was aware of them; he'd listen to the nightshift arriving, to the men's voices and the sound of their machinery. That had been the best, to drift toward sleep, with the voices of the mill men like a protective talisman.

Now it was silent; the giants were themselves asleep.

*   *   *

"It's so good of you to visit me because now they'll believe me when I tell them you're my nephew. You know," said his aunt, nodding toward the door, "many of the patients here imagine they're related to someone famous. But I really am. We'll set them straight, won't we?"

"Yes, Aunt Ruth, we sure will."

She sat forward in her chair. "I have fine doctors taking care of me, David. Very conscientious men."

Her color was waxen, and there were dark circles under her eyes; but the eyes themselves were sharp and clear. She had been the artistic one in the family. What books he'd read as a child she'd given to him. For his First Holy Communion she'd given him a silver dollar; he could still see her bending down to him on the sidewalk in front of the church. Now she was so much older, across from him, in a chair by a barred window, and there was an unpleasant smell in the room, not the smell he remembered from boyhood when she'd hugged him as he came in the door. That smell had been lilacs, from the big bush beside her kitchen window. Lilacs, and then the smell of olive oil and simmering garlic.

". . . the best doctors and the very latest medicines. I've been assured of that."

She'd always been glad to see him in her gray, old house; he'd been her favorite nephew. And this memory stood out: He'd been playing in her kitchen one day, racing little cars over the linoleum. She'd looked at him, and he'd felt that she was a complete stranger, that she wasn't Aunt Ruth at all, her thin face becoming more angular, her gaze suddenly alien and cold. Beyond her through the window the wash blew on the line, the leaves moved in the trees, and a grave doubt had entered his mind about the world.

"I feel quite well, actually. The grounds here are very beautiful and I can walk in them every day. Would you like me to show them to you?" she asked, in her quiet, medicated way.

"I'd like that very much, Aunt Ruth." He gave her his arm, and they walked down the hall, and into the visiting room where the other women on her floor were watching TV, knitting, playing cards. Again he smelt the peculiar odor, much stronger now. It enveloped him as they went deeper into the room, and he felt he was going to choke; his whole body seemed to be rejecting the smell, as if it were an atmosphere in which one could not possibly breathe—the odor of madness.

Aunt Ruth introduced him to the group gathered at the TV set, and they listed all the movies they'd seen him in, including some he'd never heard of. Aunt Ruth watched, nodding proudly at her handsome nephew, the famous movie star, who spoke to her friends and signed their copy of *TV Guide*.

He joked with them, and found himself answering with ease their oracular jibes and disjointed questions. The level of communication in a madhouse, he reflected, was not much different from that of a typical press conference, except that the questions here seemed more intelligent. But on the outer rim of the activity were other women, too lost to know him, or themselves, women softly sobbing or staring blankly into nothingness.

Aunt Ruth led him away, but then it was the nurses who had to meet him, and he saw their eyes were strange too, with strange questions in them, a little mad by habit, but he wasn't uncomfortable with them either. An atmosphere swarming with visions, paranoia, and dark compulsions seemed somehow related to every movie set he'd ever been on.

Finally Aunt Ruth took him down the long corridor that led to the grounds. The day was bright outside, and she talked about the family, about the old days, her memory perfectly clear. "You were such a talented child. And you were a dreamer, David. You played very seriously. You gave your heart to what you did. That's essential, of course. One must give one's heart."

He looked at her, and wondered what she was doing in a mental institution. There was nothing wrong with her; he'd take Aunt Ruth out of here, find her an apartment, something with a soothing view, and everything she wanted close at hand. The woman was clear-minded, she could cope. He'd give her back the remaining years of her life.

She led him around the grounds, past rose bushes on which shiny red pips hung in profusion. "A dreamer and a seeker, David. I saw it. You couldn't be other than you are. I remember the things that fascinated you—I bought you dueling foils, do you remember? Because you wanted to be a musketeer? I receive my messages by the garden wall, from the CIA." Her voice hadn't altered, the same gentle flow directed it.

"Orders are given to me from the hidden microphone. I'm an agent, you know." She stopped, turned toward him. "Who ever would have believed, David, that they would have selected me. But then—" She slipped her arm through his. "—you were selected for something very special too, weren't you."

*　　*　　*

Caspian sat in the living room of Ed Cresswell's house, surrounded by Cresswell's collection of childhood memorabilia: the round globe of a bubble gum dispenser was at his elbow; behind him was a vast library of Better Little Books, starring Captain Midnight, Spike Kelly, Terry Lee. The coffee table belonged to old, windup Disney characters in tin—Pluto the Dog, Mickey and Donald, and a Mar Toy airplane that would roll over just before it taxied off the table's edge. Throughout the house, in every cupboard and alcove, were mechanical banks, penny slot machine games, and fleets of vintage toy automobiles. Caspian had gone to Cresswell's to work on their script and the two of them had spent the evening playing with Lionel trains, which filled the dining room and included every accessory Lionel had ever made—log loaders, milk cars that shot tiny cans all over the floor, signalmen who waved lanterns in the dark.

Cresswell sat across from Caspian now, still wearing his gray railroader's hat, after having put the last train of the night into the roundhouse. "How were things in Pittsburgh?"

"I was seeing a mad aunt."

"Certified?"

"She gets messages from the CIA."

"My uncle gets messages in his hearing aid. Some of it makes good dialogue, I use it whenever I can."

Caspian sipped Coke from a bottle that a big red machine had belched out at him; in his other hand were stale Planter's peanuts from another ancient vending device that stood like an icon in the living room, lit by a baby spot from above. "My family has more than its share of lunatics," said Caspian, setting the bottle on the coffee table. "It seems to come down through the women. But it's skipped across the line, I think."

"Are you feeling psychopathic?" Cresswell held up his own Coke bottle. "It could be this soda, the sugar in it is probably thirty years old."

"It happened when I was a kid," said Caspian. "Can I tell you about it?"

"Wait till I get my notebook open."

"I'd had my appendix out and some complications developed. They gave me penicillin, to which I was allergic, though nobody knew it at the time. So every day they'd inject me, and every day I'd start to feel like I was dying. They finally wised up, but by then I'd pushed through into a low-grade psychosis. By the time I got home I felt I was making up the world as I went along—making up the car, making up our house, making the air up. Finally, of course, I concluded that I was making up me."

"Go on," said Cresswell, scribbling in his notebook.

"Well," said Caspian, "I was left with the total certitude that I had no being. I couldn't tell anyone, it was too obscene to communicate. So I lived in a constant nightmare of nothingness. I had to stay up as late as possible every night, clutching the sheets and shaking, trying to calm myself. I was like that for years."

"And?"

"I knew the world was a made-up place. I knew that some godawful conclusion was due any moment, in which everything would collapse, so I refused to take part in anything. I was like those kids in that Cocteau film, living without rules in a world of their imagination, in a room filled with sacred, unreal objects. And do you know what those childhood objects were?"

"Bubble gum dispensers?"

"Nazi souvenirs. My father brought them back from the war. A helmet, an Iron Cross, a Death's Head ring. That Death's Head ring always said to me—you know the truth, that the world is a skull, floating in nothingness."

"This," said Cresswell, "is a weird childhood." He had laid his pen down and was staring at Caspian.

"I tried out for a play in high school. When I found myself on stage, making up myself and being applauded for it, the nightmare left me. I've been doing it ever since."

"And the Nazi souvenirs—" Cresswell tapped the script which lay on the table in front of them. "—is that why we're writing this Berlin romance? This German theatre piece nobody's ever going to buy, if I may quote your agent?"

"I like their films. They know how to use a camera."

"Well, I've always said Eva Braun would have been a lot of laughs." Cresswell went to another of his dispensing machines and inserted two coins. A pair of tiny wax bottles, filled with a red liquid, came out. "Remember these? You drink the juice and then chew the wax?"

"It's coming back to me."

Cresswell held one of the bottles up to the light. "Within this bottle the quintessence of our twisted youth is contained." He turned back toward Caspian. "So do you ever have relapses? Into the void?"

"I was working as an extra in Prague, and staying in a student youth hotel. The Hotel Solidarita. It's on the outside of the city, next to a public crematorium. The wind usually blows east toward Russia, but one day it blew the other way, and the smell of the smoke from that crematorium did it to me. The world became a made-up place."

"I never travel," said Cresswell. "I stay here in L.A. with my gumball machines."

"And as a matter of fact," said Caspian, "just lately I've been having some bizarre interludes."

"Drink this," said Cresswell, handing him the little wax bottle.

They drank, Caspian spitting his out instantly, spraying red liquid onto the rug, while Cresswell grimaced, swallowed, and looked at Caspian, a furrow still on his brow. "The chemistry has settled, hasn't it?"

"To pure red dye number five."

Cresswell took the little bottle out of his mouth. "This, perhaps, should not be chewed, much as I'd been looking forward to it." He tossed the bottle into an ashtray. "The past can't be recaptured."

"Not entirely."

"I paid a fortune for those wax pieces of caa-caa."

"It's part of your search for enlightenment, Ed."

"I've bitten into more stale candy than you can imagine." Cresswell pointed to the antique glass display case that framed one corner of the living room. Lined up within it were rows of forty-year-old sweets in faded wrappers.

"You're bound to find what you're looking for sooner or later. That one perfect bite."

"Yes," said Cresswell, a faraway look coming into his eye. "Somewhere there's a Mary Jane, hard as rock, with my genii inside." He shook his head. "What a disgusting obsession."

"At least it isn't Nazi souvenirs."

Cresswell cocked his head, put a finger thoughtfully to his nose. "Wait a second, wait a second. I just—" He crossed the room, to a table on which a pile of scrapbooks was stacked. He started thumbing through them. "Recent acquisitions from an auction. They belonged to an old guy who spent his days cutting out ads for women's stockings." Cresswell held up a page, filled with the neatly cut and pasted ads.

"Definitely a leg man," said Caspian.

"Yes, but he tucked other things in here and there, and on one of these pages—" Cresswell kept riffling, then stopped suddenly, pulled out a little transparent envelope and handed it to Caspian.

Caspian opened the envelope and tapped out a reddish-tinted postage stamp from the Third Reich, of an idealized Hitler in military greatcoat, with swastikas waving from tiny buildings in the distance.

"Take it," said Cresswell.

"Thanks anyway," said Caspian, returning it to the envelope and handing it back.

Cresswell tucked the envelope into the album again. "I wonder if this old guy was a Nazi spy. These legs are all pretty chunky. Real fräulein stuff."

"*Schönheitstänzerinnen.*"

"I beg your pardon?"

"Beauty Dancers." Caspian looked at the pages of crossed, kicking legs. "A regular chorus line."

"We all have our obsessions," said Cresswell. "This is how I'll wind up, I suppose."

"Cutting out women's legs?"

"Old candy bar ads."

Caspian thumbed back through the album; he stopped at the page where the Hitler stamp lay, and though he had no wish to, found himself removing it from its envelope, revealing once again the Führer's idealized face, double chins covered by the high collar of his coat. "Nazi Germany was a made-up world." His fingertip touched the edge of the stamp. "Made-up sky, made-up buildings, made-up Führer. And everyone bought it." He turned to Cresswell. "And maybe we're still making it up. Made-up you, made-up me, made-up America. Maybe the young David Caspian was right."

"Like every American," said Cresswell, closing the album and putting it away, "you just had too much penicillin."

*   *   *

He dug in his garden near the terrace; beside him two little fruit trees were waiting to be planted, their roots wrapped in burlap. Carol worked close by, on her hands and knees in a flowerbed. Ed Cresswell was seated in a lawn chair near them, a portable computer on his lap. His fingers tapped on the keyboard for awhile, after which he stared mournfully at the sky, and dropped his arms limply beside him, knuckles on the ground. Carol said softly to Caspian, "He exudes control, doesn't he."

Cresswell stared down at the script, groaned, and put his face in his long bony hands. After a short while his tapping began again.

"He's like the last lonely woodpecker." Carol adjusted her gardening kneepads and crawled forward, digging tool in hand. "I've planted flowers all through here, I can't remember just where, but do be careful." Her part of the garden was bright, chaotic with weeds, wild flowers, and herbs. "I think this is that witchy stuff I planted. For over the door, to keep the golems out."

"Let's try some." Caspian bent down and pinched a few twigs off the plant.

"I didn't know you were the witchy type." Carol continued crawling forward.

Alicia appeared through a row of pink rhododendrons, saw her mother and father, and stopped in her tracks. Clearly, she had not expected to come upon them at such close quarters. She looked over her shoulder through the rhododendrons, then looked back at them, and took a hesitant step forward. "I'm in *big* trouble," she said, fixing them with her wide-eyed stare, which discomfitted adults who didn't know her and thought she'd just uncovered their darkest financial or sexual indiscretion. She played nervously with one of her pigtails, stroking its wavy, brown tip over and over, a thing she did to soothe herself whenever situations became doubtful.

"What's wrong?"

"I perfumed the cat."

On cue, the cat padded out through the rhododendrons, tail lifted regally in the air.

Carol sniffed as it brushed past them. *"Diva.* A hundred and seventy-five dollars an ounce."

Alicia and the cat walked off down the path, the cat still holding her perfumed tail proudly in the air. Caspian called after his daughter. "Honey, come back here."

"You mustn't scold her," said Carol.

"Why would I scold her? I'm going to offer her something more rewarding than perfuming a cat."

Alicia had turned on the path and was approaching, hesitantly, the cat purring against her leg. Caspian waved her over to him. "Alicia, I've been thinking about a hobby I bet you'd really like."

His daughter looked up at him, expectantly. He looked back down at her. "I'm going to get you an ant farm."

"An ant farm?" interjected Carol. "Are you crazy? Why don't you get her a tarantula ranch? How about a flea factory?" Carol put her hands on her hips. "That's all we need is an ant farm. It'll get broken and there'll be ants crawling all over me."

"It won't get broken. It's fascinating. Alicia can watch the workings of a complete little civilization."

Alicia put her hands on her hips, in perfect imitation of her mother's stance. "I want an ant farm, *and* a tarantula ranch."

"Well, you're not getting them," said Carol. She turned to Caspian again. "An ant farm. Of all the crazy ideas. How about a Japanese beetle hotel? So they can eat the leaves off all the trees in the neighborhood."

Alicia grabbed hold of her father's hand. "Can I, Daddy? Have a beetle hotel? I'd take care of it, I promise. We could have every color beetle, and have beetle races on the table."

"You see?" Carol looked at Caspian. "Beetle races on the table. We'll have beetles in our food, and when they get tired they'll creep into bed with us."

"I'm not suggesting we get beetles. I merely suggested—"

"—an ant farm," begged Alicia, clapping her hands as she

danced around her father. "Please, please, I'd love an ant farm more than anything."

"Your mother doesn't want you to have one."

"Mommy—"

"Absolutely not. You had a turtle and it died behind the refrigerator."

"I'll feed the ants every day," said Alicia, marching in little circles, as if to solidify her position. ". . . and water them, and read to them, and tell them the facts of life."

"There's an ant hill at the bottom of the yard," said Carol. "You can tell them the facts of life."

"But that's not the same as my *room*," said Alicia, sticking out her belly.

"See what you've started?" said Carol, turning to Caspian. "Where did you learn child-rearing, in a field guide to insects?" Carol took Alicia's hand in hers, and talked to her softly. "Alicia, you can go into Mommy's room and take a dollar from her purse."

"Make it two dollars," said Alicia.

"All right, two dollars. But you must never mention ant farms again, honey, because it gives Mommy the creeps. Do you understand?"

"Yes," said Alicia, and cast her father a conspiratory look before walking off, which suggested the subject of ant farms would be raised again at a more opportune time.

"Please understand," said Cresswell, calling across the garden to them, "I realize *Star Rover* is a better vehicle for you. I've created a real part for you, but I understand, you'd rather pilot a rocketship to Mars."

"I had a dream once that I went to Mars," said Carol, "in a container of leftovers."

"No apologies needed," said Cresswell. "Do you know where the writers are seated at the Academy Award dinner? At a table by themselves, farthest from the dais. Next to the kitchen."

"So your food will be warm," said Caspian.

Cresswell pointed to the screen of the computer. "Do you want a sex scene with the German baroness?"

"No," said Carol, "he doesn't. We think sex in films is so obvious." She shuffled forward on her pads.

"Make it tasteful," said Caspian.

"Sex is always tasteful." Cresswell pressed the computer INSERT key.

"If you write him a sex scene," said Carol, "I'll never feed you again."

Cresswell canceled the INSERT key.

Caspian picked up the little pear tree and carried it to the end of the garden, where he bundled the sapling into the ground. "Grow," he said, packing the soil in around it, "and one day you'll be a member of a pear juice consortium."

He continued talking to the tree, telling it how lovely it was, and then going into detail, about sap, flower bud, calyx, corolla, leaf metamorphosis, things he had made himself learn, in the cherished belief that a plant had as sophisticated a knowledge of itself as any botanist, and that it appreciated refinements of address. In a similar spirit, he'd installed patio-blaster speakers in the garden, waterproof and airtight, to serenade his plants. They appeared fond of Sachdev, Hindu master of the bamboo flute.

In the wooded valley beyond his property, the crows were calling feverishly, had been nervous all week, owing to an owl who'd moved into their territory. Caspian could see its enormous head and hunched wings visible at the top of an oak, and the crows circling over it, their voices filled with a nagging, territorial edge. He glanced toward the adjacent property, saw his neighbor was out. The neighbor returned his wave and joined him at the fence.

"Did you hear the police last night? They rounded up some goons out there." The neighbor pointed toward the hills with the end of a bamboo rake. "They were sacrificing a goat." He lit his pipe and puffed thoughtfully. "We live in strange times."

Caspian managed a reply, and continued chatting, but his eyes returned to the owl. His neighbor was speaking, but he was drifting off in his thoughts, remembering those etherlike trances of his childhood, when the world lost the meaning family and teachers had given to it, when the sun seemed a hostile eye in the void, and he its only knower.

The neighbor resumed his raking, and Caspian walked to the stream, and crossed over. The owl heard his footstep and flew off, wings flapping audibly in the still canyon air. He watched it go, the crows chasing after it, their shrill voices fading beyond the hills as the owl led them on.

He walked until he came to the bridle path, and there he followed the imprint of hooves in the finely beaten dust, out into the hills, where the atmosphere underwent a distinct change; he could feel the forces hostile to man—coyotes, rattlesnakes, and the air itself, hot enough to drop you. Here was the place to sacrifice a goat, were you so minded. The high volcanic hills seemed to be listening to the arcana of the earth. He felt the mind of the jagged rocks, felt their indifference to the footsteps of ritual killers, coyotes, and movie stars; other matters, of deeper significance, concerned them—hidden fires, rivers of lava, the core of unrest.

He continued along the bridle path, its slow curve taking him to the center of the canyon, where chaparral and a few scrub oak trees graced a clearing.

Heat waves shimmered from the baking clay, distorting the air. He heard the crack of a rifle shot, and turned his head. A figure in black walked beside him, in bright, polished military boots, hand gesturing with a cigarette. *"The pleasures of this establishment are unique. My mistress is only twelve. Do you think me perverse?"*

The heat waves shuddered violently, the cracking rifle sound came again, and the figure vanished. Caspian stared down at the dry earth, his body drenched in sweat, his temples pounding. A few cautious steps backward brought him out of the clearing and onto the shaded bridle path. He remembered: a smoking tomb he'd dreamt of as a child, through whose door one must never, under any conditions, pass.

He walked along the bridle path until he came in sight of the community of houses in the canyon. In childhood it had been this way, when he'd run home, filled with nothingness.

He crossed the little stream in the canyon and climbed the hill to his own back gate. The yard was empty, the air so still he could hear the insects rustling in the leaves. The house stood before him, silent, massive, a solid chunk of reality. The terrace door opened and Carol stepped out. "Ed's waiting for you in the den. He's had lunch and is feeling more secure."

Caspian entered, into the cool shaded living room. Cresswell laid down the script, and lit a cigarette.

"No," said Caspian, coming forward. "Don't—"

"Who are you, the Surgeon General?"

"I mean you—you suddenly looked like someone else." Caspian broke off, for with the cigarette in his hand Ed Cresswell was the person who'd just walked beside him in the canyon.

*   *   *

Carol read in the boudoir chair beside the bed, the lamp casting soft light on the pages of the book and on her lavender nightgown. Her legs were crossed, one knee rocking impatiently as she read. "I'm on page four and already there are three women, two men, and a dog."

Caspian lay on the bed, the screenplay for *Star Rover* on his lap, his lips moving as he tried a line here and there. Carol began thumbing quickly through the chapters of her book. "I just don't relate any longer. I'm twice the age of the person who wrote these sultry thoughts."

Caspian read on. It was monosyllabic but not the crap he'd expected. "This isn't bad."

Carol nodded, paying no attention, was skipping to the last page of the novel and reading the conclusion. "The St. Bernard did it." She closed the book in her lap. "What were you saying, darling?"

"This is a good script." He tossed it onto the night table. "But the studio will turn it into a doughnut."

"Don't be so gloomy." Carol slipped onto the bed beside him. "Your problem is you're in a business where you are the product." She lowered the strap of her nightgown. "And now I'm going to show you something I learned while I was held prisoner by a Japanese camera club."

*   *   *

From out in the hills came the first nervous bark, as the pack began its descent. The moon edged over the canyon wall, and he stood at the window looking out into the garden, where silver-hued plants answered the moonlight shining on their luminous bed. The coyotes came closer, their nervous barks growing louder. The neighborhood dogs began to whine, and somewhere in the rising tumult he heard the pack strike.

He saw his cat tiptoeing through the silvery plants, ears cocked, tail twitching as it disappeared beneath the spines of a cactus. He moved the curtains aside and looked up to the canyon rim, its edges sharply etched in the moonlit sky. He could feel the pack, climbing toward the peak; they would dine, then raid the next canyon and the next, until sunrise.

He let the curtain slip closed, and turned back toward the bed.

The room was not his own.

The walls he looked at were cracked, the plaster bare. A single bulb hung from the ceiling, and smoke from a woman's cigarette rose up around it. Her voice was an echo, her body made of moonlit substance, as was the room, a substance in which he was stabilizing, against his will.

"My suitcase is in the corner." She pointed toward a battered piece of luggage, and swung her legs off the unmade bed, her silvery nightgown whispering negligently against the sheets.

"For the love of god, stop dawdling. Do you want a rope around your neck?"

His voice was strange to him, his actions inexplicable. Yet another part of him knew what this building was and why they must leave it at once.

He stepped out of the room into a dim hallway. The stair rail was broken, the steps twisted and dark.

The street, it's late, she has no time to spare.

His conflicting thoughts were manifest in his body's rubbery movement down the hall. He reached a window that gave onto the street. A black Mercedes was pulling in at the curb. Two men in black overcoats stepped out, their breath billowing in the night air. He hurried back to the room, flung open the door, and stepped through.

"They're here!"

"Who's here?"

Carol sat up in bed, holding the sheet to her breast. He spun around, looking for the cracked walls, the bare, dangling bulb.

"I might as well pee," said Carol, and with a sleepy sigh, heaved out of bed and shuffled on by him.

He drove down into Westwood and on to Wilshire. The boulevard rolled by, until the car rental lots held only Rolls Royces and he was in the heart of Beverly Hills, turning left onto El Camino. He drove through high bronze gates into the cobblestone courtyard of the Beverly Wilshire. Pear trees and gas lamps lined it, and white-gloved Asians received his automobile and whisked it away to the parking lot below while the doorman showed him into the hotel.

The thickly carpeted corridor ran past shops without price tags, British-tailored clothes on one side, Ming vases on the other. A South American couple came toward him, and he could feel their cattle, their horses, their solid gold bathroom fixtures. He stepped beneath a Louis XVI chandelier and entered La Bella Fontana. The maître d' led him through the fluted columns that supported the Pompeian grotto, to Myron Fish's table, shared by Victor Quatrelle and by Myron's first wife, Fay Roper, now a studio executive. Twenty-five years ago, when she'd been a beautiful young actress, her marriage battles with Myron were legend; she'd once driven his Jaguar into their swimming pool. Now she had mellowed, her hair dyed ashy blonde, in a shade so close to silver it did not seem as if she were trying to look younger. Her hands were still attractive and she used them well, with amusing jewelry, blatantly costume but not cheap; on her blouse she wore a big plastic palm tree. She examined Caspian closely. "Your eyes are bloodshot, are you getting enough rest?"

"I'm fine."

"Myron, is he getting enough rest?"

"On my orders, he's struck with a rubber mallet every night at nine." Fish was looking at the menu. He turned to Quatrelle. "You'd better have a fruit salad."

Quatrelle patted his great pot. "I was born to raise fat." He ordered pheasant.

"David, what about you?"

"I'll be in a skintight spacesuit soon." He turned to the waiter. "Fruit salad."

The three-tiered fountain at the center of the restaurant bubbled, a cherub riding its crest; the meal came, and Fish played host, continuing to banter with his ex-wife. "Doing business with each other has given us something our marriage never had—a deal memo, everything spelled out clearly."

"The studio knows I'm the only one who can negotiate with Myron. I anticipate his moves."

"A little blue spot always lights my eyes," said Fish. "I can be trusted."

"Of course you can, darling. You're faithful as a Labrador retriever."

The sunlight fell through Belgian lace, and the maître d', looking like an Italian count in his drawing room, came by to supervise tiny details of the meal. The cherub watched from its bubbling spray, and Caspian ate quietly, content to absorb the mannerisms of his neighbors, to feel them, analyze them, and file them away. The way a man moved his hands while he talked indicated the role for which he'd cast himself in life's comedy; the way his pants hung revealed his defeat, depression, despair. Caspian had invented a hotel in his mind, with many rooms, and in the rooms were characters he'd created—old men, young men, men of every kind, to which he was always adding little details of dress and demeanor. They lived on in the hotel, dining, scheming, waiting, dreaming. In the hotel of memory, he'd stored decades of observations, and they were always there, behind carefully marked doors, waiting to be used.

"I bailed Alan Modesto out of the drunk tank again," said Quatrelle. "They found him on the beach in the middle of the night with his arms wrapped around a sturgeon."

"Such a good actor," said Fay. "But lately he seems to be talking through a piece of Swiss cheese. I mean, doesn't he?"

"Well," said Quatrelle, "it's a blow, a star one day and the next day they find him hiding in someone else's Mercedes. But in his prime he was the greatest cold reader in the world."

Fish put his hands on Quatrelle's and Caspian's wrists and squeezed gently. "You boys have weathered success. I like to think I've provided a role model for you."

Fay turned the conversation to a property she and Fish were developing. Caspian half listened, gazing at her. The absurd thought struck him that he knew her better than she knew herself, as if some dreamlike perception of her lying at the back of his mind had suddenly risen into view—Fay of other days, Fay of another era. It was, moreover, intensely erotic, a lovely tingle running through his perception, as sometimes happened when he dreamt of a woman he knew socially, and the dream carried them deep into intimacy. Had he been dreaming of Fay? It seemed so, but he couldn't remember, could only discern the sensuous afterglow surrounding her.

During dessert, she made a date with Fish, for supper later in the week. "Six o'clock," she said. "And when I say six I mean six."

"When you say six it could mean anything."

Caspian could not quite grasp what it was—but Fay seemed like an old flame of his, around whom faded tenderness remained. She noted his glance. "Why, David, how sweet."

He felt himself reddening, and then Fish leaned forward. "What's sweet, what have I missed?"

Fay called for the bill, and fitted a pair of little reading glasses to the end of her nose. She checked the arithmetic carefully, then handed the check to Fish. When they got up from the table, she took Caspian's arm and said quietly, "Sometimes with the old jokes you don't know, do you."

"I'm sorry, I didn't mean—"

"Don't apologize, darling, let me cherish the moment."

They filed their way out into the long hall and down it, to the cobblestone courtyard, Caspian still puzzling over Fay— in all the time he'd known her he'd never considered her as an erotic partner, but today it was as if he'd just gotten out of her bed. He wondered if this was another grotesquery of the middle age libido—unexpected surges of sexuality, projected onto whatever woman is seated innocently across from one. If so, all he could hope was that it might prove useful in front of the camera.

Fay's car was brought up, and white gloves opened the door for her; she did not place a tip in them. "Goodbye, my dears—" She drove smoothly off, with Myron Fish waving after her. "I used to say jump and she'd say when and how high." He turned to Caspian and Quatrelle. "Where did I go wrong? Well, here's my car—" He stepped toward his beloved vintage Jaguar which Fay had long ago driven into his swimming pool. He climbed in and the door was closed behind him. "Remember the motto—" He put the car in gear. "—abandon all taste, ye who enter here." He drove off, leaving Caspian and Quatrelle on the cobblestone drive, as Quatrelle's car nosed up the ramp.

"I'm popping over to *Edwardo's,*" said Quatrelle. "Why don't you come along?"

Caspian climbed into Quatrelle's car, and Quatrelle guided

the big automobile along Rodeo Drive, to a men's boutique, where he parked three feet from the curb. Hi-tech metal manikins graced the window of the shop, against a backdrop of shimmering metallic beads lit by a hidden moon. Electronic music came from the doorway, sounding the soft echoes and fading trails of outer space. "Just a mom and pop store, isn't it," said Quatrelle as they walked through the entranceway.

Edwardo stood inside, extending his hands. "Amigos—" Caspian had known him when he was a ballroom dance instructor, selling lifetime rhumba lessons.

"I have the gift you ordered," said Edwardo to Quatrelle, and led them through the store, and up a spiraling metal staircase to his office. He turned the key in a door as heavy as that of a bank vault.

"Impressive, yet unaffected." Quatrelle gestured as the massive iron door clicked shut behind them. The office walls were trimmed in chrome, and indirect lighting glowed softly from a white acrylic banquette that ran around the base of the room. Sofas and pillows in midnight blue were bathed in the glow. Edwardo sat at his desk and unlocked a drawer. From within it he removed a black lacquered box. "My grapevine tells me you two are going to do a film together."

"Yes, a little trip to Mars." Quatrelle adjusted his paunch as he sat, settling it more comfortably around his belt. Edwardo opened the box and took out a clear cellophane bag, its snowy contents in dramatic contrast to the polished black of the box. "A booster for your rocket." He handed the bag to Quatrelle, who handed him back a roll of bills. Not counting them, Edwardo slipped them, and the box, back into the drawer. Quatrelle smiled. "You have the air of a man perfectly at home in his own safe."

"Man who lives in bank vault has no cause for alarm." Edwardo stood, looked at Caspian. "How about you, David? Something for the long voyage?"

"I've already got something," said Caspian. Edwardo put

his arm around him, and ran a professional hand down the breast of Caspian's jacket, touching the Walther. "Carrying heat? That's not like you. But let me get you something less conspicuous. A little derringer, fits in what looks like a wallet. Someone asks for your money, you extend the wallet and blow him away."

"If the Handgun Association has finished its meeting—" Quatrelle dipped a tiny coke spoon into the cellophane bag, and passed it around. Caspian breathed the clear, clean power into himself, felt the familiar surge of confidence come on instantaneously, and saw, as always—everything was action, lighting, and scene change.

They left the office, Edwardo leading them along the balcony, past a row of chrome pillars. Their forms were reflected in them, curved, elongated. Caspian felt his mind shift one notch more, out past where the coke user wants to go. Edwardo's face was rippling in the pillar, and Caspian felt the walls shift within him. So little is needed for the worlds to move.

I was chosen for something special, said Aunt Ruth.

He reached for the balcony railing; a leading man does not freak out in a Rodeo Drive boutique.

He followed Edwardo and Quatrelle down the gleaming spiral staircase, to the main floor, and on to the back of the shop. "A preview of the new merchandise," said Edwardo. "Right through there, gentlemen."

Caspian pushed aside the folds of a plush red curtain, the heavy material lying momentarily like a cape on his shoulder. He heard the whisper of the fabric as it slipped away behind him, and he stepped ahead into darkness. "Where are the lights, Edwardo?"

"Lights?"

A faint bulb came on, in a room filled with large broken cartons, a headless manikin, a dust-covered pile of shoe boxes. The air was moist, and the smell musty. He turned. The man standing in the parted fold of the drape let it fall, and came toward him.

"My store is a ruin."

His hair was disheveled, his manner hesitant and fearful. He pushed aside the broken manikin, and opened the front of an old dented safe.

"Can you get me stockings? I can sell as many of those as you can find me."

Caspian tried to speak, tried to reconnoiter, to catch up to the alien stream of events he'd slipped into. There was a faint snapping sound in his neck, and he realized the man before him was speaking German.

". . . and lingerie, of course. That too I can sell."

The snapping sound echoed, in some interiority of the body, some arcane quarter of it, and he started to come to his senses. He was a German, of course. He had business with this man before him; Herr Heiss was a merchant, and as for himself, he was—Felix.

"There's your money, Felix. I'm grateful." Heiss handed him an envelope filled with bills.

Where was I? thought Felix. What a strange dream, with my eyes wide open. "For just a moment, Heiss, just now, I was a thousand miles away with you. You owned a shop, but everything was gleaming and new."

Heiss frowned sourly. "A thousand miles, yes, it would have to be that far off if it was gleaming and new, for everything in Berlin smells like sulphur bombs and falling plaster dust." He led the way through the stacked cartons. "What about stockings? Can you get me some?"

"French," said Felix. "Awarded *Pour le Mérite,* for daring display." He slipped the envelope into his jacket. "But prices are going up. Things are getting more difficult."

"I understand," said Heiss. "Whenever your shipment arrives, I am here." He opened the back door and Felix stepped into the alleyway behind the store. He walked toward the street. Just before stepping out into it, he adjusted his gray fedora, leaned on his cane, and fell into a practiced limp. In his pocket was a forged draft exemption, along with matching ID card, police registration, and driver's license, everything necessary to allay the suspicions falling on a man not in uniform; it was quality work, but should it be looked at too long, should the watermarks and pigments, seals and signatures be examined by an expert, then, reflected Felix, I will hang by my thumbs from a hook at Gestapo headquarters.

And what an odd dream that was in Heiss's shop, of myself in a far-off land.

The street was glistening from an earlier rain, and the afternoon was cool. His shadow rippled on the wet pavement, the shadow which makes one thoughtful, shadow of a black marketeer. A man could do worse in time of war, much worse; he could be under the boot of a troop sergeant in some godforsaken platoon of some ill-fated infantry regiment, freezing somewhere in Russia while the Führer ate cake in Berlin. He'd rather take his chances outwitting the Gestapo. He crossed Baselerstrasse toward a cigar shop. A trolley bearing a swastika on its side was approaching on Curtiusstrasse. On the windows and doors around the little tree-lined square the blood banners hung. He entered the shop and purchased a paper. Here too the blood banner was displayed, draped upon the awning of the shop; he had to lower his head to pass beneath it as he left, and that was as much recognition as he gave to it.

He continued along the street past the Lichterfelde station. Its windows had little flags stuck in them and patriotic slogans were attached to the glass. Soon little flags would be attached to everyone's forehead. He followed the route of the trolley tracks, around the corner, to where The Weasel was waiting for him, hunched behind the wheel of a car.

The Weasel put it in gear and drove toward him. Felix jumped in; on the visor before him was another forgery, a paper which made of The Weasel a Gestapo agent, on special assignment, signed by Heydrich himself—the sort of paper which, when waved angrily about, would cause the Kripo to quickly withdraw, on the sound principle of not arresting anyone who looks like he might arrest you.

"Heiss liked the goods?"

"Enchanted by them." Felix lit a black market cigar.

In the back seat were boxes bearing a counterfeit seal of Civilian Administration and Supply, and containing French underwear, cognac, and other luxury items.

"Mueller wants to see you," said The Weasel.

"Where?"

"At the café. He'll be there in an hour." The Weasel's features were pointed, his movements sharp and quick, and on occasion, deadly. He'd taught Felix how to survive outside the regime.

Their route took them into the theatre district, where the leading ladies were their regular customers. "It would be a curious thing, wouldn't it," said Felix as The Weasel pulled in at the curb beside the Metropol Theatre, "to die over French underwear."

"People die every hour." The Weasel stared out through the windshield. His eyes were small and cold. His hands, motionless on the wheel, were gloved in black leather. Citizens looked the other way when his gaze fell upon them.

Felix unloaded a box from the back, draped his cane over his arm, and carried the box to the stage door, where he was met by an elderly watchman, to whom he handed the box. "The show will go on."

"They complain of low wages," said the watchman, winking at him, "but they must have their fancy panties." He handed Felix an envelope thick with money. "Fräulein Schaffers is asking for you."

Felix walked on down the stage door corridor, through the familiar shadows of the theatre. Before the war, when he'd been at loose ends, he'd acted there himself, in bit parts, a line or two; he'd had a similar career in films, at the UFA lot at Neubabelsberg, Felix Falkenhayn's face anonymously preserved in a crowd scene in *The Loves of Pharaoh*. Now the backstage gloom received him as an old hand; he remembered his few lines still.

He knocked upon a dressing room door, and entered, greeted by a woman's face, reflected in her lighted mirror. "Why are you leaning on that cane? Did you turn your ankle?"

"My costume for the week. A poor, draft-exempt tubercular, with knee-joint problems."

"And what was it last week?"

"Last week, I was a foreign laborer, suffering from a highly contagious disease. The police hand you back your papers in a hurry when they read that."

"What a scoundrel you are." Fräulein Schaffers smiled into her mirror, as she patted rouge upon her cheek.

"I'm a pacifist, dear Gerta." He put a kiss on the back of her neck. "I don't believe in modern warfare."

"When are you coming back to our revue, Felix dear?" Fräulein Schaffers touched at her ash-blonde hair; it needed dye, the gray roots starting to show, the tint scarce these days, scarce as good underwear; but across the footlights she was ageless, her figure still good. Felix removed a pair of sheer blue stockings, from his inner coat pocket. "Compliments of the house."

He'd been employed part-time in her repertory company, and had been a part-time lover in her life. But as he gazed at her now, as she ran her hand through the sheer stocking and held it admiringly to the light, he had the odd feeling that he knew another Fräulein Schaffers, from some other time and place—and there they'd been friends, and done business, beneath tropic palms. "I'm dreaming as I look at you."

She parted her dressing gown, and slipped the stocking up her smooth, shapely leg. Fastening it to her lace garter, she looked up at him. "You really should return to us, there's a scarcity of leading men."

"I'm a businessman now."

"You had a different quality on stage. I'd never cast you as a businessman."

"Without my business, you'd be going around in army shorts."

"Still I miss you, darling." She returned her hand to her hair; upon her fingers were pieces of costume jewelry. He looked at her hands, which like her gray roots gave away the secret of her age, but her hands too in stagelight were transformed, so that she'd remained the troopers' sweetheart from war to war, and even if Berlin were reduced to rubble, she'd still be singing in its ashes. "I should have been a businesswoman," she said, applying liner to her eyes, and then placing a little red dot in the inside corner of each eye, to make them come alive beneath blue carbon stage lights. "Don't you think I would have been good at it? At least as good as you are?" She sat back, studying the effect, then leaned forward again. "I'm tired of kicking up my legs. I'd like to assist some industry fascist in augmenting his fortune. Know anyone?"

"Stick with your cavalry captains."

"They want to make love with their boots on. I want a pleasant little man in a nightshirt."

He gazed at her, the odd sense returning again, that he knew Gerta Schaffers in some remote time and place, where she was—a businesswoman. He'd dined with her, in tropical surroundings, while a cherub danced in a fountain. "This theatre plays tricks on one's mind. So many scenes must still linger here."

"The old memories—" Her hand closed upon his.

"I must go."

"Yes, go peddle your silk." She pulled her hand away, turned back to her mirror, and he regretted his abruptness. "Certain individuals can't be kept waiting, Gerta, please forgive me."

"Don't get yourself killed," she said, pressing on false eyelashes.

He put his hands on her shoulders. In a time when everyone was spying on their neighbor, Gerta was loyal. "I feel safe in your theatre," he said, bending down, with his lips by her ear. "But I must go."

"Charming brute." She affixed her other eyelash, fluttered them in the mirror, and allowed him to withdraw in good grace, her eyes following him in her mirror as he backed toward the door. He opened it, closed it gently behind him, then traced his way along the dressing room corridor. In the wings of the empty theatre, he paused, inhaling its magic; he stepped out on the big stage into the unlit scenery. He'd had talent, perhaps, but not enough to be exempt in time of war.

He left the theatre, climbed into the seat beside The Weasel, and tossed the money on the dash. It was a small amount to risk one's life for, but both he and The Weasel liked actresses, and they could usually be counted on to hide one in a pinch.

"I saw Gerta."

"How is the old warhorse?"

"She once told me my acting had no passion." He looked at The Weasel. "In place of a heart, she said I had cut crystal."

"I never caught your performance," said The Weasel, pulling into the street.

Felix turned the corner of his fedora down, looked out from underneath the brim, and said, in good English, *"The ghost of Caesar hath appeared to me, two several times by night."*

The Weasel drove carefully through traffic, for they wished no attention upon themselves; should the situation become difficult, there were pistols in the glove compartment and a P-38 under the seat.

"I have passion, goddamnit," said Felix. "What is the woman talking about?"

"The apprenticeship of a good servant is long," said The Weasel. "You never learned her favorite position."

"Gerta's favorite position is next-on-line at the bank teller's window."

The Weasel's eyes went to side mirror, rearview mirror,

back to the street, in a regular, constant round. "Gondolph is making us a new document. It's a copy of something called Assistance with the Defense of Berlin. Whoever holds it is guaranteed cooperation from Party, police, and Gestapo."

"In childhood," said Felix, gazing out the side window, "I was fascinated by dragonflies. Their wings are the most delicate thing in the world. The quick and slender bug—" Felix gestured with his hand. "—hovering in the sunlight of a summer day."

"I was raised a Protestant," said The Weasel.

"No army, no empire ever held the perfection of a dragonfly. A great truth, my Weasel."

"The Gestapo on Prinz Albrechtstrasse have a new device. It sends an electric current from penis to anus. That is a greater truth."

Felix tipped his hat back, showing his high, handsome forehead. "A bug, hovering over a pond, its wings quivering with the faintest hum—"

"A broom handle, inserted in your rectum, by the Gestapo chief in Milan." The Weasel turned onto Motzstrasse. The neighborhood was a seedy one—cabarets, dance bars, cafés. The Weasel drove a ways, then pulled up at the curb. "Remember to tell Mueller he owes us two-thousand marks."

Felix stepped out, cane in hand, pistol in pocket, and limped toward the doorway of a cabaret. He entered, glanced around. Here too the blood banner hung, swastika draped over the bar piano. All tables were empty save one, at which an army officer sat; he was portly and jovial, his round paunch resting against the edge of the table. The medals on his chest showed him to be an Old Fighter, his party number low; they'd met in Vienna years ago, at a meeting of a mystical outfit called the Luminous Lodge, which had proved too religious for Felix; he'd thought it was going to be a society of stage magicians. But he'd kept in touch with Mueller, and since that time, Mueller had risen in politics and war, and made a fortune in the piracy of private property. His second fortune was being made in the black market, with the assistance of Felix and The Weasel.

"They always empty the place when you're here?" Felix sat down beside him.

Mueller's smile broadened. "In return I refrain from carrying them off in the night." He chuckled. "But you should come here in the evening. The show is most amusing, dear boy."

Felix saw the owner pulling the doorshade down and turning the CLOSED sign outward. This was done in a silence so deliberate, so frightened, it seemed metaphysical.

"Now," said Colonel Mueller, tapping Felix gently on the wrist, "I have a new proposition for you."

"Parisian silk? With satin fringe?"

"Coarse German wool. A warm green, which fades to gray." He lifted his cap, spun it slowly on his finger. "You must leave Civilian Administration and Supply, you are too visible. I have a much better place for you on my staff. There are other objects at my disposal now, worth more than silk underwear, though of course—" He smiled. "—we know such things are priceless."

"Sorry," said Felix, "the army is not my goal." He pushed his chair back and started to rise. "And you owe us two thousand marks."

"Oh, sit down." Mueller shook his head with a smile of exasperation. "The world is falling apart, have you forgotten? There will soon be no more Germany and the wise are making plans accordingly, by doing a little business. I'm doing a little more than most, and I need you in uniform, so you can move freely." He lifted his wine glass. "Do you want to escape all this—" He nodded to the red banner over the piano. "—a rich man? Or an underwear salesman?" He signaled the owner, who brought another glass in haste, placing it down with the same air of gravity that had sealed the cabaret, as if he were a spectre removed from any possibility of overhearing or understanding the words spoken at the table.

Felix studied his host, who, in his field gray uniform reminded him of a blood-swollen tarantula. A spider who dined on—dragonflies? But it requires a strong web to catch that swift flier, and even when caught it is capable of fanning its wings and breaking free. "You could fix me up with an officer's stripe?"

"You shall have a meteoric rise through the ranks."

"And The Weasel?"

"I could not bring him into the circles to which I shall introduce you. Our Weasel, delightful though he may be, must remain where he is." Mueller finished his drink, and rose. "You won't have to go around posing as a blind man with a cane."

The owner of the cabaret hurried before him toward the door, to open it, close it, put a brick through it, whatever his guest might desire. Felix accompanied the colonel into the street, where his limousine had arrived. The sunlight broke the afternoon clouds; a pale yellow wash came across the colonel's form, as if a projectile of gas had exploded nearby. Felix looked around; the street was pale yellow and all motion had stopped.

He looked back at the colonel and saw the colonel's face and body frozen in grimace and gesture, as if time had ceased in that instant; he read with clarity the colonel's eyes, seeing every nuance of his greed and wile, along with his indigestion, lust, fatalism, and private pockets of ignorance, and fear; all of this was in the frozen face which gazed out inanimate from behind the thin yellow veil.

Felix turned, and now his was the only figure moving in a petrified landscape. His movement made the yellow veil quiver, causing a ripple to move along the street with a faint whispering sound, which was, he realized, the magnified sound of the sleeve of his coat in motion. All else in the world was silence.

His body suffered a jolt at the core; he'd known such a moment long ago, while watching at the edge of a pond as the dragonfly hovered in stillness above it, and he'd become the all-seeing bug itself. Now, upon Motzstrasse, once more the world had stopped, and he was again the dragonfly.

A second jolt hit Felix's body; time was resuming its march, the street was being reborn.

". . . I think they hired the director from the construction crew.

As insecure as they come. They took him away in an ambulance suffering from the last stages of St. Vitus Dance. Walk this way, David, there's another shop I want to visit . . ."

Caspian was staring at Victor Quatrelle, who, a moment before had been on a street in Berlin, in a lost dimension, a colonel in the German army.

"Where the hell are we?"

"In Emerald City," replied Quatrelle. "Where they put real stuffing in the teddy bears. What's wrong? Too much snow? Edwardo's cut is very pure."

"What were we talking about?"

"How should I know, call the continuity person, have her check the script." Quatrelle strode along, large, whale-like, down Rodeo Drive, Caspian beside him, gazing sideways at his own reflection in a shop window, making sure who he was.

Doctor Gaillard's office was in his home on top of Gloaming Way. His office window looked out on the green, sloping valley, where here and there the peaks of other roofs rose up from the thick vegetation. His office walls held large brush-painted Chinese panels; on the mantelpiece were statues of Egyptian gods. A pair of armchairs faced each other across a low round table at which he and Caspian sat. Eyes closed, head lowered in concentration, he listened to Caspian's tale.

"He's smooth," said Caspian. "An operator. But he's slightly off center. He doesn't fit in. You know, his dragonfly thing."

"Yes, the dragonfly." Gaillard spoke softly, placing his fingertips to the bridge of his nose. "Large compound eyes. Necessary for a predatory insect that captures its victims on the wing."

"Meaning?"

"No meaning. Just a footnote." Gaillard opened his fingertips, smiled. "Go on."

"He's a Berliner, a good-timer. The war crossed him up, but he's taking advantage of it."

"And what sort of feelings does he have?"

"About women?"

"About anything."

"He's a guy living in Nazi Germany. That's a pretty special feeling all its own."

"Yes, it is. What's relevant in it for you?"

"Relevant? What's relevant is that I *wind up there.*" Caspian leaned forward, traced his finger along the circular edge of the table. "What's relevant is that I lose real time. I go through the looking glass. Alice down the rabbit hole. That's what's relevant, singularly relevant."

Gaillard closed his eyes, and fell silent. He was tall, lean, with a hawkish profile, his nose strong and sharply arched. A drunken Chinese sage staggered through moonlight on the wall panel behind him. To his left was a bookcase, holding books whose spines were old and worn. He opened his eyes again. "Tell me more about Felix. Do you admire him?"

"Not particularly. But he seems to have brains."

"Go on."

"Felix is having his problem too. Because his world stopped, on a street in Berlin. Suddenly he was in the waxworks."

"Felix had a similar—lapse."

"During which I broke free. But until that lapse I was walking around in his body. I'd completely forgotten myself. His identity was uppermost, and I was like some nagging little thought far in the back of his mind."

"And what did you learn from being Felix?"

"That there's somebody else who's broken through the veil. That Felix Falkenhayn, a Berliner who lived during the war, broke through time. And his form connected with mine."

"And why are you the only two people in the world who know this?"

"There's always somebody who sees things first. Galileo. Newton. Lenny Bruce. You've gotta suffer if you want to play the trombone."

Caspian traced his finger along the circular edge of the table again. "You're suggesting I'm caught in a delusional system. Fine, I'll buy that. Just get me out of it."

"The way out of it might be to go through it."

"That's why you want to know what Felix means to me. But he doesn't mean anything, really. He's like a million other guys walking around L.A. trying to hustle a dream." Caspian paused, was himself silent for a moment. "Do you believe that Felix is real?"

"It doesn't matter. The point is—what does he hold for you that you must know?"

"I have two answers to that. The first one is that Felix and I, decades apart, discovered one of the fundamental equations about time. The second is that Felix and I are the two halves of a split personality, and we hold nothing for each other except terror. Every exchange with him is self-destruction."

"Both those views are extreme. Let's work for middle ground."

"Which is?"

"That something psychological has spoken in you. Tell me more about Felix."

"He's capable of murder. That goes with the war."

"You find this an attractive quality?"

"Useful, perhaps."

"Go on."

"What strikes me most is the similarity of his childhood to mine. He suffered reality loss. While watching his dragonflies. The world just slipped away."

"Tell me some more about your own childhood. You had the trauma with penicillin. What else?"

"I was always an actor. I acted sick, and managed to stay home sixty days out of every school year. I'd play on my bed with my soldiers, and the battles would take me out, so far out

I seemed to be over the clouds. I'd be shocked when I heard my father coming home; the day'd gone by without my even noticing it."

"Go on."

"And I invented a friend. I used to talk to him—in the mirror."

"Who was he?"

"He had my reflection, but he was different from me. I told him about things in my life, and he told me about things in mirror-land, where everything was in reverse. It was just silly kid stuff. I'd tell him I batted right-handed, and he'd tell me he batted left-handed. And then we'd take a batting stance and I'd see it was true, he was left-handed. It gave me a strange satisfaction, to know about this land. If my parents were around, and I caught a glimpse of the dining room mirror, my friend would be looking back, and we'd exchange secret smiles."

"And now your friend has returned."

"Except he's not my friend." Caspian leaned forward again, his eyes narrowing as he gazed at Gaillard. "Your manner is completely professional, Doctor, and I'm reassured by it, but you can't have had many patients who fell into the fourth dimension, can you?"

A clock chimed in the hall. Doctor Gaillard rose slowly from his chair. "You'd be surprised at the places people fall into."

*   *   *

Ramona Guazu, the Caspian maid, was walking toward her boyfriend's car at the foot of the driveway; she had finished work for the week and, as always, Nino Carillo had come for her. He was a small, slightly built man, in dark sunglasses. "A criminal," said Carol Caspian, quietly, seated with her husband in the garden. "He offered to get me Valium at a discount."

"Always treat him well," said Caspian.

"I worry about Ramona."

"I'm sure Nino is very protective of her."

"Nino is probably the one who hocks my diamond earrings."

"You always get them back."

"But I wonder whose lobes they've been in."

"They haven't been in anyone's lobes, they've been in the pawn shop."

"Look at him," said Carol, as Nino Carillo stepped out of the car and came around the front of it to open the door for Ramona. "He has such a sinister way of moving. Like some feral creature."

"He's careful, that's all."

"I think you actually like the little creep," said Carol.

"A person like Nino could be handy to know someday."

"Yes, if we need to murder anyone." Carol tilted her head thoughtfully. "Which is always a possibility." She lifted her arm and gave Nino a friendly wave. He waved back, removing his sunglasses. His beady eyes squinted toward them.

"I know him," said Caspian.

"Of course you know him. It's Nino."

"No, I know him from somewhere else."

"The donkey act in Club Tijuana?"

Caspian stared at Nino Carillo, as the gangster slowly raised his sunglasses. A faint popping noise sounded in Caspian's ear, and the camera of his soul rushed to a closeup of Nino Carillo's face.

The smile was frozen, the little black eyes gleaming like marbles. Felix gazed at The Weasel, wondering about the peculiar attack of *déjà vu* he'd just had—The Weasel's head tilted just this way, his smile just so, and behind him palm trees, he and The Weasel in that tropic land together.

"I've had strange dreams lately," said Felix, as they got into their car.

"I never dream," said The Weasel, putting the car in gear.

"Never?" said Felix. "Too bad. There are doorways in dreams."

"I had a dream once," said The Weasel. "When I was young." He drove along Hermann Göringstrasse, past the SS barracks on the corner.

"One dream? That's all? In an entire life?"

"One is enough," said The Weasel. His hands were sheathed in black gloves. His overcoat was black, like Felix's, and their trousers too were black, to match their suit jackets; each wore a plain, somber tie against a plain white shirt. The Weasel drove carefully, slowly, along Hermann Göringstrasse, in traffic that might have seemed normal, except for the occasional dispatch rider on motorcycle, or armored personnel carrier.

"Mueller has offered me a commission. I could be a senior officer tomorrow."

"You can carry a wooden ruler marked Blood and Honor."

"He made it sound attractive. Of course I won't do it."

"Of course," said The Weasel.

They turned, to smaller streets, heading east. The Weasel told Felix his one dream.

"It is that of an antisocial malfactor," said Felix.

"I keep it always near my heart," said The Weasel, coldly, softly, as he sent the steering wheel through his gloved hands.

They entered Lichtenberg, a worker's neighborhood, the street lined with small shops on both sides. The Weasel nodded. "There it is." He pulled in behind a long, black hearse. He and Felix climbed out, and walked toward it.

"A No Parking zone," said The Weasel with a smile. "But no ticket on the windshield." He nodded toward the coffin inside. "The dead are left alone."

He and Felix climbed in. The Weasel started up the hearse and pulled into the street. The lid of the coffin lifted, and the corpse sat up. "It's comfortable, but time passes slowly."

"We should have given you a magazine," said Felix.

The corpse rubbed the back of his neck. He was a large, robust man, dressed in a winter jacket and hiking boots. "I must stretch my limbs or I'll never make it. Can you stop somewhere?"

The Weasel looked in the rearview mirror, turned the hearse into a side street of the district, free of shops. He pulled in at the curb. "Make it fast."

"Much obliged to you." The corpse climbed out of the coffin and Felix hurried around to open the back door. The corpse jumped down, and moved briskly in place on the sidewalk. "Everything's in knots."

Felix looked up and down the street, then saw a young boy staring at them from the entrance to an alleyway; the boy's mouth was open, his eyes bulging in horror as he watched the corpse dance around in back of the open hearse. Felix walked over to the child, and pointed to the stretching, bouncing corpse. "They didn't put enough embalming fluid in him. Understand?"

The boy's eyes bulged further. His knees were shaking. Felix leaned closer to him. "Want to help us hold him down?"

The child bolted, and Felix waved the corpse back into the hearse. He jumped in after him and closed the door from the inside as The Weasel drove off. "That will have to hold you. Now—" Felix tapped the soft lining of the coffin. "It's filled with food. Just tear through to it. Also water. You'll be in the box for forty-eight hours." He knelt beside the coffin, the corpse kneeling with him, nodding his head at every word. Felix opened his coat, removed a sheaf of papers, which he handed to the corpse. "You and your coffin will be carried off the train at Überlingen, and taken to a place where you can cross the border on foot." He handed the corpse a Luger and ammunition. "Clear?"

"Quite."

"Into the box, then, I've got to screw you down."

The corpse looked morosely at Felix, and then climbed back into the satin folds of the coffin.

"Before you close that—" said The Weasel.

The corpse sat up again. "Yes, of course, here you are."

He reached into a corner of the coffin and withdrew a small sack. "Gold napoleans. It's all there. I'm grateful." He lay back inside and Felix proceeded to screw the lid of the coffin down. Upon finishing, he brought his hand to a piece of brass filigree work fastened near the head of the coffin. He pulled it and a small, square section of the coffin lid flopped open on tiny, invisible hinges. "Open this when you run out of air," he said down into the dark hole, from which two eyes were staring out.

"I'm losing my nerve."

"The Gestapo has devised new uses for the simple soldering iron," said Felix. "First they insert it in your nose."

Two fingers reached up through the small opening and drew shut the tiny lid.

Felix crawled up into the front seat beside The Weasel. "Who is this fellow?"

"Chemist, I. G. Farben. He opened his yap."

Felix turned around and rapped on the coffin lid. "You should have learned to juggle. And to talk without saying anything."

A muffled comment came from within the coffin. The Weasel drove on, back through the outlying districts into the heart of Berlin, to the railway station. "You know," said Felix, gazing over at The Weasel's small, deadly calm figure dressed in black, "you should have been an undertaker."

"Instead," said The Weasel, drawing a gloved finger across his throat, "I work as the middleman." He brought the hearse around to the side of the station, to the freight reception area. The coffin was unloaded by the Reichsbahn crew with practiced efficiency, onto a dolly, and wheeled to the platform, Felix and The Weasel walking beside it. "There are a great many soldiers here today," said Felix.

"Heydrich's passing through," said one of the workers. "He'll be boarding the same train as your stiff." The worker nodded to the coffin, and Felix looked at The Weasel. The platform was swarming with Field Security Police, SS, and Gestapo. "We're going to be stopped," Felix said in a whisper to The Weasel.

"Just remember, you're a Bavarian crook." The Weasel's little eyes narrowed further at his little joke, the corners crinkling up, and Felix felt that what chance they had was all in the little man's unperturbable manner. Which, reflected Felix, comes of having had only one dream in his entire life.

They accompanied the coffin to the freight section of the train. The Weasel presented the conductor with ticket, death certificate, travel permit, and a letter bearing the forged signature of Himmler, for extra measure. The conductor nodded and waved the crew aboard with the coffin. Felix and The Weasel turned, to face black leather overcoats—an inspector from the Gestapo, and two of his assistants. "Papers, gentlemen."

Felix and The Weasel handed over their identity cards, police registration, labor registration, and driver's licenses. The inspector examined them carefully, as Felix watched the current of human traffic making a wide detour around the little gathering. Beyond them, the soldiers and officers of the SS were making their own fuss, in preparation for Heydrich's arrival.

The Weasel had gone on the offensive. "Herr Kriminalrat, we have just had the honor of carrying a hero to his final transport. Our firm is an old and honored one. I should like to extend to you any professional help you might need."

"I?" said the inspector. "I have no dead to bury."

"One never knows," said The Weasel, in cold, funereal voice. "His Angels are everywhere."

The inspector looked closely at The Weasel, who gazed back at him with eyes like dead oysters, eyes that seemed to measure one for a coffin. "Our firm has assisted at many funerals of State. Permit me to show you a commendation we received from Deputy Führer Hess regarding our service to him at the time of his father's decease."

God help us, thought Felix, as The Weasel reached into

his jacket pocket for a paper Felix knew was not there—but the inspector had already shoved the original papers forward, back to The Weasel. "That won't be necessary." He turned to Felix. "Why are you not in uniform?"

Felix bent down and rapped on the spare ammunition clips strapped to his shin. "Artificial limb, Herr Kriminalrat." He straightened slowly, his eyes on the platform steps, beneath which he'd have momentary cover, while he heaved the stick grenade that hung inside his topcoat. "Also a rotting lung, sir. Tubercular, I'm afraid." Felix coughed, moistly, toward the inspector, who narrowed his eyes suspiciously but nonetheless drew back.

The space between them widened. The Weasel removed his black derby hat and performed a solemn, funeral director's bow. The Gestapo inspector turned away abruptly, with his two assistants, to look for less complicated prey. The Weasel replaced his hat, and watched the Gestapo team walk off. "That was Olsommer. Does a good business in black market himself. On a dark night, I once sold him a truckload of butter at five hundred marks a pound." The Weasel walked on, back to the hearse, as the motorcade bearing Reichsprotektor Heydrich appeared at the front of the station.

"I'm taking Mueller's offer," said Felix.

"As you wish."

"There's more money, and less risk."

"You'll eat cream pie every night," said The Weasel softly, as they reached the hearse.

Felix looked across the hood at his colleague. From the railroad platform orders were being barked out, as the way was cleared for Heydrich. The Weasel turned his head, and the angle, the light, the color of the sky, all combined to produce that *déjà vu* in Felix concerning the tropic land.

". . . anything you want, Mr. Caspian, you understand?" Nino Carillo's thin, cold smile was unchanging. "How much acid can one man lick, right?" He opened the door to his car, in which Ramona the maid was already seated. Carillo slipped behind the wheel, his small, wiry frame graceful, each of his movements precisely made. He backed the car around, and pulled away, leaving Caspian standing mutely in the drive, as Carol came forward, suspicion in her voice. "What were you talking to him about? You're not buying controlled substances from that creature, are you?"

Caspian turned toward her, his reality slowly putting itself back together. "I—was in Berlin."

"You'll be in jail if you take up with Nino. David, did you just medicate yourself with him, you look terrible."

"I was on the bench back there with you, wasn't I? How did I get here on the drive with Nino?"

"Oh god, he did give you something. Your color is awful."

He breathed deeply, tilted his head back slowly. "Carol, very weird things have been happening to me lately."

"You're not drugged?"

"I'm—I'm trapped in time."

"You're on Cold Canyon Road. People never get trapped in time here. There's zoning against it."

*　　*　　*

The party goers had gathered at Julius DeBrusca's house, within the gated colony of Malibu. Caspian stood near the hot tub in Julius's massive den, knowing no one must sit in it, for DeBrusca was sensitive about who shared his waters.

". . . been suing me for years," DeBrusca was saying to Myron Fish, from his white plush lounge near the empty bubbling tub. "The last appeal was reversed. They win, I win, meanwhile my lawyer's looking at *yachts.*"

Seated on the bench alongside the hot tub was Roma French, whom DeBrusca had just signed to play the female lead in *Star Rover.* Beside her was her latest lover, an eighteen-game winner for the Dodgers. His pitching hand was dangling in the Jacuzzi. Carol Caspian, standing next to her husband, frowned at the hand in the water, and said softly, "Doesn't he know about Julius's rule?"

Roma wore an orange batik dress that left a shoulder bare and then wrapped tightly around her breasts. Caspian had seen her in only one film, where she'd had her blouse torn off; he'd forgotten the point of the film, but he'd never forget Roma.

"She's only twenty years younger than you are," murmured Carol. "Did you see what happened to the last older man she took up with?" Carol pointed to one of DeBrusca's Roman statues—a headless, limbless torso. "That's all that's left of him."

The studio vice-president in charge of advertising and promotion who'd drunk himself into a stupor at Caspian's party was drinking himself into a stupor at this one, and approached, a drink in each hand. "I wish I were home building furniture."

"Could you make us a nice transitional Queen Anne Chippendale side chair?" asked Carol.

"I worked with Armas on *The Man From Planet X*. I told him he'd made a fine exploitation sci-fi flick. He said was I kidding? Didn't I understand? *The Man From Planet X* is *Jules and Jim*." The studio executive swayed, sipped from one glass, then the other. "Isn't that obvious? *Jules and Jim?*" He sighed and gazed around the room, his baggy eyes resting on a gray-haired man standing by DeBrusca's fireplace. "That was once the hottest agent in this town. Now he runs a restaurant. I never go there, I'm afraid I'd be eating one of his old clients."

The studio executive blinked slowly, burped quietly, and shuffled off to say a few words to Roma. She eluded him with the grace of a matador, and he found himself wandering in empty space, while Roma came toward Caspian. "I'm so glad we'll be working together."

"Pleasure's mine," said Caspian. "I've seen everything you've done."

"You'll love acting with David," said Carol. "He knows four kinds of hand kissing. On the wrist, up the sleeve, turn it over—"

Roma gave her a quizzical glance, then continued on her

way across the room. Carol watched the rolling contour of her perfectly sculpted hips. "She's just a little large across the beam."

"Yes," agreed Caspian quickly, "she'll soon need two chairs to sit on."

"Thank you, darling." Carol smoothed down the collar of his shirt. "You'll be spending two months on location with her."

"Adultery is not one of the movie's themes."

"It's one of Roma's themes." Carol turned toward the lonesome Dodger, who now had his pitching elbow submerged in the churning water. "I'm going to ask him to tell me some locker-room secrets," said Carol, and walked toward him. Caspian watched her sit down beside the ballplayer, and suspected the young man was going to have a confusing next few minutes. He began his own trek through the mansion, circling among the other guests, and continuing on out of the great den and into the sprawling living room, where more of the party had gathered, including a number of starlets who were destined for small parts in *Star Rover*. Roma would have a $100,000 dressing room van and they would have something resembling a Port-o-San. One of them broke from the group, and stepped in front of him. "Hi, I'm Selena Silvi, I hope you don't mind me introducing myself."

"How could I mind?"

"I've seen all your pictures. You're a first-class actor. I've only got a small part in this one but I don't care."

"Keep beating the door down."

"Actually I'm into other things."

"Such as?"

"Tarot, astrology, pendulums. I think they've helped me get ahead."

"Good photographs will help you more."

"I know you're right. But if I'm going to make it I will, and if not—"

"—then you need a better agent. It's been nice talking

with you, Selena. I've got to get back to my wife, she's in the next room with a coked-up ballplayer. Good luck in your role."

"Hey, don't run away, I want to look in your eyes. I get messages from people's eyes."

Her own eyes became almost expressionless; but underneath, he could see the flicker of psychosis. She stared at him, her gaze as unrelated as the attentions of a snake. Then suddenly, her eyes snapped back to normal. "Say, you're into some very heavy stuff, aren't you. Wow, I never would have guessed. I thought you were just another dumb star."

"What did you see?"

"Well, I mean *evil,* you know? Do you know what kind of toads are running around in you?"

"Maybe."

"I'm impressed. What are you, a warlock?"

"No, just a dumb star." He walked on by her, out of the living room, and entered another wing of the house. Selena Silvi had put him into anxiety; he felt as if something was chewing on the inside of his chest.

Slow down, you're all right, you've had a few drinks, you're a little bombed, that's all. Look at the nice pictures on Julius's wall.

The long hall held a major part of the DeBrusca art collection—Picasso, Chagall, Degas. He thought of Julius strolling by them, a bicarbonate of soda in his hand.

At the end of the hall was a rose mirror, reflecting the distant living room in its coppery depths—where Roma French had established herself now, with her court around her—ballplayer, hairdresser, business manager, and a lawyer prepared to sue the angelfish in the adjacent bowl should it prove necessary.

Roma's image was burnished copper, and he was suddenly aware that she had another identity in the mirror's depths, which shimmered before him, rose-colored, undulating. Like the mirrors of his childhood, it contained a secret. He was slipping, could feel the crack opening in himself. Terror gripped him, as he found himself looking at a dragonfly. It flew over a coppery lake, its flight beckoning him, and he was forced to follow.

"Your friend Marla is waiting for you," said the host at the cabaret, and pointed down a long row of tables to where Marla sat in shadow, her legs crossed, a drink on the table before her.

Roma, whispered a voice in Felix's mind, and he wondered at the odd dissociation he'd just felt, of having disappeared and gone to the tropical city. I walked there, and spoke with people. We were at a party together, and Marla was another woman, unknown, from that tropic land. One thinks of things, marvelous things, but then they are gone, like the dragonfly.

Marla had not yet seen him, and he decided to let her wait a little longer, to flare her temper into the old-remembered form. He walked toward the bar, through the sweep of a coppery stage light; on stage, a young woman was performing a naked *tableau vivant* with a Grecian harp. Smoke gathered in the spotlight beam, so that she seemed to wander in mist, while at the far end of the stage a three-piece band dully thumped out her theme, indifferent to her naked artistry.

The bar was occupied mostly by women, several of whom had voices oddly deep. "Felix, I must have new stockings, look . . ." The deep-voiced woman lifted her dress, revealing torn nylons upon a calf like a drill sergeant's. "Do you have something for me?"

"You, my friend, are the bravest man in Berlin." Felix tipped his hat to the woman.

"Because of my costume? Because I love to dance?" The deep-voiced woman laughed. "Do you know what we call Deputy Führer Hess? He's our very own Fräulein Anna. He's one of us, my darling."

"Even so," said Felix, "you're asking for a one-way ticket to a health camp. You ought to go to Paris."

"And leave my beautiful Berlin? My favorite haunts? Lehrterstrasse, by the football field? The times I've had there. Not to mention the Hitler Youth Hostel on Prenzlauer."

"Someone will turn you in, and we shall mark your empty place at the bar." Felix removed a package from his pocket and gave it to the queen, who slipped him some bills. "You're a pal, Felix. If you ever need a favor from my side of town—" She put the package under her arm and sauntered with it toward the ladies room to change.

Felix turned toward the stage. The naked artist now pantomimed wading with her harp into a stream. The illusion was given depth by the drummer overturning his beer stein and flooding her part of the stage.

Felix put his gray fedora on the bar, its brim illuminated for a moment by the traveling spotlight beam that followed the naked girl's progress on stage. He turned his gaze toward the door of the cabaret. Through it came the regular denizens of war, love, crime, and bizarre theatricals. He saw Colonel Mueller's limousine arrive, and his silhouette in the street as he stepped from the car. The colonel waved the driver on, the limousine vanished, and then the colonel too was gone, into the shadows of the street.

Felix finished his drink and crossed the cabaret floor, toward Marla's table. She seemed at home in the cabaret of souls whose identities, for whatever reasons, were elusive. She'd removed her beret, and let loose her long auburn waves. The coppery rose spotlight swept over her, momentarily highlighting her perfect profile. She'd taken the night off from the chorus line at the Scala, so that he might put her on to something good, but he saw she had become suspicious.

"Well," she said, as he approached, "what dirty business have you been up to?" Her suit was shiny blue, with a red silk blouse beneath it, a soft sheen following the shape of her bust as she opened the jacket. She leaned back, putting an elbow on the low backrest of the chair, her breasts outlined for an instant as the stage spot swept by again, shining through the thin silk.

"You attract the light," he said, putting his hand through its smoky beam.

She swiveled sideways, uncrossing her legs, and he noted that her stockings bore the elusive charm of a run along both calves, disappearing up under her skirt. Her shoes too were worn, the low heels rounded and the leather wrinkled at the toes. As if sensing his appraisal, she put her hand to her hair, fluffing it out, for it at least was in full repair. "You've already kept me waiting," she said.

"I can get you out of the chorus line."

"Into what?" Absentmindedly, she traced the run in her stocking with her fingernail, an unconscious gauge of her fortune.

"I have a friend who's interested in your working for him."

"What sort of pig is he?" Marla opened her purse, removed a cigarette from her pack.

"He can do more for you than anyone else you are liable to meet at this hour."

"What will I have to do to entertain him?"

Felix lit a match on his thumbnail and held it out to her. "I'm not a pimp. This is government business."

He called the waiter, ordering a Berliner Weisse for himself and Marla. "Beer with a dash of raspberry syrup, Marla— we drank it on our Sunday picnic in the forests of Grunewald."

"Could that have been us?" Marla raised a brow; she was hard, like the arching line penciled above her eye. Once, recalled Felix, we were quite different; once we trusted in the world; once we trusted each other. Now we are indifferent insects, coldly carapaced.

The waiter set two sturdy bowl-like glasses down, the drinks topped with red foam, penetrated by a pair of straws. Felix sipped his, nodded appreciatively; the waiter had remained at his elbow and now leaned down, speaking softly. "The colonel will see you backstage. There is a room there. Half an hour."

Felix nodded, still sipping his beer, the taste returning him to those Sundays with Marla in the sandy forests and the parks. They'd wandered together in the crowds, in the sunlight.

"Watch," he said, pointing toward the cabaret stage, "here comes the tasteful end." The naked nymph was concluding her act, closing the curtains around herself, leaving only her round *derrière* visible. A moment later it vanished, to scattered applause.

"You come here every night for that?" Marla gave him a wry smile. He returned it, and put his hand gently on hers. "Didn't we get engaged on one of those Sundays?"

"We may have. But those two people are gone." Marla idly turned a bracelet on her arm. "They've vanished forever into their Sunday. To the place where all happy times go."

"You're just what my friend is looking for."

"And why is that?"

"Because you know you're alone. There is only Marla. A dark and poignant secret."

"You talk like an underwear salesman."

"Fine French lace." He lit a cigarette. "Through it all is revealed."

The curtains on stage parted, and the next performer stepped out, a heavyset creature with a long flowing wig and a bosom enormously padded. She asked the drunken drummer if he needed a crutch to keep him upright, to which he replied with a drum-roll. The performer stepped forward, her bare legs showing the same muscular development as the half-women at the bar. The drummer slipped off his stool, and collapsed on the floor; the performance was momentarily interrupted while his colleagues revived him with a pitcher of water in the face.

Felix smiled, and turned back to Marla. "The dragonfly, ever seen one? Such a beautiful insect. A bright blue livery—" He ran his finger along the shiny blue collar of her suit, and onto her red silk blouse. "—on a fiery red ground. But within just a few hours of death, all their beauty is gone and they turn a dull brown."

"Well, then I'll look like a storm trooper, won't I," she said, flatly, and he saw that she'd already made certain adjustments of her own concerning the game of war.

"My friend is an army colonel. Uniforms jump when he shouts at them. Use your head and you'll soon be enjoying many privileges."

"I don't like soldiers."

"The world belongs to them at the moment."

"The world belongs to chaos." She laid a lock of hair over her small, perfectly shaped ear. "How have you managed to escape a uniform, by the way?"

"It has not been easy."

"No patriotism in you, Felix?"

"Not a scrap. These armies are just grinding noises heard in the dark."

Marla raised her glass to her lips. "This colonel, he runs your underwear business?"

"Don't despise it, Göring himself buys truckloads of nylons. Everyone is doing business if they can. Official vehicles deliver an extraordinary number of geese and ducks to generals' doors." Smoke poured from his flaring nostrils. "There are art objects, important pieces floating around. And big industrial contracts."

He studied her face for some reaction, for any sign of weakness. But she was calm, and indifferent. She set down her empty glass. "Does your colonel know anyone in films?"

"Don't aspire to act in any of the films they're making now. No one will ever want to see your face again when the war is over."

The door of the cabaret opened again, and some *landsers* entered, hobnail boots clattering on the floor. They had seen the front, and their manner was wild. Men who know they're already dead, thought Felix; the best of soldiers. He watched them stagger toward a table, and felt their wolfish power. He turned his gaze back to Marla, who was maintaining her cautious scrutiny of him. He smiled at her. "You'll be valuable to the firm, Marla. There are two-hundred thousand pairs of shoes to be sold."

"I'm an actress, not a shoehorn."

Exasperating woman, reflected Felix to himself.

On stage, the jovial chanteuse was displaying her rolls of sausage, body naked except for a great brassiere and a garish pair of panties. Coyly, she began to drop the garment, but at the climactic moment the spotlight went out. Catcalls increased, except from the bar, where several ladies with shadowed chins were clapping.

"You're a sublime actress, Marla. Cruel fate alone has caused you to be overlooked and consigned to kicking up your heels at the Scala. But your guardian angel Felix has come to your rescue."

"Do you know anyone in the Propaganda Ministry?" asked Marla. "There's lots of work for an actress there."

"You can hold a golden torch." Felix snuffed his cigarette out in the ashtray.

"The dream dies hard."

"I prowled the UFA lot too," said Felix, removing his fedora and gently creasing the crown. "I wanted to be a citizen of that dream world. One afternoon I played a Teutonic knight in a tin suit in which I nearly suffocated."

The waiter signaled him, toward a doorway at the rear of the club. He rose and led Marla across the floor, through the smoky light, and for an instant he felt they had reached the realms of Pluto. The *landsers'* loud voices were near, death in them; glasses tinkled, the band played off-key.

The waiter nodded down the hall toward a dressing room. They walked to it and Felix knocked lightly on the door.

The colonel opened it with a smile, welcoming them into

a room filled with old bedraggled costumes—magician's capes, magisterial wigs, dusty tophats. "Nothing grand, my friends, but a poignant charm nonetheless. Here the illusions we adore assemble themselves. Marla, how exquisite you are, even more beautiful than I had judged with my opera glasses at the Scala."

"What is your interest in me, Colonel?" She looked at her watch. "I am due back at the theatre—"

"Well, then, before you rush off, please accept this little pledge from me—and my firm." Mueller reached down to a dressing table, from which he removed a small black box. With a slight bow, he handed it to her. Marla opened the box, her eyes softening at its contents—pearls, a diamond clip, a necklace of sapphires. She looked from the jewels to him, and back again to the plush-lined box. "You have employment for me?"

The colonel picked his riding crop off the table, flicked it against his boot. "Some shoes, a thousand tons of tea, one thing and another." He took a card from his pocket, handed it to her. "On the hills east of town, this address, tomorrow night."

She put it, and the jewel box, in her purse. "I must return to the theatre now."

"My limousine will take you," said the colonel, stepping with her to the door. He took her hand, kissed it lightly. She cast a look at Felix, and then was gone, down the backstage hall.

"Well," said Mueller, "she will be right, I think."

"She'll play her part."

"One would think her father was a baron, not a pants' maker."

"You've done your research."

"It is the style nowadays. You yourself, my dear boy—" Mueller took a folded document from his breast pocket and handed it to Felix. "—now have Aryan blood guaranteed uncontaminated back to 1750."

"And I have no intention of spilling it for the Fatherland."

"Have I asked for sacrifice? But pay attention—" Mueller

picked his gloves up from the table, drew them carefully on, one finger at a time. "For what we are engaged in now we can be put against a wall."

"You'll find no one more careful than I."

"Oh, there's always someone. Let us trust his path never crosses ours."

The colonel bumped a low-hanging bulb with his head, and the dressing room mirror flashed with the reflected, swinging light. Felix heard a dragonfly's wings, and with a jolt he saw the depths of the mirror turn coppery. And standing in that coppery world, gazing back at him, as if across a ghostly distance, was Marla.

He reached for the light bulb, to stop its swing, but his hand passed through it. And Marla was joined in the mirror by an entourage of men and women, and she had changed, was regal, a leading lady at last, with clothes and wealth and her name was . . .

. . . *Roma* . . .

Caspian swayed in the hallway, beneath a cubist painting, of a guitar, disassembled by the painter's eye. Roma French was gazing at him, from the end of the hall. He looked at his hands; a coppery wash was vanishing from them. When his eyes met Roma's again, he felt their souls were like an old photograph taken in a dream, on a Sunday afternoon in Germany . . . drinking beer in the park . . . with a swirl of raspberry in it.

"But why am I going to Nazi Germany?" Caspian sat across from Gaillard, the morning sunlight between them, shining upon the circular table. "Can you understand how that feels? To be walking along in your own life, and the next thing you know you're a Nazi?"

"It's the problem of the shadow." Gaillard finished the bit of tea in his cup, and set the cup back down with a delicate click into its saucer. "Here's David Caspian, a man like any other; he's not a saint, but he has his principles. And suddenly he's turned into something very dark. He becomes, in fact, just about the worst thing a man could become—a Nazi." Gaillard gazed at him, the expression in his eyes gentle, a gaze of reassurance. "If we look at it psychologically, we might conclude that the unconscious is trying to give you a feeling for evil—an evil which you had no idea you carried."

"And I'm the only one who carries it?"

"Everyone carries it, but we project it onto our boss, our

neighbor, the Russians, or, in the case of the Germans—the Jews. They're the evil ones, and we're the innocents. It's the problem of all human culture. We refuse to accept our capacity for evil, and instead lay it on somebody else. But to become whole, we need both halves of our nature."

"You've seen this before?"

"Dreams of Nazis, of being a Nazi, or being tortured by the Nazis, are common."

"Except I'm not asleep. I'm completely awake, and then pow—I'm the worst possible thing anybody could be. In the middle of my sweet, successful, moral American life, I'm suddenly faced with the fact I'm part of the bloodiest regime the world has ever known." Caspian paused, closed his eyes. "You couldn't get a movie star to *play* a Nazi. Dirk Bogarde tried it once, and it almost ruined his career." He opened his eyes. "And here I am, forced to *be* one. And you say it's some kind of moral enlightenment?"

"Jung called it the integration of the shadow. Usually it begins with understanding little pettinesses, hatreds, jealousies. But you've somehow leapt straight into the great shadow of the race. It's not an ideal progression for therapy, because it forces so much on you all at once."

"And that's why I totally lose myself?"

"How long were you gone the last time? From the De-Brusca party."

"An hour or so. And during that time my wife apparently spoke to me, and I answered her."

"As Felix?"

"I was over on his side, and he was on mine."

"When you were on his side, in the nightclub, did you know that you were David Caspian?"

"I was Felix completely. There was a faint sense of someone else in the back of my mind, a vague floating entity. But everyone has that, don't they? Don't you?"

"Did you enjoy yourself as Felix?"

"Look, it wasn't like I was on vacation. I didn't know I was me being Felix. Do you enjoy being yourself? You just are. I was Felix, and I was dealing with it."

"And what exactly is the *it* of being Felix?"

"A chess game existence. Every move made with care."

"Unlike David Caspian?"

"I have an agent for those things."

Gaillard smiled. "During your lost hour, your wife talked to you? Did she notice anything odd?"

"She said she joined me in the hall where the mirror was, said I was very self-engrossed. Apparently I told her I was thinking about my role in *Star Rover.*"

"*You* told her?"

"Felix told her."

"Roma French, fill me in on her."

"Roma's a good actress. I saw her in a rerun last night, and she has a very odd quality, something slightly off-center. I'd been laboring under the illusion she was just a pair of tits, but I was wrong."

"Any attraction there?"

"Until I saw her rerun, it was just your fundamental male response to that kind of beauty."

"And now?"

"Now I don't know."

"On the other side of the coin, she's the German woman, Marla?"

"Yes."

"An old flame of Felix's."

"There's still some wine left in that bottle. Felix is drawn to her, he hears carousel music, a park they used to go to. He walks with her there, in his memories. Maybe she's his weak spot, the kind of woman he could wind up getting killed over."

"You speak German, don't you?"

"I acted in Germany for a year or so."

"And you collected Nazi regalia in childhood."

"I didn't collect it. It came to me. That's the weird part, as if the stuff sought me out. As if I were part of some—pattern." Caspian paused, looked down into the valley. "As if I was being set up."

"By whom?"

"By something disembodied, something stationed at the swinging door between the realities."

"And why David Caspian?"

"An easy subject."

"Why?"

"A weakness somewhere, a tear in the fabric."

"We're all subject to unconscious influence," said Gaillard. "Artists deliberately open themselves to that influence and not infrequently get more than they bargained for."

"Got any other actors living half their life in Nazi Germany?"

"I've heard a great deal in this room."

"So what do I do?"

"You're doing it. If David Caspian could be taught one lesson by the universe, what would it be? Felix has something to do with that lesson."

"You're still maintaining he's a dream figure, a bit of repression or something."

"He could be the Devil himself, for all I know." Gaillard paused, gazing absently toward the bookshelves that lined the far wall. "Did you ever hear of an easy quest? Jung felt he was being crushed by a mountain of stone."

"But did he go through the veil?"

"As a matter of fact, he did."

"And what did he find?"

"He fell thousands of feet. He found Salome and Elijah. They were independent entities and he held long conversations with them."

"And what did he make of it?"

"He made the foundations of depth psychology." Gaillard leaned forward. "What are you making of it?"

Caspian remained silent, his eyes shifting back to the tree-tops of the canyon. The sun was burning off the last of the morning mist, and the moist warbling of the song birds was increasing. "We're living in a schizophrenic universe, that's the lesson as I see it. A maniac must have created it." His breath came rapidly, and his chest began to heave. A fire had started in his diaphragm, and he suddenly sobbed, a dry choking cry.

"Good," said Gaillard softly, "spit it out."

* * *

The Myron Fish swimming pool was S-shaped. Diving boards at either end gave it the look of a dollar sign, and Fish frequently received his greatest inspirations floating there on a vinyl raft; he floated there now, sunglasses to the sky, one hand trailing in the warm water.

"You'll be shooting in Death Valley and DeBrusca runs a tight production. If only half of a door is seen in a shot, only half that door will be painted."

Caspian floated face down on a raft beside him, gazing into the water toward the tiled floor of the pool. "Are you saying I'll be staying in the Death Valley Holiday Inn?"

Fish lifted himself on one elbow and looked toward the poolside patio, where his latest starlet was stretched out. "That girl has more talent in her little finger than—" Fish gazed at the phenomenal female, whose breasts were mushrooming out of a harlequin bathing suit, which divided her torso into a dark half and a light. "I feel privileged to be guiding her career."

"So many young girls owe so much to you," said Caspian.

"And I owe so much to them, mostly in alimony payments."

Fish paddled slowly off, his little pot belly offered to the sky, a martini balanced on it, idly anchored by two limp, pudgy fingers, as his other hand stroked lazily through the water. Caspian's daughter Alicia met him at the edge of the pool. "Can we take a meeting, Uncle Fishface?"

"Alicia," said Carol, in a warning tone.

"Dear Uncle Fishface," said Alicia.

"That's better."

"Dear Uncle Fishface, what's your new girlfriend's name?"

"Valerie," said Fish, reaching up to the edge of the pool for a copy of the *Los Angeles Times,* which he opened and laid over his face.

"She's awfully pretty."

"Yes, she is."

"When I become pretty will you be my agent?"

"Should there be a need for it, of course." Fish's voice was muffled by the newspaper. Alicia got in behind his float and pushed it gently along through the shallows. "I thought we should discuss my career."

"Come to my office," grunted Fish, his voice growing heavy with sleep.

Caspian rolled off the raft and swam a lap, the water cleanly creased by his stroke. He reached the ladder and pulled himself up it, toward the diving board. Ed Cresswell was seated nearby, bean dip in one hand and bread in the other, while a cigarette smoldered in a saucer. He lifted the bean dip in greeting.

"I've decided on an important course of action."

"You're not quitting our project, are you?" asked Caspian. In spite of a somewhat odd personality, there was no screenwriter he'd rather work with than this lean, bony, melancholic seated before him, bean dip in hand.

Cresswell lowered the dip, reached for his cigarette, and tapped the long ash in Myron's pool. "I'm going to begin tap dancing lessons."

"May I ask why?"

"I feel I'm a Fred Astaire sort of guy."

Caspian looked at his hunched, graceless, paranoid friend. "Right, Ed. You and Fred are a pair of crickets."

Cresswell placed his cigarette back in the ashtray. "I was hoping you'd take lessons with me."

"I'm already taking more lessons than I've got time for."

"An actor should know how to tap dance."

"I've taken fencing lessons, singing lessons, breathing lessons, karate lessons, riding lessons, mime lessons, and juggling. I've studied elocution, concentration, divination, and masturbation. I've had enough lessons."

"You could use the exercise." Cresswell pointed at Caspian's naked waist. "You're getting an unwanted pregnancy."

"What a vicious thing to say to a friend." Caspian sucked in his gut. "An inch, that's all I've gained."

"Think how impressed Carol would be when you came tapping your way down the stairs."

"We don't have any stairs."

"We'll find some and surprise her. She'll look up from her shopping and there we'll be, tapping our way into her heart."

"I see this is a well-developed fantasy."

"I feel I've been turning in on myself. I want to get out into the light. I want tap shoes." Cresswell, still seated, made faint slapping sounds with his rubber-thonged sandals.

Caspian turned back to the diving board and scaled the ladder leading up to it. He'd taken crash courses from a violin virtuoso, a Swahili scholar, and a brain surgeon, to look proficient in scenes that'd lasted only a minute, but they'd been authentic minutes. Tap dancing and Urdu would doubtless come in their own sweet time.

He climbed up onto the diving board, and looked out over the wrought-iron fence toward Myron Fish's nearest neighbor—an Arab who was converting an entire hillside into a concrete slab, reason unknown.

He walked to the end of the board and dove off into the bright mirror, cutting through the water to the bottom, fingers skimming the blue tiles. He glided over them, then turned and swam back upward, toward the rippling, sun-bright surface.

He broke through, and the droplets of water hung lopsidedly in front of him, their descent arrested. Light was reflected from them and he seemed surrounded by a shower of tiny transparent moons. The day had gone; the sun was a spotlight over a pool and the pool was indoors, in a cavernous room filled with people. A party was in progress and it was night in Berlin.

How far away I was, thought Felix. The warm land, so tantalizing, and those faces, almost familiar.

Felix turned lazily in the pool, gazing at the high dark windows of the mansion, through which stars shone delicately, splintered into thin webs of light.

The ragged edges of giant ferns were cast against the windows, hanging with a tropic indolence that mocked the situation of war, but a spirit of melancholy brooded over the party, as if this were the last bright gathering before eternity.

He swam to the edge of the pool and climbed out, into a robe held by an elderly servant, who escorted him to a screened dressing room. He removed his robe, and toweled dry. Upon his forearm was the tattoo of a falcon, wings outspread, a memento from younger days. He rubbed it now, and reminded himself, as always, that one of these days he must have it removed, for identifying marks were so useful to police agencies. Hanging upon a hook was his uniform; he put its form-fitting shirt and trousers on, then the jacket and tie and high black boots. He clicked his heels with a resounding crack: Member Abteilung II, Interstate Contacts for Economic Development, under the command of Colonel Joseph Erhard Mueller, special deputy dealing with southeastern Europe. Lieutenant Falkenhayn stepped from behind the screen.

Enlisted men bearing trays were offering champagne and brandy to the officers' wives; the elderly butlers proffered similar offerings to the civilian guests—a few businessmen in evening wear. They were engaged in conversation with the colonel's staff— young lawyers, economists, investors in uniform—and their first concern was the economic development for which their group had been formed. They discussed not Panzers but the peat-cutting industry in Dorohueza. Felix walked slowly past them, on the fringe of their conversation, their voices strident, confident, as they derided some other officer, not present.

"He made a mess of that mineral water business."

"And the Polish brickworks, most of which were in his head, hello Falkenhayn, getting along?"

He responded quietly, correctly. He knew his lines, and for once his papers were almost in order. He walked along the edges of the great room. The mansion belonged to their brigadier, with whom Colonel Mueller sat on a couch, a tea table before them.

"The turnover for last year was five million marks. We shall hide army interest in it and allow Herr Ziegler to remain on as titular head." The brigadier nodded toward a middle-aged businessman who was being entertained by Marla while his leather company was being incorporated into the army cartel. Felix could see the man's thought forming: here is a woman of considerable loveliness, and a thousand-pound bomb might fall on my factory no matter who runs it.

The brigadier was putting plum puree on a cracker. Felix looked to the wall above the brigadier, where hung old family portraits—field marshals and prelates in noble poses, beside whose gilt frames candelabra burned as if in ceremony to their souls.

He wandered on, his course bringing him nearer the scrutiny of two plainclothes agents of the Gestapo. Their dour stare made him uncomfortable, and he quickly crossed the floor to blend with a group of fellow army officers; they were discussing another gentleman standing by the brigadier's white concert piano. "They say he's a relative of the Duce."

"He was a doorman in Naples."

The officer flicked a wrist toward Marla. "She's straight out of the chorus line."

"But," said Felix, "she's the Countess von Blaustein. The colonel introduced me to her."

"She could dance for thirty-six hours on benzedrine with a number attached to her back."

Felix gave Marla a sign to join him by the punch table, where, after excusing herself from the shoe magnate, she met him, her long gown trailing over the toe of his boot. "I've been making quite a success," she said, taking a glass.

"A perfect performance. But a little softer, you're reaching the back row." He nodded toward his fellow officers.

"Herr Ziegler is enchanted." She smiled across the room to her magnate.

Felix dipped punch into another glass. "That soldier over there. Do you know him from somewhere?"

"No, why do you ask?"

"He seems to recall seeing you, Countess, in a dance marathon."

Marla softly touched her punch glass to his. "You were a good partner. Didn't we take second place?"

"We held back the night." He withdrew his glass. "Can we hold it back now?"

Marla adjusted the bodice of her gown, resettling it around a naked expanse of bosom. "I must say goodbye to my shoemaker. Are they really taking his company from him?"

"Every bootnail."

"And he's so cheerful."

"He has you."

"He'll not have me long." She set her glass down, as the shoe magnate rose, and she accompanied him, toward the door, Felix watching from the punch bowl.

"Well, how are you holding up?" Mueller was behind him, helping himself to a cucumber sandwich.

"The Gestapo are eyeing me," said Felix, his gaze again meeting that of the two plainclothesmen across the room.

"They want to frighten you, they want to frighten everyone."

"I have a card in their files," said Felix, reaching for a little green gherkin, whose head he bit gently off. "It's marked violet, for a grumbler."

"I've never heard you grumble," said the colonel, and then in lower tones, "Do you think those two petty shadows mean anything to me? They are here to feather their own nest, not take apart yours. Our danger lies in higher spheres."

"And these are—?"

The colonel drummed his fingers lightly on Felix's shoulder. "You said you were an actor. Well, act the part. What sort of acting did you do?"

"He was in a play at the Circle Café," said Marla, coming up behind them. "He got the tail of his coat caught under the leg of a chair on stage, and when his cue came to rise, he couldn't."

Colonel Mueller pressed her hand. "I want you to visit with the Italian air attaché, over there by the piano, beneath the ostrich feather. We wish to land at one of his fields and he's been withholding cooperation. Set his reel of red tape in motion."

Felix heard the air raid sirens begin, and the far-off rumble of bombers. The butlers discreetly pulled down light-tight fabric blinds on the windows and skylights, but the party continued. Marla walked toward the Italian attaché, through the now-dimmed light playing upon the family heirlooms and on the walls, and upon her silk-sheathed form. The attaché straightened to attention as she approached. Mueller smiled to Felix. "Executions every half hour."

"If he has connections in the Italian cinema, we'll never see her again."

The colonel took his elbow, turned him slowly. "That gentleman over there, white mustache and wire glasses. He would serve you to the worms if it got him one extra meal and a trolley transfer. We're installing him as vice-assistant mayor of Cracow. You'll be responsible for his safety in getting there, and you'll conduct a little personal business for me."

"I know little about politics."

"My dear fellow, surely you recall Zuckmayer's play about the little shoemaker: Unable to get a passport out of the bureaucrats, our shoemaker buys an army surplus officer's uniform and orders a unit of soldiers to the townhall, where he arrests the mayor, and issues himself his own passport." Mueller gently tugged the sleeve of his jacket. "It's simply theatre, Felix. Just play the part of the little shoemaker in the right uniform, and nobody will dare trouble you." Mueller indicated that their conversation was finished, and Felix went over to his lance corporals, who were standing at the other end of the banquet table, gazing pensively at Marla and her attaché. "I'm sure I've seen her at the White Mouse café. She was in a revue, Fan of the Chinese Dancers."

"We're leaving for Poland," said Felix, from behind them.

The lance corporals withdrew and Felix walked to a table at poolside, to retrieve his cigarette case. Seated beside the table now was a tall officer with the pallor of a clam. He took a cigarette from the silver case extended by Felix. "Thanks, Falkenhayn, you do manage to get excellent cigarettes, don't you."

The subject changed to business—iron foundries, textile mills, Klinker Zement. Felix said, half jokingly, "I hear we're even getting into jam-making."

"My dear fellow, we're already in a hell of a jam." The sound of distant air raid sirens punctuated the officer's sentence. He held a snifter of Danzig Goldwasser in his hand, swirled the gold-flecked liqueur around with a twist of his wrist. "Colonel Mueller told me you were a man who knew café life."

"I've crawled through a few."

Their eyes turned to the pool, where a young woman in a harlequin bathing suit was slipping into the water. "The brigadier's mistress," said the officer. "I like younger women myself. Very young, if you catch my drift. I know a place, a private club actually. You might enjoy it."

The officer flicked an ash in the pool. Felix gazed at it

floating on the shimmering surface of the lamplit water, then turned back toward the officer.

"What are you staring at?" asked Cresswell. "Is there something wrong with my shirt? It was hand rolled in Hawaii." His bony arm drooped down toward the surface of the pool, ash falling from the tip of his cigarette.

Caspian leaned back in his deck chair. The sun struck him with its full force, the afternoon golden, treacherous, and shimmering—a snifter of gold-flecked liqueur in which a Reich party dreamed.

"The obsessions of a psychopath never change," said Dr. Gaillard. "They're fixed, and that's the tragedy. But Felix is fluid, and has already changed. He's joined the German army."

Caspian sat across from Gaillard, and tried to take assurance that a deep psychic layer was revealing itself, and that it was purposeful in spite of its schizophrenic style. "His joining the German army brings me little comfort."

"We're only dealing with its symbolic value. Felix has become legitimized."

"Meaning?"

"He had an uneasiness about being an obvious criminal. He must conform, must join the Party. He's raised up in order to be more useful." Gaillard closed his eyes. The silence was not an empty one, Caspian's mind pressing in the darkness with

Gaillard, toward some kind of insight as to Felix's real purpose in his inner cosmology.

"Yes," said Gaillard, opening his eyes, "he's eager for power but he has to come closer to consciousness in order to gain it. He isn't content with his underworld existence any longer."

"Why not?"

"The restless urge to selfhood." Gaillard paused, and gazed at Caspian. His eyes had an odd way of changing when he spoke. "Felix is an ascending part of you that wants the ego to move over. The ego is the real tyrant, you know. Gives all the orders and hates change. Actors, owing to the insecurity of the profession, and the adulation they receive, have egos like solid steel."

"But Felix is an ego too."

"He's a partial ego. Only available now and then."

"He's getting more regular."

"You're dwelling on him night and day. But let's go back to Felix's motivation. He's a power drive of yours, I feel pretty certain about that."

"Let me be immodest for a moment and say I already have more than my share of power and all that goes with it."

"But it's never finished, you know. That game goes on forever. Hercules fights an endless battle against phantoms in the underworld. You were a poor kid, you fought your way to the top of an elite profession, and you wore jackboots to do it. There's ugliness in that somewhere, and your soul is burdened by it. Enter Felix."

"Agreed. I'm aggressive. But Felix's world is as finely detailed as the reality on Wilshire Boulevard. He's not a dream figure."

"The case isn't yet in on what constitutes reality. Some wise men have said that Psyche created the world."

Caspian drew back from the wrestling match. The hour was valuable and he was wasting it. And something had just occurred to him. "So long as I keep saying that Felix is his own entity in his own world, and I'm an entity in my own world, we remain split apart. And if I can see Felix as part of me, we start coming together."

"Good. But bear this in mind—we may never know who Felix really is. Because at bottom he may be something more universal than any individual can comprehend. But what we can do is dismantle the components of his image, and at least find out why the god has clothed himself in these ways in order to appear to you."

Caspian nodded, and rubbed his forearm, which, somewhere during the hour, had begun to itch. Now it was tingling like a brushburn; he pulled back his sleeve. His eyes widened, and he thrust the arm out toward Gaillard.

Appearing faintly, from beneath the skin, was the tattoo of a falcon.

*　　*　　*

He walked past the sound stages, their steel domes blindingly bright in the cloudless sky. Trucks, vans, and station wagons passed him, each one bearing some part of the dreamer's art; few people walked on the blazing tar of the studio complex, and he was alone when he stepped onto the back part of the lot, into the make-believe streets.

He liked the city of no people, where only the wind was a resident, blowing through the empty neighborhood—a winding suburban street with colonial and brick federal houses, buildings perfectly made in outward detail and hollow inside, with beams and planks carelessly strewn about in back, where the camera could not see. The lawns were landscaped, the sidewalks curved gracefully, but no one came down them, not a dog or a cat or a living soul. He thought of it as the safest neighborhood in L.A.

He continued through the ghostly neighborhood, its illusion capturing the eye and promising that all was normal, that a car would soon approach and kids tumble out—but the wind rustled leaves over dusty doorsteps and through the unfinished hallways, where klieg lights stood, great glass eyes staring at the emptiness within.

He turned the corner in suburbia, and was in a frontier town, dust blowing along past hitching post, saloon, and general store. A World War II fighter plane had been dumped up against the jail, as if it had sought to land there, out of its own dimension.

He stepped around it, into New York City. Its stoops were deserted, no shoppers or apartment dwellers to be seen. He passed the facade of an employment agency, perfect in every detail, including a patched broken window with chipped lettering on it. Next door was a Chinese laundry, dusty paper parcels heaped in the window. He stepped into its shaded doorway and thought about the fact that he was going mad.

Beside the laundry was a lucky staircase for him, on which he'd performed with a gang of street hooligans in a turkey called *Street Wise Angels*. He'd come out of it with a swimming pool in his backyard and a Porsche 928, and that, he'd concluded, had to be street wisdom.

"Hey, buddy!"

A studio cop was looking at him from the corner of East 157th Street. "You from the tour? If you are, you're lost. You're supposed to be over by the submarine." The cop pointed courteously, like no cop you'd ever find in a real city, and then came slowly forward. As Caspian stepped out of the shadow of the stoop into the sunlight, a look of recognition came over the cop's face. "Oh, I'm sorry, I'm new on the job. You're Tom Van Horn, right? Sorry I bothered you. I'll just fade out." The studio cop tipped his hat and walked away.

Caspian remained where he was, as the draught of insecurity circulated through his veins. To be mistaken for Tom Van Horn, an actor at least five years his senior, who now only played older men—kindly uncles, senior business partners, aging scientists—and played them badly—to be mistaken for him was deeply depressing.

He withdrew further into the shade of the doorway, and fought off venomous feelings toward Tom Van Horn, who was actually a very decent fellow. Caspian saw him in his mind's eye, but the portrait was distorted, Van Horn's face made slightly grotesque; and a small hump was forming on his back. And oh yes, one other little detail, his nose was falling off. And nobody would hire him.

"Well," Caspian muttered to himself, as he stepped back out into the sunlight, "what can I tell you? Every actor, somewhere in the ugly recesses of his soul, hates every other actor, especially those who resemble him, however faintly."

He continued along past Carlucci's Cafe, the office of the *World Telegram,* and Klein's Department Store. A few yards beyond the Manhattan street corner, he entered a medieval village. Upon the battlements of yon castle, stuntmen had performed some of his most daring feats.

It was empty now, the wind moving an arched door back and forth on a squeaking hinge. He gazed at it, wondering if some Nazi warlord was about to manifest. It was just their kind of cue.

The door moved open violently and Myron Fish stepped through it. "They told me you were out here. What're you trying to do, give yourself a stroke? It's a hundred and twenty degrees."

Caspian shielded his eyes from the sun and squinted at his agent. "Myron, have you ever thought you could be a Nazi?"

"I've often thought I was working for Nazis." He turned, shielding his own eyes as he surveyed the vast studio complex. "Why? Have you been offered a part in one of those German films they only show at Harvard? You'll ruin yourself. Leave this town for five minutes and they redecorate without you."

Caspian put his arm around Fish's shoulder, enjoying the

strongly rooted feeling of the diminutive theatrical agent. A man like that cannot be dragged into the fourth dimension.

*   *   *

Victor Quatrelle gazed out from the balcony of his beach apartment, and listened to Caspian describing events of the past month. "Sounds to me, David, as if you've been using too many drugs. Of course, there could be other factors. A columnist I know thought he was receiving an illumination in his office every day when he faced his chair to the window. A brilliant surge of power went through him. Actually, it was an electric cord that'd rubbed itself raw underneath the rug. He was slowly electrocuting himself."

Caspian sat on the railing, a drink in his hand. "My shrink says it's some kind of archetype realizing itself. But I go to this place, it makes perfect sense, and I come back."

"I wouldn't mind getting away myself," sighed Quatrelle, hands folded over his paunch. "Five years of sitcoms is enough to make anyone want to join the Nazis."

Caspian looked at his friend. "Well, you're there too. On the other side."

"I am?" Quatrelle chuckled and turned back toward the ocean. "Who am I?"

"A colonel in the Wehrmacht."

"Not my kind of part at all."

"Felix isn't my kind of part either."

"Who's Felix?"

"He's the guy I become."

"And what does he do over there?"

"He's in the army too. He works—for you."

"David—" Quatrelle drummed his fingers softly on his stomach in a slow, patient rhythm.

"I know the difference between drugs and the fourth dimension. Past and present are one reality. You and I live here in L.A., but we also live in Germany, in the Third Reich."

"You're telling me I'm a closet Nazi?"

"Oberst Mueller."

"Well, I suppose I've been told worse." Quatrelle got up and went to the little bar just inside the terrace doorway. Caspian watched Quatrelle's moves carefully; Colonel Mueller was hidden, no trace of the imperious aesthete evident in Quatrelle's gentle, jovial manner. "Here," said Quatrelle, handing him a drink. "You need to relax. You're starting to sound like Bertrand Russell."

"This is the forty dollar stuff you use only for seductions."

"You need something pure in your system. You've probably had too much carrot juice lately."

"For the first time in my life, I've been practicing moderation in all things."

"A terrible mistake. Throws the system completely out of whack." Quatrelle sat with his own cognac and sipped at it slowly. "Next thing you know you'll be flying in jets and wearing emerald earrings."

Caspian tipped his glass toward a streak of sunlight falling on the terrace floor. "Shadow and sun are a doorway. Take nothing for granted. That's how I see things these days."

"Sure," said Quatrelle, "once you have enough money to loosen up, you find yourself focusing on spiritual things. I've been through changes myself. I went to a pet store and nearly bought a parrot. I felt he was giving me assurances about Christian marriage."

"People have been spacing out since time began," said Caspian, "and formulating their experiences into dogmas. But this thing wouldn't make good religion. Who wants to meet their other half, the Nazi?"

Quatrelle drained his cognac. "Shall we go for a walk? I keep feeling I should air you out."

Caspian stood, set his glass down. "I haven't been able to tell any of this to Carol."

"No," said Quatrelle, "she's not shaped for this kind of information."

They left the apartment, descending the back stairs down to the brightly blazing beach. They strolled along it, past the bathing beauties, the surfers, the life guard's tower. The sun glared back from the water. "It's with us now," said Caspian, nodding his head toward the brilliant surface, where molten splinters of light were forming into a twisted cross.

The swastika, after all, said the voice of Dr. Gaillard, *is a leftward turning device, down, into the unconscious.*

"I'm not so sure I want to hear more," said Quatrelle. "I don't think it's wise to encourage you."

"And I think you're afraid of that world."

"Afraid of *your* fantasy?"

"The fourth dimension exists," said Caspian softly.

"Then I'll get to it in my own good time, won't I."

Caspian stared at Quatrelle, seeing Mueller there in his friend's eyes, but discreet, hidden behind a veil of third-dimensional assumptions.

They walked past the marina beach houses, past Washington Boulevard, and on into the park along the water's edge. They came to a wire enclosure, where weightlifters were lifting brutal loads. Quatrelle mimicked a lifter's contorted expression as the athlete squatted slowly with a huge weight across his shoulders. He rose again, veins bulging dangerously in his forehead, and Quatrelle exhaled forcefully. "I always feel better after someone else has a workout like that."

On the sidewalk further down, between sand and palm trees, a television cameraman knelt, photographing a little girl on rollerskates. A woman was coaching the child on how to skate past the camera. The cue was given and the sequence began, the little girl skating up the sidewalk. "Don't look at the camera!" screamed the woman and raced after the child, grabbing her and shaking her violently. "What's wrong with you! You're supposed to be a *professional!*"

"Ours is a wonderful art," murmured Caspian.

They continued along together, beneath the rows of palms.

"Years ago," said Quatrelle, "I had a dream. In it, I was wandering around in beautiful farm country. When I woke I felt I knew where that farm was, but I just couldn't place it. A long time afterward, I did a film in Denmark, and we finished it off by driving across Europe. In central Germany, near Johannesberg Castle, I found that farm. Down to the last detail."

*   *   *

He sat in his study, staring at the German pistol.

He looked toward the driveway, where his Porsche was parked, and his Mercedes, and his wife's BMW.

I'll sell them. And get a Hungarian half-ton.

He rose, the Walther in his hand.

I'll go to the canyon, and bury *this* goddamn thing in the sand.

He tucked the pistol in his belt, covered it with his shirt, and walked down the hall. The tiles clicked beneath his light step, but the familiar embrace of the foyer had no charm for him anymore. The house was a thin bubble against the wind in which Felix moved.

He stood in the massive wooden doorway. The front garden was glowing metallically, the spines of the cactus glinting like bayonets. Carol and Alicia knelt amongst them, working on the smaller, more delicate succulents. Apprehension came over him to see them encircled by glistening points, as if they were held captive. He adjusted his shirt, hiding the pistol.

"A toad!" cried Carol. She crouched down, searching. "He got away."

"Toads have places to go too," said Alicia, soberly.

"Where?"

"To see their agent." Alicia crawled along, dragging a little garden pail behind her.

Caspian took the lower path, dropping out of sight at the end of the garden. He went out the back gate and crossed over to the hills. As soon as he stepped off the road into the chaparral, he felt his obligations slip off him, replaced by a green cloak, the weave of the instincts. Out in the hills, human voices were lost, and the gods of the vegetation spoke, their tongues softly murmuring in leaves the hot wind stirred. He became conscious of how his feet touched the stones, how his body angled its way through the underbrush, and how he blended in, just another creature moving in the hostile but beautiful desert land.

He climbed, bits of volcanic debris sliding behind him. He climbed without stopping, sweat soaking his shirt to his skin; he was fast, his legs were strong, and high up, one's perspective changed; or perhaps one's thoughts clarified from immersion in the naked sunlight, from its thick caress, its suggestiveness—smells of dried mud, baking stones, and flowers that were deliberately perfuming the air, calling to their visitors, come to us, come. And always there were death's emblems— hawk's eye, snake's rattle. He crested the first peak, and beyond it was another, and then another, spire after spire, in a line extending up the coast of California, a vast range of mystery. Neither mine, nor Felix's.

The coyote appeared a few yards to the left. It was staring at him, tongue out, eyes glowing.

He reached slowly for the Walther. The animal stopped and regarded him, head cocked, ears up.

"You see this?" Caspian spoke softly as he brought out the automatic.

The coyote's eyes narrowed, and its snout closed, but it held its ground. Caspian felt its intelligence in a palpable wave, a current of force that came from its eyes and entered his own. The coyote gave a low whine and disappeared back into the brush.

There was the scuffling of paws over loose ground, and then the yapping of the pack began. They broke from the brush and charged him. The leader's eyes were glistening. The Walther was steady in his hand as he pressed the trigger.

In the space between action and its advance he went into

the bullet's whine, singing out with it toward the coyote. The coyote's eyes grew brighter and larger, becoming enormous globes that froze before him, their animation gone, their radiance a cold, unliving light.

. . . unter der Augen einer Polizeistreife . . .

Er kommt direkt aus der Stadt.

Brilliant headlights flashed. I was dreaming, thought Felix, of that world again, and of a wolf who gazed at me. Where is that warm land?

"Your buyer will come from town and meet us at the hotel. Will that be satisfactory, Lieutenant?"

"Yes," said Felix, "that's fine." He nodded at the white-moustached vice-assistant mayor of the occupied territory, and they walked toward the headlights of the Mercedes. His lance corporal was at the wheel, and a second corporal beside him.

"The hotel," said Felix, getting in, the vice-assistant following. The vice-assistant adjusted his trouser crease, his coat. Felix gave him a sidelong glance: I know your operation well, my friend, Felix can smell the black market ten kilometers upwind. You supply canned goods to the army and every sixth gross goes into your own cupboard.

"This man we are meeting," said the vice-assistant, "you may find him filled with suspicions. These Swiss think they can afford to insult us."

It would be prudence to approach you with suspicion, Herr Vice-Assistant, thought Felix. I am far from Berlin and the rat holes I know so well, into which a man may safely disappear.

". . . an art dealer, so they say, but he may be an agent of Swiss Intelligence." The vice-assistant stroked his white moustache and returned Felix's glance. "I've tried to keep tabs, and your own Intelligence Section has been most helpful." He ran two fingers down his gold watch chain, thoughtfully. "Be on your guard."

"I appreciate your concern."

"It is part of my duty, naturally."

Felix watched the city pass, his own thoughts passing with the dark facade. Resistance was in the air here, he could feel its shadow moving through the city. He adjusted the pistol at his waist; a submachine gun and light automatic rifle were beside him. His lance corporal at the wheel glanced into the rearview mirror, his eyes meeting Felix's. "Checkpoint ahead."

He looked toward the next corner, where rifles were being raised by the Cracow police, who, on occasion, had been known to shoot holes through German officers' heads. His other lance corporal was already opening the glove compartment and removing their traveling papers.

All is in order, said Felix to himself, repeating the most precious phrase in Europe at the moment.

The window in the Mercedes was going down, and Felix laid the submachine gun across his lap. The auto pulled to a stop and the lance corporal thrust the papers briskly to the policeman in charge of the checkpoint. The vice-assistant leaned across Felix, speaking softly. "I am known at the checkpoints. A bottle or two now and then cheers these weary men." He showed his face at the window, and the police sergeant nodded.

"All is in order." He signaled to the gate, and the swinging barricade was opened.

"Of course," said the vice-assistant mayor to Felix as they drove through, "no position is truly safe these days. Many people in my city don't understand the goals of our administration. They are impatient."

"They wish to use you as a bulletin board," said Felix, "with lead pushpins." He smiled, watching to see whether the politician paled. He felt certain the vice-assistant mayor had gotten where he was by giving brandy to some and embalming fluid to others.

The vice-assistant did not flinch. "I have a bit of food waiting for you, and some acceptable wine. As well, I took it upon myself to arrange for some friends—actresses, actually—to join you after business for a little party." He rubbed his gold watch chain.

"You've made an indelible impression, Herr Vice-Assistant."

"Your brigadier is a wonderful host. My hospitality cannot equal his, but I have tried, Lieutenant Falkenhayn."

"Should your city be reduced to matchsticks by the Allies, Vice-Assistant—" Felix took a cigarette from his case, lit it. "Should the ends of war, which are never simple, find you in difficult circumstances, I will remember you as one who did a kindness." Smoke poured from Felix's nostrils as he glanced again at the vice-assistant, from whom parting would be so pleasant, owing to the accompanying certainty that they would never meet again in life. In hell, perhaps, in that newly occupied territory, but on this earth, Vice-Assistant, you are the sort of man I go out of my way to avoid. I feel the knife of your duplicity pressing against my ribs each time you speak.

"And here is your hotel, Lieutenant."

The Mercedes drew into the curb, Felix checking the street for signs of the underground forces who loved the Germans so. The street seemed clear, and the party stepped from the car. He spoke to his corporals. "Wait in the lobby. I'll call down to you when I've finished business."

The lobby doors were already swinging open, held by the owner of the hotel, who bowed deeply for his honored military guest, eyes beseeching him to limit himself to stealing only the smaller pieces of furniture. "Delighted, sir, simply delighted." He handed Felix and the vice-assistant over to an elderly bell-hop, who'd gone beyond the age of caring who pillaged whom.

He opened the metal fencework doors that enclosed the hotel lift, and they stepped inside. The vice-assistant held his hat in both hands, drumming it softly over his stomach. The elderly bellhop stared downward, lost in an old man's reflections, which Felix somehow felt, and which disturbed him, for up to now he'd been almost enjoying his army uniform and the respect it engendered; but the old man's watery gaze had reflected the truth for a moment, of having seen many uniforms come and go, and they meant no more than the striped pants of a bellhop, and a bellhop was more useful.

The lift stopped and the old man opened the doors again, then showed them down the hall to the bridal suite. "Your guest is waiting."

The suite, over-decorated in lace, was occupied by a Swiss who exuded the aura of a Zurich vault, a close hush seeming to surround him. Felix signed to the vice-assistant that it was time for him to go. The vice-assistant indicated by a gesture that he would be in the lobby, balancing a ball on the end of his nose. When he closed the door behind him, Felix opened his suitcase with two swift snaps and laid it on the bed. A goddess by Botticelli looked back at them. The Swiss collector bent over the painting with a magnifying glass, his gaze seeming to glide into its inner spaces; he lifted his head. "Tests must be made."

"There's no time for that."

"And I suppose there is no previous owner?"

"Here is the painting. That is all you need to know." Felix made as if to close the suitcase, as when reluctant buyers looked at French underwear. Was an Italian masterpiece so different? The Swiss's hand reached out, to stop the closing of the case.

Felix let him bend over the jewel of the Florentine school once more, for which he'd flown from Switzerland into occupied territory. He would not leave without it, and both knew it.

The collector now let the frame slip casually from his hand. "A hundred thousand, Swiss."

"I have no time to bargain." Felix closed the case with a definitive snap.

"You have some other price in mind?" The collector's magnifying glass now dangled from its string, as he gazed with mock surprise at Felix.

"The other price is a half-million, as you well know."

The collector's eyes narrowed, and one eyebrow lifted, just slightly. "Under different circumstances, we might enter that lofty region, but I too have no time for bargaining, nor does the world. I will give you a quarter million for something fragile, and inedible in the hour of starvation. Take it or leave it."

Felix handed over the suitcase in which the virgin rested, her legend so revered that armies sent their minions to bear her to her next lover. "Congratulations."

The collector gave his own suitcase in exchange, in which the quarter million already counted, was enclosed. "I wonder— will this night and your face haunt my dreams?" He took the army suitcase and walked to the door, as Felix picked up the phone, connecting with his corporal in the lobby, who spoke briskly.

"Your party is here, sir. Actresses."

"Bring them up, Corporal."

Felix laid the phone quietly back in the cradle, and placed the suitcase of money in the closet. The temptation was to follow his Swiss visitor across the border, money in hand; in the other direction, back through Poland and into Germany, was a net of Party informers, Field Security Police, Gestapo agents, and Bund Maidens, any of whom would be so happy to catch an officer bearing a private fortune.

He went to the liquor cabinet and mixed himself a drink. A light knock sounded at the door, accompanied by women's voices. He raised his glass to their muted sound. "My honor is true." He drank up, and opened the door for his corporals and three young ladies.

"We are simple soldiers," he said, bowing to them, "and we wish you every comfort. My name is Falkenhayn."

The doorway filled a second time and the aged bellhop wheeled a cart in, on which silver tureens sparkled. The lids were lifted, plates were filled, and the company seated itself at a long candlelit table by the window. The actresses spoke nervously, the one beside Felix cautiously inquiring as to what branch of the service he represented.

"The Office of Antiquity Removal." He gazed into her opalescent eyes, which glittered in the candle flame. Just beyond her was the window and the lamplight of the square, faintly twinkling. A military van passed through the square, shadowy forms seated within it.

"And how long are you in our city?" she asked. He noted that she and the other girls were eating with rather more gusto than was ladylike.

"We have until morning," he said, and poured more wine, but the conversation was interrupted by the phone. A thousand pardons—could the lieutenant come to the lobby for a final word with the vice-assistant.

He hung up the phone, excused himself, and went out to the hallway, where the elevator was already waiting for him. He entered it feeling some impatience, but understood that the vice-assistant had business to discuss, and preferred the wide space of the lobby, where the walls could not listen. Felix found him in the middle of the large room.

"Lieutenant, you will forgive me, there has been a call relayed to me from the Armaments Inspectorate. A new contract for the manufacture of uniforms is to be awarded here. Your brigadier's family has a textile company near our border." The vice-assistant smiled. His chauffeured car was pulling up outside, at the curb. He continued speaking as he led Felix out through the doors, to the even safer region of the street, where none but the lampposts could overhear them. "I can make introductions for your brigadier's family. The contract will be virtually guaranteed, and it will not be an insignificant one. Please inform him of my eagerness to assist in this matter."

"Uniforms, Vice-Assistant. I shall carry your message to the brigadier."

The vice-assistant clapped his hat upon his head, and turned toward his limousine. "Occasionally," he concluded, in a confiding tone, "one is the right man in the right place." The vice-assistant touched two fingers to his hat brim. Another automobile turned the corner, accelerating suddenly. The vice-assistant raised an arm, as if to issue a traffic warning. A long, thin gun barrel glinted at the window of the car, and automatic rifle fire exploded out of it.

Felix flattened himself to the sidewalk, pistol drawn. The car lights were on him and he fired directly at them. The lights altered, their cold luminescence becoming warmer. The lights were eyes, in the head of a wolf.

The creature stared at him from a dark hillside, its blazing eyes bearing human intelligence. All around him was the pack he led.

Who are you? asked Felix.

I am Head of the SS, said the wolf.

The animal whined nervously and turned, and the pack turned with him, vanishing over the hillside. David Caspian lay with his arm outstretched, the Walther clutched in his hand. He rose slowly, the gun dangling from his fingers, and turned toward the slope up which he'd climbed.

A soldier was standing on it, staring at him; he carried a rifle, was raising it. Caspian's arm came up, the Walther extended at the end of it, the soldier's heart in his sights.

"Hold it, Jesus Christ, don't shoot!" The man's hands went in the air.

Caspian lowered the Walther and walked toward the man. What had seemed a soldier's cap was a gray tennis visor; his uniform was a striped jogging suit. His rifle was a stick, now fallen to the ground.

"I'm sorry," said Caspian, jamming the pistol into his belt. "We've had prowlers around here recently."

The man was pale, his lips white, and his eyes still wide with fear. He was overweight, sweating, and was looking at Caspian as if at a dangerous lunatic. "I'm visiting a friend on

Cold Canyon Road. Guy named Sabitus, produces records, you know him?"

"Yes," said Caspian, "I know him."

The fear and suspicion in the man's face were not diminished. He half turned, backing down the slope. "I've climbed high enough. Yeah, plenty for today . . ." The rocks loosened beneath his feet, rolling down the slope, and he followed them, as quickly as he could. Caspian watched, as the man took the first opportunity to get into the thicket, where, with a loud rustling crash he managed to hide himself, and disappear.

Caspian faced Gaillard across the analyst's low table. "I almost killed my neighbor's house guest. Do you understand that? I was within an ace of pulling the trigger. I had Felix's killer instinct, his calm, his resolution. It was all still lingering in me, and so was the sense that I was surrounded by enemies." Caspian sat back in his chair. "I just thank god the guy waved his arms, or I'd have been hiding his body in the hills." He paused again, leaned toward Gaillard once more. "You've got to help me before I *do* kill somebody. Maybe I should be locked up."

"Don't dramatize."

"This thing is destroying my life."

Gaillard put his feet up on the battered hassock. "Did you ever hear Hemingway's double *dicho? Man may be defeated but not destroyed.* The reverse of it is, *Man may be destroyed—*"

" '—but not defeated.' What does it have to do with me?"

"We inevitably suffer defeat in life. It's important to accept this, to accept our weakness, to accept that our consciousness is a dicey thing, and that our real bedrock is the vastly more powerful unconscious, which does with us as it will. It defeats us again and again; if we bow to its superior force, it stops just short of destroying us, and ultimately can reveal the totality of itself, which includes a sense of something we can only call an eternal soul. So, in the end, man is defeated but not destroyed."

Gaillard picked up his pipe, rubbed its polished bowl in his fingers. "Hemingway preferred the other half of the *dicho*. He believed man could be destroyed but not defeated. He fought against defeat, resisted it with all his might, repressed any hint of weakness, and, finally, he chose destruction before defeat." Gaillard opened his tobacco pouch, filled the bowl of his pipe. "Now what has our friend Felix been up to since we last met?"

Caspian related what he could remember of his most recent interlude as Felix—of going into Poland, of holding a Botticelli in his hands. He described the Swiss art collector, the hotel, the assassination of the vice-assistant mayor on the sidewalk.

"Tell me about the bellhop again, the old guy at the hotel, the one who sees through all the elite army horseshit."

"You like him, huh?"

"He's the sanest one we've met so far."

"Well, there's nothing at stake for him. He's a fixture at a good hotel."

"But the quality he carries, that's important. Doesn't care about masterpieces, German officers, vice-assistant mayors. He just lugs the bags and wheels in the booze."

"A normal person?"

"Who says I want you to be normal? Normal is an illusion, she's just another one of the goddesses." Gaillard leaned forward. "Our infirmities make our soul. I'm not trying to lift you out of your pathology. I'm trying to make you comfortable with it."

"With losing reality?"

"The old bellhop speaks clearly to me. I'd seek his counsel."

"He's just a cynical old man in a sinecure position."

"Carrying luggage is no sinecure."

"It is when other people are carrying bazookas."

Gaillard paused, stared at his own toe rising out of his dark sandals. "Who's this Swiss art collector?"

"I don't know. Maybe it was C.G. Jung. Didn't he have trouble with the Nazis?"

"So they say."

"Tell me about it," said Caspian.

"He dealt with Nazi psychiatrists during the war. Tried to hold neutral conferences in the profession. He also made the mistake of publishing papers on the structure of the Jewish psyche, at a very bad time. Afterward he said he'd 'slipped up.' In Swiss German, it's *usg'schlipft*. An interesting word. Literally, it means to slip, as on a dance floor." Gaillard went silent a moment, staring out the window. "During the dance, while the music was playing, and the crowd was waltzing around." He looked back at Caspian. "I don't know. Nobody knows. The great man's shadow. But we were talking about you."

"Let's talk about Felix. You know, he's not ideologically a Nazi. He does not, so far as I know, fuck people over."

"The black market is not known for its fairness to the poor."

"So he's shady. But at least he's not—" Caspian paused, as a sickening thought crossed his mind. He stared closely at Gaillard. "If the task is to integrate a piece of the world shadow, things could get much worse, couldn't they? I could become, not a Felix, but an Eichmann. Instead of being just a shady individual, I could wake up a Beast of Buchenwald. And how do I integrate that?"

Gaillard nodded, slowly. Behind him, the Chinese sages, in their brush-stroked panels, wandered through a stillness of eternity. He leaned forward, his voice calm, deliberate. "Jung has said—to look upon the face of naked evil is shattering."

"From which we can conclude that he saw it."

"Presumably."

"Do you think it could come to that with me?"

"To integrate such a monstrous shadow, a man would have to have already gathered enormous light. We're increasing your light a little bit each week, so you can deal with Felix. I think that's all we have to worry about for now. You say that you and Felix look alike?"

"Yet he isn't me, for at moments when I'm going out and see his face, I know—he's the other."

"What is that like?"

"It's a swift, psychological blow."

"And then it starts to weave you in."

"I feel this is it, there isn't any point to struggling, this is the way things are." He looked at Gaillard. "Give me a drug that will flatten me out and stop it from happening."

"Treat the body and screw the soul."

"Do you know how fast I'd ram a needle in my arm if I thought it would help?"

"We drug people in asylums, but then we have zombies. Is David Caspian's next film going to be *Zombie Nightfall?*"

"The film is what I'm worried about. How is it going to look if I flip out in the middle of a hundred people, with cameras running, and money going down the toilet at the rate of a thousand dollars a minute?"

"I want to hear more about the way it weaves you in."

"I feel my center slipping. I don't hold the coordinates of my personality anymore. The things that were me seem like a dream somebody was having; over on Felix's side is the real me."

"What if you resisted it?"

"I'd be in limbo. I wouldn't be anybody. I'd be a lamp-post. Local color."

"Tell me about the Nazi souvenirs your father brought home."

"They scared me. The only thing I liked was the helmet. It had a dent in it, bullet-size. I'd put it on and think about the Kraut who'd been wearing it that day it stopped a bullet, and he'd say to himself, *Gött im himmel, dot vas close.* And he'd fight on, while I lay in the summer grass, staring at the sky."

*　　*　　*

A gentle breeze played over the enclosed screen porch, where soft yellow light shone on bamboo chairs and table. Carol Caspian was studying a portfolio, over late night coffee. "This is what's called a tweed mink, ten thousand dollars, look at the motion in it, that's one of our better ads, very schnitzy." She turned the page, to a couple in furs. "This is their marketing director, that's the vice-president, I got them to pose, and *that's* a good ad." She flipped the page. "Here's another terrific one, the new Bitch of the Month, in chinchilla."

"I'm going to have to hammer you to sleep."

"I'll schtup myself with Valium. Just look at this sable, it speaks for itself, it's not like selling ice in winter, but don't you think we brought something unique to it?"

"Unique doesn't do it justice."

"The client flipped. I took control, they were responsive." She sat back in the bamboo swing, pushed herself with her bare foot. She swung toward him, touched his knee with her toes. "I had my impact statements ready."

"I'm sure you did."

"The ad reeked of credibility. Turn the page, look at that next one—sophisticated couple near the sea, woman wearing twenty-five thousand dollar coat. We know what she had to do to get it, the question is, does she swallow it?"

Caspian stared at the ad, his mind drifting. He'd been thinking about the double *dicho.* The way the words of the *dicho* reversed themselves—each time he said it, each time he switched the saying around, he felt something move in himself, like a sculptured figure with two heads, one facing forward, the other behind. The heads kept turning, like the *dicho,* round and round.

And he'd come up with another *dicho:* A man may vanish yet still be visible.

And—a man may still be visible yet vanish.

Carol put her legs across his thighs, resting them there as she swung gently. "Have you been listening to me? Or am I getting glib and shallow? What time is it? I don't usually start getting glib and shallow until midnight."

"It's only eleven-thirty, but you're gaining momentum."

"I've got to take a peek at Alicia." She stood up, in peach culottes, with matching top, which she modeled for him momentarily, turning, hands in the front pockets. "You didn't comment on my new outfit."

"It couldn't have cost less than a thousand dollars, by Givenchy."

"Twenty-five cents at the thrift shop on the way home. Thelma's Clean Clothes Cheap."

"Remarkable."

"Listen—" Carol took him by the elbow, got him up from his chair. "The teacher says Alicia has been crying again."

"Did she say why?"

"Some other kid was punished and Alicia spent the day crying for her."

They walked into the hall and down it to Alicia's bedroom. Her ceiling was painted with silvery stars and moons; her bed was surrounded by her favorite stuffed animals, and her night-light burned with a gentle glow. But he could see from the way she was huddled in bed that she'd fallen asleep troubled as only a child can be. Carol tucked the sheet around her shoulders, and laid a kiss on her cheek.

They backed out of the room, and retraced their steps to the kitchen. Carol sat at the counter in front of a bowl of fruit, took an orange and peeled it, while outside the coyotes began their howling. She turned toward the darkened living room window. "They get on my nerves."

Caspian gazed out the window, toward the moonlit hills.

In the foreground, cast upon the glass, was his own pale reflection, in the filmy kitchen light. "If you listen, you can understand what they're saying."

"They sound like encyclopedia salesmen."

He continued staring at his reflection. Carol said softly, "Alicia cheats."

"On tests?"

"In the games the children play. Teachers notice these things." She toyed with the sleeve of her blouse, adjusting it, then smoothed out the seam in her secondhand culottes; he felt the mute question in her manner.

"And she thinks it has something to do with us?"

"In her own snide way, yes, she hinted that Alicia's trouble might have to do with us, that perhaps one of us was cheating on the other. She was dripping with understanding and feminine sympathy, the bitch, by the way, are you cheating?" She gave him a scrutinizing look, and he returned it with his actor's mask, calm and impenetrable. "You know I'm not."

She studied him closely, looking for a tiny crack in the mask. "Roma French?"

"Good god, no."

"I feel I'm going to eat a lot of pastry tonight."

"I'll tell you what I think is troubling Alicia, but you're not going to be able to make much sense of it."

"Try me."

"The house is haunted."

"David, I have enough trouble falling asleep."

"It's not the house, exactly. It's me. There's something stalking me."

"Who? What?"

"A dead Nazi."

"You're playing a part, right? An assignment from that three-hundred dollar an hour acting teacher you go to?"

"You know those stories about sorcerers using other people's bodies?"

"Tell them to use a hamster. David, this isn't like you."
She gave him her hand. "It's midnight, I'm a glib, shallow being, and dead Nazis don't buy ad space. Now let's go to waterbed, as we say in L.A."

He walked with her into their bedroom. A night-light burned, a brass Pierrot and Pirette. The bed was massive, bleached oak. She walked barefoot through the thick pile of the carpet. Everything was in place, everything tasteful in their perfect life. She took off her blouse and culottes, and stood naked for a moment in the interior light of the closet; a pair of mirrored doors reflected her in profile, creating an infinity of gamine forms. She brought out a nightgown, dropped it around her. "So why does Alicia cheat?"

"There's pressure in the atmosphere. She's trying to out-run it."

"I refuse to live in the Twilight Zone."

"Well, then just call it a distortion in my personality. Anyway, that's what she's picking up."

"She cheats because she's unhappy. She's unhappy because both her parents are egomaniacs. I suppose that's probably it."

"I don't think you have any responsibility for it."

"You're going to bed with your clothes on?"

"I'm going for a walk."

"Tell your ghost I said hello, I'll be in here plotzing myself to sleep."

He knelt at the edge of the bed, and stroked the hair gently away from her brow. "Use your hypnosis tape."

"I could never let myself be hypnotized by a man with a Texas accent."

"How about the subliminal one, with waves breaking on the shore?"

"There are people muttering underneath it, and I don't trust them." She rolled over and reached for her pills. "You should take one. Or maybe two. Give one to the ghost." She reached for the water. "I'll be comatose in five minutes."

"Goodnight," he said quietly, but she already had her eye-pads on, and was burying herself in the sheets.

He stepped out through the bedroom door, onto the deck. His dog moved silently out of the shadows to join him, and he recollected the words of the dog's trainer—*if there's anything raggedy goin' on, a Doberman will find it.*

The dog followed him, through the garden and out the gate. The coyotes had already disappeared, retreating back into the hills. He walked along the road, stopping to look down at the only light burning in his house—the soft glow of the nightlight in Alicia's room.

He continued along the empty road through the canyon. The Big Dipper hung down over his house, emptying its dark contents onto the world of Earth.

His thoughts, as he walked, were of himself and the universe. But nothing was revealed. The nuclear furnaces burned overhead. The road wound on through darkness.

The Doberman walked beside him, its long black snout pointed at the ground, nostrils working excitedly over the scent of the coyotes, its eyes flaming little rubies. The road curved, deeper down into the canyon; his canvas shoes were silent on the roadbed, the Doberman's nails dangerous-sounding little clicks. He turned off the road, into the brush, and the Doberman followed, nose working over the dry, sandy soil.

They were in the floor of the canyon, ringed by the dark, humped shapes of the hills.

"I'm here to meet you."

His voice echoed in the dark, empty ring.

"Come on. Let's have it out."

The hills received his voice, swallowed its echo, and returned to silence.

He continued on across the canyon floor.

Sachlichkeit, said a voice through the canyon's veil.

The Doberman's lips drew back in a snarl. A pair of uncanny human eyes were reflecting the moonlight just ahead. He saw the shadowy form of the head and body, and fear pressed against his heart—but a moment later the figure stood fully revealed beneath the station lamp, and it was just Corporal Sagen.

"Sagen, you startled me," said Felix. "Your eyes were like two mirrors of the moon."

"I've not been drinking, sir."

"Don't bother to explain, Sagen. Lead on."

They marched along the length of the platform and descended a flight of stone stairs to the freight yard where, at one of the sidings, the contents of a freight car were being unloaded into a light field truck. Felix stood beside the open doors of the freight and hurried the transfer. If the Field Police came nosing around, a number of embarrassing questions could be asked, the answers to which one gave by nodding one's head, into a basket. "Quickly, we haven't got all night."

The soldiers speeded their efforts. Corporal Sagen folded the railroad invoice, filing it in his clipboard with a number of others. Should someone in the hierarchy wish to know exactly what had arrived this night by rail, they would have this slip of paper, which showed tins of sausage and little else—certainly not caviar, snails, cigarettes, Dutch cigars, and chocolate. Sagen pointed to the load in the truck. "To Colonel Mueller's estate, sir?"

"No, the shipment goes to Armee Oberkommando, to General Siebecker." Felix made his own notation in a small black book, indicating the exact contents of the gift. He pointed to the cases of escargot. "Put one of those in my car."

Sagen stood by as Felix watched the last of the unloading. "Will that be all, sir?"

"We have a flight going out, with that special crate that came in last night."

"The paintings, yes sir."

"How do you know it contains paintings, corporal?"

"I don't know, sir. It was an idle comment, and will not be repeated."

"Each sparrow that falls is counted, but not by you, only by God and Colonel Mueller. Is that clear?"

"Perfectly." Corporal Sagen drew himself into statuelike immobility, with a blank stare to match. He had been at the front, and never, so long as breath moved in his body, did he want to repeat the experience.

"Should anyone question you, anyone at all, you know nothing, and the matter is referred directly to me. Is *that* clear?"

"Yes, *sir.*" Of all things, nothing could be more clear to Corporal Sagen. If someone was going to swing for whatever was in the mysterious crates that passed through his hands, let it be Falkenhayn. Sagen had a case of snails safely hidden in his own jeep, along with five hundred cigarettes, and that was enough for this night's work.

Felix crossed the freight yard, to where a soldier was just closing the back door of the Mercedes. Thin fog played about the station lamps, but no passengers entered. He slid in behind the wheel. The muted dash lights came on and the car purred softly; the leather upholstery whispered at his shoulders as he turned the automobile; another turn brought him through the station lot and into the street. The only thing for which there was no black market was weapons. People were sick of them. A silk shirt was worth more than a six-barreled mortar. In great demand were escape vehicles, even motorcycles, and the gasoline to propel them once the country collapsed. He'd made a good profit selling those particular items to high-ranking officers preparing to flee; in response, the Gestapo had intensified its investigations, and drawn its net tighter around the black market.

He drove the unlit thoroughfare, the play of his headlights sweeping shattered windows and skeleton doorways of houses struck by British Lancasters. His eyes automatically searched the skies as he drove, scanning for those high-moving shadows that carried the first decanate of fire in their bellies, aggressive and new. He took an out of the way road, past untempting targets, through the abandoned streets of the Jews tonight. He checked his rearview mirror, where only the empty road showed in the dark curtains of a clouded night.

This other, this faintly sensed spectre from the far tropic land—yes, I felt it strongly back there on the platform, that aroma of flowers and reddened fruit.

The spectre played at his nerves, with its warm, lovely breeze from nowhere. Had he seen a rathole in the fabric of the world, a tunnel blasted through the stuff of existence? Or was it the strain of his chess game played with the Gestapo; he and Mueller were in so deep, in every corner where money could be had, that an escape route through the stars seemed one's final move.

He entered the unbombed sector, down Ku'damm, where Marla now occupied a townhouse. Her papers identified her as one employed in Intelligence, where a number of "countesses" were at work for the Reich.

He parked, and a servant answered her door. He was shown in, and climbed the stairs to her sitting room. An antique atmosphere prevailed, with decor provided out of Colonel Mueller's own collection—a Roman marble horse in the entranceway, a seventeenth-century still life on the wall, lit by centaurs bearing soft-shaded lamps. Marla, in a black satin robe, lay stretched out on her long couch. "Darling Felix." She looked at him without interest, but laid aside her magazine. He sat across from her, taking a cigarette from his silver case; she'd had it inscribed for him the same way, DARLING FELIX, with the same indifference.

She uncoiled her legs and gazed at him over the surface of her onyx table. It and the Louis XVI chair he sat in had been part of a Danish estate that had broken up unexpectedly, the property graciously accepted by the army, in exchange for a handful of train tickets.

"Your new life seems to suit you," he said, lighting his cigarette.

"I once rode a paper moon in the chorus," she said. "I know how long illusions last." Her leg rocked beneath her robe, a gold slipper edging out from below.

"And how is your Italian attaché?"

"We're finished with him. I'm with a Polish baron now, helping him put his factory in a hillside. He wants it safe for the duration."

"Prudent fellow."

"He's made Mueller the principal stockholder." She rang for the maid and had her bring champagne. "And what have you been up to, darling?"

"Delivering snails and caviar." He took the champagne from the maid, popped the cork, and poured for himself and Marla. "You have many and beautiful possessions."

"I trust possessions."

"So did the Dane who owned that couch."

"Did you come here to discuss morality?"

"Our old theatre was bombed."

"Pity," said Marla.

He touched the toe of his boot to the onyx table, whose surface reflected candles hanging above it, in a Flemish chandelier. The pillaged objects seemed once again at home. Their natures, he thought, are colder than their owners. But the splendor of a well-appointed townhouse is not compromised by provenance.

"I brought you money." He laid an envelope on the table.

"From Mueller?"

"A secret admirer."

She examined the envelope. "This is your stationery."

"For your wardrobe. From your underwear salesman."

Marla slipped the envelope between the cushions of the sofa, and turned back to him, her expression softer now. "You always threw money away."

He placed his cigarette in the ashtray, where it burned, a slender stream of smoke rising from it. "Do you remember—I once thought to buy us a little chalet? In the north? We stayed at a lake, Steinhuder Meer."

"I hardly remember those two people." She swung her legs off the couch.

He retrieved his cigarette, watched the smoke curl around his fingertip. "We sailed on the lake, carried by the charm of the wind. But you're right, Marla, we're not what we used to be."

She stood, closing the robe at her ankles. "Do you know a man named Emil Weiss?"

"He's a Gestapo wheel."

"What did you ever do to insult him?"

"I? Nothing. Mueller and he don't get along." Felix inhaled nervously. "Why do you mention Emil Weiss?"

"He has risen in the world of the State Police."

"He's talked to you?"

"All very delicate, with an icepick in every word. He intimated that people who receive their orders from Mueller are under suspicion. In the most charming way, he quoted several articles of the penal code to me."

Felix stared down at the glowing onyx tabletop. The cold surface had a tomblike quality now, of a polished gravestone, and the same cold stone seemed lodged in his heart. Marla walked toward the fireplace. Above it hung a gold-framed mirror. She spoke to his reflection. "Have you prepared an escape for us?"

He stood, and smoothed down his collar. "Have you ever thought you could go through a mirror? Like the fabled Alice of England?"

Marla gazed at the glass, and spoke softly. "I've been going through it for years."

He went to her, touched her lightly, his palm running down the length of her smooth hair. "Emil Weiss may wake one morning, much to his surprise, with a bullet in his neck."

"The war is lost," said Marla. "We should get out now."

"There's lots of money to be made before the end comes. Give all your attention to the Polish baron and his hillside factory." He kissed her lightly on the cheek. "Keep your nerve. I'll get you out in time."

"I shall have to trust you." Her eyes expressed her doubts.

"A little bribery at the border, Marla. I've done it for perfect strangers. Won't I do it for someone I once loved?"

"Felix never loved anyone but Felix."

"That is where you're wrong, dear queen. I loved you on a particular Sunday. You were wearing a floppy felt hat. I wore an old suit, well pressed."

He put his lips to hers, and she closed her eyes, her body becoming soft against him; their kiss lasted a long moment, as the Danish clock ticked on the mantelpiece. He parted from her, and the maid appeared, to open the door for him. He descended the stairs, his gloved hand skimming the polished railing. At the stair's end was a golden globe, borne by a faun. He stepped on past it to the door, the street, and his Mercedes.

He started up, steered carefully through the pockmarked street, where the shadows went axle-deep. He patted the dash. Good leather, white gloves, I shall live through this night.

Buildings passed, lampposts bent their shadows across his gleaming hood. From over the rooftops, a siren began to sound. He parked on the Ku'damm, beside a row of boarded-over restaurants. The sky was vibrating with bombers, the warning too late as always. He was in the midst of it, bombs already exploding with a flash that lit the clouds.

Good boots, fine uniform, I shall live through this night.

He dove toward a cellarway. The roar of the Lancasters was answered by antiaircraft artillery, and the great searchlights were playing against the, clouds. The ground beneath him rumbled, a soldier's song passed through his brain:

A bullet came whistling,
for you or for me?

He huddled in the cellarway. The sky was filled with roaring and the rumbling in the street came nearer. An armored scout car turned the corner, its dark, slitted eyes searching with the warlord's face; the 2-cm cannon sniffed slowly around, until it was pointed directly at him.

He floated out of himself like a paper bird on a string.

He turned in the air, saw spirals of fog ascending over the city. Those are the dead, muttered the frozen scout car, its machinery still growling.

Ghosts bearing machine guns sped by, fighting on in illusion. He saw, amidst the spirals of the dead, a familiar spirit, spiraling toward him. It merged with him, changed his direction.

Caspian heard the snap in his neck, so sharp he thought it was broken. Slowly he lifted his head and found himself kneeling before his daughter's window.

The head of the institution sat across from Caspian, his office a cheerful one, the walls a bright peach, the windows giving out to the spacious grounds below.

"Your aunt has taken a turn for the worse, I regret to say." The doctor spoke softly, his voice like that of someone speaking to a skittish animal, to soothe it and calm it. Caspian had noted that the man talked that way to everyone—patients, nurses, orderlies, as if to him the entire world was slightly mad. "It was quite unexpected. I thought, with the medicine we had her on, she'd stay as she was. I'm sorry you won't be seeing the person you saw on your last visit." An orderly was summoned, to lead Caspian to his aunt's room. He found her seated by the window, staring through the bars. Her body was slouched, but her head was jutted forward.

"You have a visitor," said the orderly.

She bobbed her head around, her frail old neck extending from her small rounded shoulders. Her face was ravaged beyond what he could have imagined—the skin of her cheeks a dark yellow, as if she were jaundiced.

"Hello, Aunt Ruth." He took the aged, wrinkled hand in his. "Aunt Ruth, it's David."

"I know who you are."

"Can I do anything for you?"

She began to cough, a dry hacking effort to get something out of her lungs. He put his hand on her back, felt the vertebrae of her spine protruding. The coughing ceased, and she lifted her head again, wearily. "They're after me . . ."

"Who's after you, Aunt Ruth?"

"I borrowed money from them and now they're after me."

"I've paid all the bills. You don't owe anybody anything."

Her small, bony hand closed on his. "Debts and lies, they've found me out. They're coming for me. They torture everyone they take."

"Nobody's going to hurt you." He stroked the back of her hand. "You're here in your own sunny room, and nobody can get in to harm you."

"They're in already. You can't keep them out. Their agents are too smart for that. I've done terrible things. Debts and lies. They wired my brain while I was sleeping."

"Who, Aunt Ruth, who did it?"

"You know who."

"Who?"

"The Nazis."

He looked at the orderly. The orderly whispered near his ear. "Yesterday it was the KGB. Before that it was the FBI. Tomorrow it'll be something else."

Caspian sat down beside his aunt, and remained there with her for the afternoon, staring out through the bars of her cell, while she told him about Hitler, the wiring in her brain, and debts and lies, and the Beast of Buchenwald.

*   *   *

The sunlight fell upon the monastery panels, where the Oriental sages stood in their frozen mountain world. Gaillard and Caspian sat across from each other, in an atmosphere nearly as still as that in the painted panels. Gaillard was listening, eyes closed, as Caspian gave the details of his aunt's mental illness.

Gaillard opened his eyes. "Every family has its own pathology and stupidity. You shouldn't think that you're carrying some kind of hereditary taint." He put his feet up on a misshapen old hassock. "In the last bout you had over there—Felix was feeling the Gestapo closing in on him?"

"Yes."

"We're his Gestapo. He feels us tightening the net."

"And when we catch him?"

"Too soon to tell." Gaillard ran his hand slowly through his hair. Behind him, on the window ledge, a scarlet-breasted bird was pecking at his feeder, the bird's sharp beak filling the stillness with a fervent tap-tapping. Gaillard looked at the bird, but his eyes did not seem to take it in. He was thinking, and following the thought he turned back to Caspian. "You put Felix on like a theatrical costume."

"To the complete exclusion of my own personality?"

"That, I'll admit, is extreme."

"Thank you."

"But not unheard of. Healthy people lose their mind every day. A woman slicing potatoes suddenly throws the knife into a wall, where it quivers ominously. She catches her breath, thanking god she didn't stick it in her husband, who's sitting in front of the TV set cheering the Rams. In your case, the weird interlude lasts longer, but you're used to that, you've acted on stage, you've played parts that've lasted all evening, and all year. You're trained, if I may put it that way, toward a certain form of personality loss."

"I'm not a Stanislavsky actor. I stay outside the character I'm portraying. I never lose myself in a part, ever. I'm always there, watching me perform. Brecht called it *Verfremdung*, alienation. The character I play is a stranger, someone I don't know fully, no matter how I get into him, and he becomes that for the audience too—an unexpected creature, alive with doubt, shadows, things not explained." Caspian broke off suddenly. "It's a sensitive point with me. Most of my fellow actors are so far into naturalism that half the time you can't understand a word they're saying."

"Tell me about your study in Germany."

"It's the foundation of everything I've done since. When the Beatles got back from Hamburg they knew how to write songs. The same year, I got back from Berlin and I knew how to act."

Gaillard ran his hand over his brow a few times, tracing the furrows that were etched there. "We can assume you've absorbed something of the German spirit."

"I used to know my way around Berlin."

"Any Nazi acquaintances?"

"A playwright whose father had been head of Hitler Youth in a small northern village. The old man was still a Nazi and the son fought with him terribly about it. I never saw the return of the Third Reich, if that's what you mean."

"A world movement doesn't vanish so readily."

"The people I knew in the theatre were pretty decent."

"A world movement," continued Gaillard, "is, in fact, in all of us. Whatever surfaces in the human psyche is common property."

"You're saying there's a fascist in me?"

"I'm saying you had to seize power, break away from Pittsburgh, leave the place of the Satanic mills. Your dreams and fantasies show you raging at all of that still. Felix is part of that rage."

"But I've won all those fights. For whatever it's worth, I *am* a star."

"No, you're a deranged ogre. You want continual affirmation, which no one ever gets because other people have to live their lives too. They can't spend *all* their time adoring you. So the power drive is unsatisfied and continues to manifest."

"All stars want adoration. As my wife says, we're in a profession where we're the product."

"And it makes for some very acute distortion. I see it a lot out here, so I don't find Felix's takeover so odd."

"Do you remember the Collyer brothers?" asked Caspian. "The two old millionaires who were found in a room piled with newspapers? I know exactly how they felt. I'm afraid to leave my house."

"Yes, but you're already in the bayous. You've got to go forward. When you panic and try to turn back, it just weakens your position and Felix gets stronger." Gaillard returned his unseeing stare toward the window, where two birds were pecking now, and fluttering their wings. He gazed past them in thought, toward the valley. "The ego can split early in childhood when it's just taking shape. A gigantic shadow may form. This is what's haunting you, this split in yourself. I don't say you caused it. But only you can repair it."

"What made it split in the first place?"

"Really, it doesn't matter. But let's just say that when your ego was forming, something may have been disturbed in the atmosphere of your home. The ego carries in it a tendency toward splitting, and yours did so."

"Felix has been in me since childhood?"

"I should say he's your ego's twin. But not as strong. He's the weaker, that's why he's ruthless. You merged with the outer world, and he aligned himself with darkness."

"But how did he gather so much identity? Such a total world? There's everything there—cars, women, armies, cities, a complete reality."

"Not quite complete."

"What's lacking?"

"You. Felix needs you in order to really live. Otherwise he's the eternal exile. You have the upper hand in the ego complex. What he wants to do is seduce you over to his side, get your ego over into his dream reality. Get himself some authenticity. Felix may seem like a powerful creature to you, but he's just a *Würstchen,* a little sausage. You're stronger."

"How can you say that, when I'm walking around with my mind hanging out of my face?"

"I see much worse in a day. You can't imagine what it's like to have a true schizophrenic on your hands, a person whose vitality is so low that they can't be made to function. Nothing will bring them into the world, because they have no reserve of strength in the ego. They're hopeless, but I nurse them along, for that's all I can do. I've got one woman, a perfect genius, her visions are incredible. But she can't make anything of them, not for herself or anybody else. You, on the other hand, are vital, active, working. Don't worry so much about being vulnerable. It's when you're vulnerable that the soul is gaining depth."

"You call this depth? When I suffer reality loss?"

"Ok, you're having full-scale loss and it's horrible. But every gain, even small ones, are made by the ego suffering loss." Gaillard paused, dropped into thought for a moment. "I'm doing the best I can for you, which is to analyze the details of your fantasy, in order to shed light on it for you. You've stumbled into the core of a gigantic problem, I don't deny that. The archetypes rule the world."

"Amazing."

"What?"

"You still see my situation as psychology."

"I can't see it otherwise. I spend my whole day listening to people's visions. If I took them all as concrete I'd be ready for an asylum myself. And what use would I be to you if I said, yes, you're being taken over by a Nazi. I'm here to strengthen what is real, not lend ectoplasm to what is not." Gaillard brought his fingertips back together once more. "You're starting to get the picture."

"Am I?"

"Psychology is like tuning a radio. We can tune in on the

whole universe. You're one of those who's found it out. It's a shattering piece of knowledge, but it can be integrated."

*   *   *

He sat under a tree on the lawn at MGM, reading *Variety*. He'd spent the morning being fitted for his *Star Rover* wardrobe, and had a few more hours to go. The remnants of a studio sandwich lay on the grass beside him. He thumbed through to the last page of the paper out of life-long habit, then laid it aside in favor of another habit—watching people walk by. The stream of people through a studio gate was always an interesting study; a man could drive a long automobile, telephone-equipped, but when he stepped out of it, his walk revealed how secure he really felt.

At the moment, a studio carpenter was swaggering by, his hammer swinging loosely in a metal loop on his belt, and every step he took indicated that he wouldn't take any shit from anyone. Starring in his own mental movie, *Blazing Hammers*.

On first arriving in L.A., Caspian had built houses himself. He knew the *esprit* of carpenters, and the strange daydreams one fell into as the hours passed. One followed one's chalk line and level, and after awhile no problem of construction seemed too much.

A red Ferrari had entered the lot, and he watched Roma French park it, and get out. Her off-screen walk was a little cautious, he observed; stride was measured, her arms held close to her body, not swinging very far either way. Baggy jeans, a loose denim shirt, sneakers. Hair perfect in every detail, but something dejected in her style.

"Roma—"

She turned her head; he stood, and waved her over. She came toward him, a little self-consciously, he thought. Contract difficulties? Boyfriend? "You look like you need to sit and listen to the birds."

He lay his copy of *Variety* down on the grass for her. She laid on it, knees drawn up, arms wrapped around them. Staring straight ahead, she said, "I just came from my acting class." She tilted her head toward him, her long auburn hair hanging down below her shoulder. "I was terrible. And everybody else was wonderful."

"Anyone I know?"

She turned away, staring straight ahead again. "They're brilliant in class but when you see them on the screen, you wonder what they think they're doing."

Caspian nodded. "The acting class geniuses."

"It's demoralizing."

They sat in silence and, as promised, the birds were singing, up in the tree and on the sloping rooftop of the studio. Roma stretched out on the grass. "It takes me awhile to shake it off. When they critique my scenes, they tear me apart and throw me away. But in the end, somehow, they really don't know what acting's about."

Caspian leaned back on one elbow. "I know an English actor. He can only play kings. Because he's so—" He arched his head into a position of royal disdain.

"I wouldn't go to the bottom of the garden to see any of them, but because we're in this class—" She opened her purse, took out a little hand mirror. "Maybe I should quit the stupid thing."

"I wouldn't. Just my opinion, but I always seem to learn something."

"I'll be feeling inferior for the rest of the day, until I get home to my cats."

Caspian watched as she checked her makeup in the mirror, a small silver antique, with the chipped enamel remnants of a pastoral scene painted on its back. After a few touches on her mascara, she returned it to her purse, and smiled at him. "I'm still there."

"No question of that."

"I've always been a klutz. I must have one leg shorter than the other. I can fall down walking across my own living room."

"Did you fall down in class?"

"We use big wooden blocks for props. I fell over one of them. Everybody loved it." Roma nodded across the lot, to where another young woman had just parked her car and was stepping out. "There's someone who's coordinated. Do you know her? The stunt girl, April O'Keefe?" Roma waved, and April waved back. "I always feel I should do my own stunts, but at the last minute I chicken out and let April do them."

"What's wrong with that?"

Roma watched, as April marched into the shadows of the entranceway. "I've got no problem with the fact that I make a fortune compared to her. I mean, I'm worth more to the studio in dollars. But when she falls a hundred feet from a window in my costume, I know my *life's* not worth more than hers." Roma stood, handed him his *Variety.* "I've got to run."

He watched her walk toward the studio, then made his own way slowly back toward the building where the costume fitting was being done. The studio streets were baking, and the asphalt soft beneath his feet.

A small moving van came by, slowed, and turned the corner just ahead of him, a load of electric cable dangling out its back end. The van cut sharply and a wheel went up on the curb; the cables shifted and one of them fell out. "Hey—" Caspian called to the driver, who glanced in his rearview mirror, and stopped. "I've got my head up my ass today," said the driver, as he climbed out.

Caspian bent to help him with the cable, and a sharp, cracking noise sounded at the base of his skull; the bright day grew dim. When he straightened up it was night.

Felix lifted the box of inks and rollers, and handed it up to The Weasel, who stood at the back of the stolen moving van.

"I heard a noise," said Felix, "like rifle fire."

"Very likely," said The Weasel.

"But from within my skull." Felix felt the back of his neck, shrugged, and returned into the building, and down the basement steps. Gondolph was coming up them, a small duplicating machine in his arms. "For god's sake," he said, "hurry."

"I think I put my neck out," said Felix.

Gondolph looked over the glasses on the end of his nose, and hurried by impatiently. Felix entered the forger's rooms in the cellar, where boxes of paper and inks stood in waiting piles—paper whose watermarks had been produced after tremendous labor, paper worth much to Gondolph and even more to the Gestapo. But a friend of The Weasel's at Prinz Albrechtstrasse had tipped them that an arrest was coming.

The little forger appeared in the doorway again, out of breath, The Weasel beside him. The Weasel looked at the boxes. "Which?"

"That one. Those pigments can never be reproduced again."

"At your service—" The Weasel lifted the box, and Felix lifted another, and went up the stairs beside The Weasel, with Gondolph following, bearing chemicals, crushed rock of a certain kind, aged coffee grinds of a particular blend. . . .

"And to think how much I paid that block warden," said Gondolph, puffing on the stairs.

"Someone else paid him more," said The Weasel.

"I forged him the most beautiful ration stamps he ever saw. I got his nitwit nephew out of the army." They stepped into the darkened street, and walked toward the stolen moving van. "Be careful with that box! If those bottles break, there'll be no more ration stamps for anyone."

"Read our advertisement," said The Weasel. "Safe Packing and Handling in Sanitized Vans."

"With the Gestapo on the way, my god, my hands are shaking. Look at that—" Gondolph held up his right hand. "I couldn't forge my own name."

"Well," said Felix, "should we clear out and leave the rest behind?"

"My business is ruined if we do." Gondolph hurried back

toward the building, and Felix followed, not exactly lingering himself. He was in uniform, helping an enemy of the State.

"Have you got a piano?" asked The Weasel, coming down the stairs behind them. "We specialize in moving them."

Gondolph rushed ahead into his old basement room, was jamming brushes and pens in his pockets, scooping up a line of counterfeit government and military stamps. "Sonsofbitches, hounding a craftsman . . . take those medical forms, and those hospital certificates." He pushed by Felix, wheezing with exasperation. "Some poor devil may need proof of a bad case of piles."

"Your new home will be safer," said The Weasel, shouldering another box.

"Where am I going to be?"

"Downtown. Bülowbogen."

"Where all the old whores end up," grumbled Gondolph. "A street walker there only gets ten marks."

"Think of all the money you'll save," said The Weasel, ascending behind him.

"I grew up on this street," said Gondolph.

"So did Block Warden Karpus," said Felix, behind them on the stairs.

"The oleaginous bastard," wheezed Gondolph, as they stepped through the upper doorway. "He's put half the neighborhood in concentration camps."

"Has he?" said The Weasel softly, lifting his box into the back of the van.

"Of the four hundred and eighty thousand block wardens in Berlin—" Gondolph set his box in behind The Weasel's. "—Karpus is the slimiest."

"I'm getting nervous," said Felix. "I can feel something moving on us."

The Weasel smiled toward Gondolph. "Felix has become a clairvoyant. Hears voices."

"I can't leave my type fonts behind," said Gondolph. "I've slaved for years to reproduce imperfections identical to the government printers." They returned to the hallway. An elderly woman had opened her door, and was looking out. "Moving day," said The Weasel, lifting his little black derby. She stared at him suspiciously, but when she saw Felix's uniform, she scurried quickly back behind her door.

"Grandmother Karpus," said Gondolph. "She spies for him. The only ones left in the building are Party members."

"And what did they think you were?" asked Felix, as they entered the forger's rooms once more.

"An explorer." Gondolph hurried to his boxes of type fonts, and handed them up to Felix. "I'll get the rest. Weasel, take the engravings. Over there. British five pound notes." Gondolph looked around. "What else, what else?"

"I presume," said Felix nervously, "you're leaving the wallpaper? Or should we peel it off for you?"

"You'd be amazed what's hidden behind it," said Gondolph. "But it's for the termites now." He shuffled back and forth, peering into other boxes, then shook his head. "Let's say adieu, my blood pressure's up."

"A moment," said The Weasel. "What's this?"

"Some very good schnapps."

"I thought so." The Weasel opened the bottle, took three glasses down from a shelf. "We must drink to Safe, Dependable Moving." He poured the liquor carefully, filling each glass. "There you are, Gondolph. A man shouldn't bid farewell to an old home without toasting it."

"Toast? We'll be toasted, they'll toast our stretched necks." Gondolph took the glass, tipped it up, and drained it down. The Weasel clicked his glass against Felix's. "Haste is the Devil's pace."

Felix drank, set his glass down. "Perhaps we should wait and offer some to the boys from Prinz Albrechtstrasse."

"For the love of god," moaned Gondolph, "let's go."

"You have absolutely everything you treasure?" asked The Weasel. "There'll be no return visit."

"I have the essentials of my trade. Bed sheets I can replace."

The Weasel picked up the end of a gray, wrinkled sheet, and held it out at a distance in his gloved hand. "Such as these can never be replaced."

"I'm leaving," said Gondolph, "with or without you." He led them back out through the door, but then turned for a last look. "I'll miss it, though."

"And it will miss you," said The Weasel.

Gondolph put his foot on the stairs, lifted his head, and froze. He brought his foot slowly back, removed his glasses from the end of his nose, and turned to The Weasel. "Military police," he said in a choked voice.

Two shadowy forms at the top of the steps descended, into the light that shone on the middle of the staircase. Their machine pistols glistened, their holsters creaked on their hips as they came slowly down.

"I know them," whispered Gondolph. *"They burnt a man to death on this block. Set fire to his prayer shawl."*

The two policemen were large, heavy-limbed, the stairs creaking beneath their weight. They came off the last step, unhurried, like the cat who has caught the mouse out of his hole. The first one put the barrel of his machine pistol under Gondolph's chin. "Going somewhere?"

"Yes, sir. Helping my sister to move."

"Where is she?"

"Just inside, sir."

"What is an officer of the Wehrmacht doing here?" He pushed Gondolph aside and stepped toward Felix.

"Friend of the family," said Felix. He let his hand drop slowly down toward his pistol.

The policeman turned to his associate. "I think we've interrupted something very interesting."

"A fine little party." The second one put a finger under Felix's lapel and lifted it lightly. "The kind that puts an officer to work breaking rock. Wouldn't you like that? Helping to build the new Autobahn?"

"If you're lucky," said the other. "If not—" He made a snapping motion with his fingers, near Felix's neck.

"Gentlemen, please," said The Weasel, stepping between them, "I can explain everything."

"Shut up, you little ass-plug." The policeman shoved The Weasel against the wall. "Let's see your identity card."

"Of course," said The Weasel quietly. He put one gloved hand to his coat, drawing it slowly open. He held his other hand up momentarily, to show it was incapable of treachery. Then he put it inside, and brought it out with a lightning thrust, upward into the policeman's gut. He sliced sideways, and whirled to his right, sticking the point of the knife through the other policeman's neck. The two giants were dead at his feet before they'd even released the safeties on their weapons.

"Amateurs," he said, with quiet scorn, and stepped away from the pool of blood forming on the hall floor.

"Jesus Christ almighty," said Gondolph.

The Weasel wiped his knife blade on one of the dead men's trousers, and slipped it back inside his jacket. "Where is Block Warden Karpus's apartment?"

"First floor, front."

They dragged the dead policemen up the stairs, to the Block Warden's door. The Weasel took off his derby, removed a piece of wire from inside the lining, and picked the lock. The door swung open and he switched on the light. "Shall we make them comfortable?"

They dragged the bodies across the living room, and dumped them on the couch. Gondolph looked around the Block Warden's place, admiring the heavy bourgeois furniture, the fine china, the thick carpet. Felix and The Weasel propped the burly policemen upright on the couch, hands folded in their laps. "An artistic tableau," said The Weasel, "but it needs something else."

Felix plucked a yellow rose from a vase and put it between one of the policemen's fingers.

"Here," said Gondolph, removing a copy of *Mein Kampf* from the bookshelf. He fitted it in the hands of the other policeman, pages open, the man's head lowered toward them. "Only the dead can understand the Führer's prose."

They backed to the door, went out, and closed it quietly behind them. When they reached the front hall, they found the Block Warden's grandmother peering up the stairs. The Weasel lifted his derby. "Your grandson won two pigs in a raffle."

The old woman stared at him, her brow lowered in a frown. The Weasel put his derby back on. "My advice to you," he said, with a slight bow, "is to join a nudist cultural group."

He walked out the front door, Felix and Gondolph behind him. The dark street was empty. They hurried to the van, and Felix brought the back doors closed.

"Rifle fire," he said.

"I hear nothing," said Gondolph.

The sharp, whistling crack was repeated at the base of Felix's skull, and night became day. David Caspian was staring into the loaded studio van, the coils of cable loaded deep within it now. "That's better," said the driver.

"Yes," said Caspian, backing slowly away, "much better."

"He was one of the real producers. We needed a dead moose and in two hours he found one that'd just been hit by a train."

Herman Armas sipped his gazpacho soup.

". . . isn't this pretty . . . silk ankle pants with a chiffon sheath. . . ." The model from Saks of Beverly Hills stopped at their table, turned in front of Roma, then Caspian, then Myron Fish, as Fish leaned toward the director. "And before that he was the greatest agent in the world. He once sold a studio a dead actor."

"And now he's dead himself."

"These things happen."

". . . notice the simplicity of this striped tunic . . ."

"When he said the check was in the mail, it meant you'd never get it, but all in all—"

"A wonderful person," said Fish. "Didn't you think so, David?"

"The best," said Caspian, having twice been forced to sue the recently deceased producer.

The waiter brought luncheon champagne, and they touched glasses. "I think you'll be glad to know," said Armas, "that Howard Hibbs is definitely going to write the score."

Caspian closed his eyes, already hearing a musical soundtrack of devastating sentimentality.

"David loves Howard's work," said Fish.

". . . and here we have a little side-buttoned turquoise jacket . . ." The model turned for them, then moved like a zombie toward the next table.

"It's a *special* film," continued Fish. "I think we're talking major myth."

"We're talking major heat stroke," said Roma. "I mean, six weeks in Death Valley?"

"Death Valley's very do-able," said Fish.

"I like the light there," said Armas.

Roma's attention returned to the fashion show. She herself wore a soft suede skirt, which hung in long folds to her calf, and the model had complimented her on the matching fringed and beaded jacket, which reflected the light in glittering little points along her arms; her blouse was loose-fitting silk, in creamy white, and it hung negligently away from her breasts.

The waiter returned with their lunch, served it, then gesticulated with the sacrament of pepper dispensed from a large wooden mill.

"You're all going to have an exceptionally brilliant masterpiece," said Fish. "Triumphant, stunning, and magnificent, in that order."

"I've always wanted my own planet," said Roma.

". . . a deeply wrapped dress, notice the open back, with slashes of pink . . ."

"It'll simply be *the* space adventure film of—" Fish paused, dramatically "—the summer." He patted his lips with his napkin and turned to Roma. "That was a terrible shame, those recent accounting improprieties you suffered. I felt as if my own daughter had been raped."

Armas nodded. "I always have Solomon and Finger warming up in the bullpen."

"Of course none of us," said Fish, "want to be locked in mortal struggle for a few extra dollars." His hand went to the chain at his throat, and the gold coin suspended there. Light from the window struck the disk; it caught Caspian's eye with its soft brilliance, its edges liquid and melting . . .

. . . *as if I were able to dream with my eyes wide open,* thought Felix, fitting a cigarette into an ebony holder. The restaurant of the Hotel Eden in Berlin was large, crowded, but he'd been seeing a much more intimate place, a smaller, darker dining room, and every detail had been perfect, and vivid, and real. He'd been there with friends, but he was a different man—a man of another sunrise.

He lit his cigarette. A fashion show was in progress at the hotel, a model coming down a raised runway, her body clad in a flaring skirt. He kept his eyes on her, though his first business was with the man seated beside him, Herr Wurm, furnace manufacturer.

Herr Wurm passed a heavily ringed hand over his bald head. He was a small man, and Felix felt he knew him from before somewhere, but his mind would not serve the memory up, its location in one of the odd dreams he'd been having lately.

"Yes, Lieutenant, only a few details need to be worked out. And, if I may say so, this is a most pleasant atmosphere in which to do it." Herr Wurm brought his pudgy hands together and applauded as the model withdrew behind the curtains and was replaced by another. He reached for his portfolio, brought out a blueprint.

"With the installation of the furnace that your section has

ordered, there is an optional ash-remover, most efficient when such large quantities of ash are being produced. If that amount were to be removed by hand, well, it would be very slow." Wurm modestly pointed out nice details of the mechanism.

"I'll give it to Colonel Mueller." Felix returned his gaze to the runway, down which the model came, in tennis clothes.

"Of course, of course." Wurm turned toward Marla. "Is the fashion show to your liking, Countess?"

Marla smiled at Wurm, but Felix observed: her interest was with another gentleman at the table, who directed films for the Propaganda Ministry. Wurm looked back to Felix. "This is my third furnace installation for the Reich," he said, confidentially.

Felix kept his eyes on the runway. There wasn't anything for him in this furnace business, a cumbersome installation at one of the Göttingen armaments plants, though Mueller had undoubtedly made something on the sale. Marla leaned toward him, said softly, "Do you see, just entering at the door. He's looking our way."

Emil Weiss, the Gestapo lieutenant colonel, was in civilian dress, but his evening wear was as impeccable as any uniform. Observing Marla's attention, he returned it with a bow; his eyes fastened on Felix, like a hawk sighting a prey too well sheltered for a strike. But I've made note of you, his hunter's manner seemed to say. I'm always circling here.

Felix returned Weiss's stare. I too am a hawk, Herr Weiss. Falcon is my name. I too have talons, and I'm not so polite either.

The officer of the Gestapo passed near their table, and Felix felt how much more pleasant the world would be with Weiss gone from it.

"Yes, Herr Wurm, I'm sure the armaments plant will be most interested in your ash-remover. As you say, the unit is incomplete without it."

"We wish to offer every possible service."

"I'll be inspecting your installation myself."

"Will you, Lieutenant? Before I forget, I've brought a small gift for you. It won't offend—?"

"Not at all."

Into Felix's courier case went one of the finest wristwatches in Europe. "Business need not preclude a mood of good feeling, Lieutenant. I myself will cherish this evening we've had together, and I like to hope you'll maintain some faint memory of me."

"I'll not forget you, Herr Wurm," said Felix, closing his courier case.

Again Wurm smiled, and ran a thumb under his lapel, in which a tiny gold swastika was fixed. A nearby spotlight, following a fashion model as she turned at the end of the runway, bathed the twisted golden cross in a flash of brilliance.

Felix saw Gestapo Chief Weiss cast in gold light, needles of it shimmering around him; Weiss's eyes pierced him, pinned him, held him fast.

. . . my net is closing on you . . .

Felix felt a soft popping sensation at the base of his skull, and suddenly he knew who Weiss really was.

". . . and I saw my commission flying out the door. David, are you listening to me?"

Caspian lifted his head, and stared into Myron Fish's face. Fish was seated at a desk in his own office, and Caspian was seated across from him. Fish leaned forward anxiously. "David? Are you having indigestion?"

Caspian looked around the room. "Myron, how long have we been in your office?"

The agent got up, came around the desk. "What weird drug did you take at lunch?"

"You're a man named Wurm. You live in Germany. You were just with me, at a Nazi fashion show."

"David, a Middle America matinee idol should not take LSD, except in the privacy of his own swimming pool."

*   *   *

Doctor Gaillard looked at him across the table. "So I'm on the other side now?"

Caspian had flown back from the desert in a hired jet to keep his appointment. "You're Gestapo Chief Emil Weiss."

Gaillard was silent a moment, his finger tapping gently on the arm of his chair. "We must be getting somewhere." He took off his glasses, polished them on his shirttail. "Tell me some dreams."

"A stupid dream. I was president of the United States."

"For a Hollywood actor, that's no longer a stupid dream."

"I'm not political."

"That's what they all say. To be president of the United States means you have all the power." He gazed down at his sandaled feet, letting the silence speak to Caspian. Then he glanced up, one eyebrow raised. "Our old omnipotence fantasy? Seems like it's still around."

"I don't want to rule the world. I'm fixated on one thing, constantly, and that's the fact that I've become a lunatic."

Gaillard pointed to the file cabinet across the room. "I've got a patient who hears voices coming from his big toe. I've got another guy who believes his thoughts are being broadcast to everybody in the supermarket. And a young woman who swears her thoughts are being stolen and used by people on the soap opera she watches every afternoon." He turned back to Caspian. "Those are my crazies. You don't qualify."

"Well," said Caspian wearily, "just what is my clinical classification?"

"That's not so easy to answer. And does it matter?"

"I feel like being a statistic today. To keep up my faith."

Gaillard pointed to the rows of case studies on his bookshelves. "You're not in any of them. I've never met anyone even remotely like you."

*   *   *

"The purpose of having money," said Julius DeBrusca, "is to sleep at night."

Caspian sat with DeBrusca beneath a large canvas awning on the set. A gleaming spaceship rested in the desert just beyond them, with *Star Rover* production people swarming over it. They'd put the skeleton ship together during the early morning hours, out of modular units manufactured back at the studio. While DeBrusca droned on, Caspian gazed at the ship, a beautiful creation that looked as if it really could lift off and penetrate the outer reaches of space—while hanging onto the skeletal other side of it were the young artist-technicians in DRINK BEER T-shirts who'd designed it.

"Money," DeBrusca continued, "is motion. Last week in Vegas I saw a dice table being hoisted up the side of the casino hotel to the room of an Arab who didn't like crowds."

DeBrusca's male secretary sat beside him, writing. DeBrusca glanced at him. "Did you get that, Robert? Or should I speak slower?" He turned to Caspian. "Robert's going to write a book someday, exposing me. Isn't that right, Robert?"

"Not at all, sir. This is a letter to my wife."

"Expose me, it's good for box office. Money breeds in books like the one you're writing."

"Here's the envelope, Mr. DeBrusca. Addressed to my wife."

"Here's the title for you. Call it, *The Dogs Were on Half-Salary.*" DeBrusca turned to Caspian. "I never pay movie animals full wages."

Caspian returned his gaze to the spaceship, and to the array of space weapons, robots, and extraordinary ground vehicles that surrounded it—millions of dollars worth of technical genius, all of it spread out on the desert in front of DeBrusca, who watched to see that not one extra nut, bolt, or dash of paint was used. He pointed with his cigar to the spaceship, and grunted.

Myron Fish ducked in under the awning and sat beside them. "I've just come from putting a woman in a show." He passed a hand over his suntanned dome. "She had a complete blackout, forgot all her lines, and had to be carried offstage."

"She wanted to be released from her contract," said De-Brusca.

"Buy them out when they're young," said Fish. "That's the only way to be sure." He wiped his perspiring dome with a handkerchief, and looked at Caspian. "If I had hair, I'd consider myself a perfect human being."

Caspian knew how the lady-in-question felt, had himself gotten involved in projects from which the only sensible course seemed to be to bail out. But he'd always stayed, believing his own hard work could turn the film around. His shock, consequently, was considerable, when he walked onto a set that looked as if it had been designed by a traveling salesman and lit in colors that resembled a Batman comic book. Then, when the dailies started looking like grandiose home movies, the actors would get nervous and begin overacting, and the director would try and compensate for this with a stream of congratulations, by which you knew, with absolute certainty, that you were in a turkey. Then you reflected on the shortness of human life, and vowed to work henceforth only in small, whimsical films, or Off-Broadway. And then Myron Fish would go to work on you, and reel you back in, using the words "millions of dollars," with great frequency. Caspian tended to listen when these three words were spoken to him by Myron.

He lifted himself from his chair, out of the stream of conversation, and threaded his way through the labyrinth of equipment covering the desert floor. He stepped into his air-conditioned Winnebago, shut the door and sat down in the cool refuge. Through the blinds he saw Roma's trailer nearby, to which her many attendants came and went.

"Roma is Marla is Roma . . ." He let the blinds fall shut. His costume had been laid out for him—the uniform of a lone wolf of the cosmos, shiny black, with silver piping on the sleeves. He stripped and got into it, looked at himself in the illuminated dressing room mirror.

A knock came on the door and Victor Quatrelle stepped through, in the robe of an intergalactical magician. "I come from Asteroid Bagel Nosh."

He lifted his robe over his knees, flopped on the couch, and glanced around at the pristine interior of the mobile home. "In the old days, we'd take advantage of a quiet space like this to smoke dope before going in front of the camera. Things that'd make a Christian man shameful." He reached into his robe and brought out a joint. He lit up, and parted the blinds behind him with his finger. "Lots of cut-rate activity going on out there."

The gaffers had surrounded the spaceship with lights, giving the hull an unnatural sheen, as if from some internal force. "Rocket to Reno, senior citizens half price." Quatrelle let the blind snap shut, as an amplified voice sounded in the desert air. *"Ready. Places, please. Have fun. I like that smile, it's real genuine."*

"He likes it, it's genuine," echoed Quatrelle, fanning his heavy, muscular legs with his robe.

Another knock sounded on the door, followed by the voice of the wardrobe mistress. "Is everyone decent?" She came in, looked Caspian over, and gave her approval to his costume. She was about sixty years old, dry and hard as a desert boulder, and seemingly as impregnable, but Caspian wondered what her secret fears were, wondered where her shadow fell, a question he found himself asking about everyone he met lately, trying to discern their formula for staying real.

She turned Quatrelle around in his robe. He peered at her over his shoulder. "I'm supposed to have a cattle prod."

"Props has your magic wand."

Quatrelle bent into an aged crouch, the smoking joint concealed in his hand, as he spoke in an old man's trembling whine. *"I've got to disco tonight and props has my wand."*

The wardrobe mistress ignored him, as she straightened the seams of his robe. "Remember to keep this pulled forward."

Quatrelle stayed in his demented crouch, following her to the door. "I want some teenage sex!"

She closed the door in his face. Caspian opened the refrigerator, brought out a container of orange juice. He sat down with it, and opened his script; closing his eyes he whispered his next lines at the ceiling.

Quatrelle looked at him. "Talking to your Nazis?"

"Not at the moment."

"Next time you do, tell them the steering column is loose on my daughter's Volkswagen."

"Did I ever tell you I gave Cooper his first haircut?" The makeup man had cornered Caspian at the edge of the set, and maneuvered him into a canvas chair; he bore a battered old kit bag, from which mirror and comb protruded, both worn from long use. "You know, you look a little like Coop." He styled Caspian's hair, wave by wave, combing, patting, spraying. "Now don't change it, don't touch one hair." He took a last critical look at the delicate coiffure, and walked off; the wardrobe mistress came by and put a space helmet over it.

Beyond them was the spaceship. "Hit all the switches."

"Got 'em."

"Higher—flood it—good."

Caspian walked toward the ship, where he was joined by Myron Fish. "Your work is the talk of this production." Ahead of them on the set was Herman Armas, conferring with his assistant director. Fish lowered his voice. "You're happy with Armas's direction, am I right?"

"Apart from not directing me—"

"He has confidence in your instincts."

"He never stretches his actors."

"What are you, a living bra? Get into that spaceship and just be yourself."

Caspian took a last look at the script and handed it to Fish, as the director came toward him. "It's a lost world you've landed in—" Armas gestured, at the vans, coffee wagons, trucks, lighting towers, through which crowds of people were moving. He nodded at the assistant director, who lifted a megaphone. "Can we have quiet work, please, quiet work."

The carpenters laid down their hammers. Caspian moved onto the sands beside the spaceship. "All right, David, you're alone, more so than you've ever been before, in an alien atmosphere. Give me that quality again, of somebody who's walked off the edge of the world." Armas turned toward his camera crew. "Roll 'em."

"Scene two, take one."

"Speed."

"Action."

The sand was hot and yielding beneath his step. The first cameraman dollied past Caspian, working his fine adjustment knobs, with which it was said he could write his name, which was four syllables long in Polish. Caspian spoke his lines, walking toward the dolly track.

"Good, David, could we try that once more, please."

They repeated the shot five times, then paused to reload the camera. Caspian stepped under a sunshade, near the cameraman, who had his arms inside a sewed-up coat, beneath which he threaded film into his instrument, a faraway look in his eyes. DeBrusca walked by, hands folded behind his back, growling to his secretary, ". . . we can thank Al Jolson's prick for Actor's Equity."

Fish, standing behind Caspian, said quietly, "I love that man. I'm talking in terms of affection."

The cameraman withdrew his hands, brought out the loaded camera, and nodded to the A.D., who lifted his megaphone.

"Places, please."

"David, let me have it one last time. You're the outcast, alone, it's *Last Year At Marienbad,* walking the halls lugubrious." Armas looked toward his camera crew. "Roll 'em."

"Scene two, take six."

"Speed."

"Action."

Caspian walked through the sands, toward the dolly track, glistening in the desert sun. He gazed at the rails, eyes traveling along them to the vanishing point, *ganz grau und aufgelöst,* all gray and merging.

The railroad tracks fell behind in silver streaks, their steel gathered into the mist of morning. Felix stared at them, and at the hypnotic fluttering of the railroad ties. He rested his arm against the back window of the train, through which he could see the world falling away, to the rhythmic clicking of the wheels.

I've dreamt of that place a dozen times now . . .

A whistle blew, and he turned toward the approaching platform, where he spied his waiting host. When the train stopped, he descended, and was greeted by the plant manager, Kessler, who showed him to their automobile.

"We've been spared so far," said Kessler, as they drove from the station. "But the Lancasters have gotten new Rolls Royce engines. We'll be hearing them soon."

Felix watched the gray, soot-covered buildings pass. Factory sounds filled the oppressed atmosphere, and the chemical smell was strong, a sickly sweet odor that forced Felix to roll up his window. "The barometer is low here," he said, and Kessler looked at him, and looked away. "Morale has not been good, and for my part I consider that sabotage. In this factory, anyone who goldbricks is a candidate for the concentration camp."

"A bit severe?"

"The Minister of Armaments has himself issued the directive. A few good examples among these shirkers will spread the word in a hurry." Kessler lit a cigarette, tossed the match out the window. "No one is excluded. There's more than one plant manager behind barbed wire now. The swine were siphoning off materials for their own use. Well—" He glanced at Felix's uniform. "I don't have to tell you about such matters."

"Yes, I know all about that sort of thing, for unfortunately it is widespread. There are many important persons who will never be apprehended." He looked back at Kessler. "Good connections, you know. The right families."

"They're all swine," snapped Kessler, but said no more, as they were entering the gates of a large compound, a city within the industrial city. Felix saw streets leading to residential houses, stores, recreational facilities. Looking upward, he spied a carapace and turret rising above the trees of an adjacent hillside. "And that?"

"The office of von Göttingen. He'll be coming down to meet you."

Kessler drove past a wire enclosure, within which rows of barracks stood, guarded by factory police. "The conscripted labor force," said Kessler, nodding toward prisoners visible on the street of the enclosure. "They're not much good, but we find use for them." He motored on, deeper into the factory complex, finally pulling up at a gleaming office building. "Here we are, Lieutenant. I can offer you some breakfast."

Kessler led him to his office, where coffee and cake awaited them. "Company policy has always been generous, we have medical and educational benefits, and a good pension. There's no excuse for blatant absenteeism, which is our greatest problem. The workers are losing their will, you see. But von Göttingen has stood by them. Wages have not been cut. What needs to be cut are a few heads, I'd say. After all, we are at war."

"No one can have failed to notice that," said Felix. "But execution for absenteeism?"

Kessler turned a cool gaze on Felix. "You sympathize with deliberate sabotage? Let me remind you that Armaments Minister Speer considers absenteeism to be ruinous to the war effort. Frankly, Lieutenant, I'd not expected this from—" He glanced at Felix's regimental insignia. "—a man in your position."

"I'd not been informed that plant managers now had the power of life and death over their employees." A Nazi with a swastika on his jockstrap, reflected Felix. Nevertheless, to bait him further could jeopardize business. *Just go down there and look after my interests, dear boy, show them that Mueller is prepared to assist in every way possible.* "Forgive me, Herr Kessler, I am overstepping my mission. I am here only to see that you are happy with the installations Colonel Mueller has been supervising. I refer to the furnaces used for burning the assembly line's waste material."

Kessler lifted an eyebrow. "I accept your apology, and extend my own. We are all under a strain. But how droll you are, Lieutenant." Kessler interrupted himself, and gestured to the window, through which Felix could see an auto approaching from the castle. Felix glanced back to Kessler. "That's a handsome machine."

"A Belgian Minerva. Von Göttingen is a collector."

Felix watched the car window as the automobile neared, and spied the aging aristocrat in its shadows. Kessler went toward the door. "I've been with von Göttingen twenty-five years. The present crisis has brought out the best in him."

The great industrialist entered, without ceremony. Felix clicked his heels, and bowed toward the old lion. "I am honored to meet you, sir."

"Your engineers have been most obliging. Tell Colonel Mueller I'm pleased, and anticipate a long relationship."

"He'll be happy to hear that, sir."

"He gets things done. No red tape. Some of these military

chaps can't supply a paper clip without everything in tripli-
cate."

"Colonel Mueller knows there is a war on."

"Without his influence on my suppliers, this plant would
be stuck. Have you finished your coffee? I'll show you around."

He led Felix on a tour that took them from one roaring
building to another. Conversation was difficult, and von Göttingen spoke with gestures, indicating where the weapons were
made, and the peacetime products. A guard bearing a rubber
truncheon moved through the ranks of the assembly line workers, most of them sickly looking women in sack cloth. Von
Göttingen's eye passed over the workers, to mechanical elements
of his factory of which he was proud. The tour ended beside a
vat of glowing steel. Von Göttingen smiled, his face yellow in
the glow, like a head swimming off a gold coin.

They walked along an iron ramp, and down a flight of
echoing stairs, which led to an outer door. "And Wurm's
furnace?"

Von Göttingen pointed, toward the barbed wire enclosure.
"It's in use there, but the area is dangerous. Disease, you know.
Those people are like rats. We were afraid of the plague. That's
why I had to order the furnace, to dispose of the bodies."

Felix paused on the outer walk of the building, unable to
move. A cloud, blended from the many smokestacks of the
complex, hung low in the sky. Von Göttingen took him by the
arm. "I have another contract for your Colonel, one requiring
his expeditious touch. It is all prepared, in the simple form
Colonel Mueller and I prefer. You understand?"

"It is for such matters Colonel Mueller has trained me,"
said Felix, stiffly.

"Good. The contract is waiting for you. None but Mueller
must see it. It's a straightforward matter, just some more equipment, but I don't want other army dignitaries questioning its
necessity here. Mueller has a way, as you know, of circumvent-
ing much bother." Von Göttingen showed him back into the

main building. "Well, Lieutenant, this concludes my business with you. Your train does not come until this afternoon. There are more pleasant parts of our establishment you can enjoy. Permit me to suggest the executive's lounge. You'll find some excellent port."

Felix made his way through a labyrinth of buildings, to the lounge—a somber study, of exposed beams and dark oak paneling. It was furnished with red leather chairs around a crackling fireplace; the wine was served in handcut glassware; a public relations man was on hand to provide conversation. His right arm was an empty sleeve. "One of our other plants. A direct hit. I ducked when I should have jumped." He raised his glass. "To victory." His voice was flat and distant.

Felix drank the excellent wine, and ate the delicate cheese. He walked to the window, and found he had a partial view of the prisoner's compound. "The company enjoys cheap labor."

"They're no bargain."

"A pity you have to look at them."

"The barracks must go somewhere." The public relations man took out a cigar, lit a match one-handedly. "It's odd how much one can adjust to. We're adaptable devils, we human beings. Cigar?"

"What will history say to this?" said Felix softly.

"History is a bog, Lieutenant. Things slip into it, the mud closes over them, and they are never heard from again." The maimed host lit Felix's cigar. Smoke from the tobacco wreathed the two men's heads.

Felix returned to the window. Attempts had been made to screen off the camp with shrubbery, but it had not yet grown high enough. Give it time, he thought. Then, suddenly, without a word he left the lounge, and returned to the street.

On the wire gate of the compound hung a sign reading, DANGER—CONTAMINATION. Beyond the wire fencing were the rows of barracks. A few lone women were performing chores between the buildings. At the end of the barracks row, he saw a young girl, moving along from building to building; she was chasing something, her movements quick and graceful as a cat's. Fascinated, he watched her coming nearer, then saw the squirrel she was stalking, the squirrel looking to eat acorns and the girl looking to eat the squirrel. Her feet were bare, her calf muscles flexing and unflexing as she moved silently near the rodent, who had found something and was turning it over in his paws.

"Come here," said Felix. The girl looked up, startled by his presence. The squirrel was forgotten, and she made her way quickly toward the fence.

She was little more than a child, her floppy dress of sack cloth revealing only the tiny beginnings of breasts, but her arms looked as strong as bands of wire, the veins standing out prominently on forearm and bicep. Her face was dirty, and decorated by sores. But she was in better health than the older women, for they were skin and bone, and she still had fat covering her muscle, probably owing to her skill as a hunter. She gazed at him with caution, but he saw, in her eyes, that she felt herself a match for anyone.

From his black marketeer's smattering of languages, he was able to address her in stilted Polish. "What work do you do?"

She was wary of entrapment, but he made no threatening gesture, and his eyes held no calculating malice. "Pour steel," she answered. Her arms bore the marks of the truncheon, and her eyes remained on his, dark eyes, a child's eyes, fierce. He thought of the furnace, and stepped closer to the wire, linking his fingers in the mesh. "I will arrange for you to be shipped out of here. Do you understand?"

She stared at him, but in such a way, he was not sure she understood. Well, it didn't matter.

"What is your name?"

"Valentina," she answered, slowly. "Valentina Povanda."

He wrote the name, and took her tattoo number. She backed away, her eyes still fixed on his, until she disappeared into a doorway, uncertain if she'd been selected for his bed or his oven.

He continued along the fence, to the men's compound—a few barracks buildings and a row of dog kennels. Within the kennels, he saw men's eyes peering out. A whistle blew overhead, and the men crawled from their kennels.

He turned and gazed up at von Göttingen's castle on the hillside, then walked around the compound as the laborers were marched off. An army guard remained at the gate, a Doberman beside him. The soldier snapped to attention as Felix came beside him.

"Where does he sleep?" Felix pointed at the dog.

"With me, sir."

"Not in the kennels?"

"No, sir, he is a trained animal."

Felix offered the guard a cigarette, and they withdrew into the small guardhouse. A brazier burned there, a coffeepot on it. Felix nodded to the window, toward the women's compound. "There is a prisoner there, number 2336787. See that she gets extra food." He handed the guard some money, which both men knew would go into the guard's own pocket. But Valentina would get a few scraps more.

"She's from the second shipment," said the guard. "They aren't well when they arrive, and they get worse."

"She'll be leaving here. Is there a doctor for these people?"

The guard pointed toward a cement block house at the far edge of the compound. Felix left the guardhouse and went toward it, but on the way discovered Herr Wurm's furnace. Camp laborers were loading cadavers on a forklift. The factory guard, seeing Felix, snapped to attention with the briskness of an army man, though he was older and long past military glory. "Good morning, sir." Then, seeing Felix's frown, he added, "Disposal, sir, of the deceased volunteers."

The naked, wasted bodies were lowered from a van, then shoveled into the furnace door. A gray plume of smoke rose upward from the stack, mixing with those from the factory buildings. "And what do they die of?"

"Bad luck."

Felix walked on to the medical building. It was small, the doctor's office ill-lit and underequipped. "I can't control things here," he said in response to Felix's inquiry about the health of the laborers. "I have no basic supplies. I have thousands of people on my hands, half of them dying, and do you know what I am issued? A hundred aspirin tablets." He looked across his desk at Felix. "Have you influence? Then use it. Otherwise the girl you asked about, and everyone else in this place, will be going up the chimney." He turned, and gazed out his office window at the compound, through which the emaciated laborers now walked, slowly, dully. "A hundred aspirin," said the doctor again, as Felix backed out of the office.

He followed the street of the compound, behind a line of women. Their wooden clogs scraped against the pavement, but no head was raised, no voice heard. He followed them to their dining hall, where they lined up for thin soup. Valentina Povanda turned her wary black eyes upon him.

"Ah, there you are, Lieutenant." The plant manager came up behind him. "I thought we'd lost you. There are a great many streets. What do you think of our morale? I'd say it's good, considering." His gesture excluded the file of creatures shuffling past him.

"These women would seem to lack for food."

The manager turned, as if wondering which women Felix could be speaking of. His eyes finally acknowledged them. "Dysentery's their problem. They're fed, but they can't retain anything."

"The soup is water."

"The clouds don't rain vegetables. There are shortages."

"You have lost no weight."

"I have lost two sons. And now it is time for us to take you to your train."

Felix looked at the girl, hunched over her bowl at the long table. Again she glanced at him, and he knew his own nakedness behind his perfectly tailored uniform. This child, these women at the table, they were real, made so by their suffering. He, and the plant manager and all the good townspeople who worked there, were the ghosts.

"We really must go, Lieutenant, or you shall miss your train."

"Does it matter? We have no existence."

"Quite possibly." The plant manager, with unexpected graciousness, took him by the arm, and escorted him to the company car. They drove to the main gate, and Felix stared straight ahead as the gate was opened. By the time they reached the railroad platform, the doors of the coaches were ready to close. He hurried aboard and proceeded to his compartment. The train left the station and he settled into the rhythm of the wheels. He'd do what he could to get the girl out of there, but the world was in flames and he a gambler at a burning table.

The succession of farmhouses calmed him with their gentle pattern, and he wished for something to read, something light, a magazine, to distract him. He noticed a dog-ear of paper, poking up from the cushions of the seat. He pulled it out and found a circular, already faded, of the German Resistance.

The circular showed a canceled swastika. At the bottom was the instruction: *Please duplicate and distribute.*

To have such a thing on one's person was a death sentence. He tore the paper in half, and continued tearing it, into many pieces, then opened the window and scattered it to the winds.

"*. . . good, David, that's perfect, we'll print that . . .*"

The camera crew rolled by on their dolly. Caspian stared at it. His director was walking toward him, all smiles. "A great take. I can't wait to see the dailies."

"Yes," said Caspian hoarsely, "neither can I."

"Sun in Gemini, moon in Pisces. You have the classic elements of the dual personality." The astrologer was an elderly man, in a battered old leather chair in a studio whose walls held a Mayan calendar wheel, prints of Chinese and Hindu constellations, and an antique Persian horoscope on parchment paper; suspended in the air above his chair was a mobile of the planets, rotating gently around a central golden ball. In his hand was Caspian's horoscope, neatly drawn, the lettering fine and precise as calligraphy. He was gazing at it, and stroking the fine wisps of his silver goatee.

"A very deep-seated duality, especially through your lunar past. The sign itself is a glyph of the heels of two feet moving in opposite directions." He glanced up at Caspian. "Gemini, of course, is the sign of the twins. One twin is true, the other—false."

The astrologer had a tape recorder running, to allow Caspian to carry away a tape of the reading, price inclusive, a very high price. It whirred quietly on the arm of his chair, as the old man continued. "You have a heavy series of oppositions. Here is the Warrior's Bundle, indicating a personality at odds with itself. It is commonly thought of as two people wrapped up in one." The old man nodded to himself, still stroking his wispy beard. "You have an early Capricorn ascendent, three degrees. This is your professional ability, your power. You have great presence, are a self-assured performer. But what is most interesting here—" The astrologer's finger left the wisps of his goatee and laid itself upon the outer rim of Caspian's chart. "A most unusual configuration, one that could not happen again for hundreds of years. Pluto is on the midheaven and Neptune is on the ascendent. I would call this the quintessence of a weird predicament." He looked at Caspian, his aged eyes watery. For a moment they seemed to be focusing on the fringe of Caspian's form, as if perceiving energy fields peripheral to the human body. Then they returned to his face, and the old man studied him carefully and silently, in an old man's way, and Caspian felt that he was no more than a bit of nature to the old man—a rock, or stream, or bird seen by an eye that has already seen so much, and for which all things have fallen into their portion of the universal Tao. Which is fine for an old man, reflected Caspian, but I'm still thrashing down here. "You were saying—?"

The astrologer's gaze returned from afar, and he hunched forward, over Caspian's chart. "A configuration that brings extreme self-transformation, especially if you are engaged in something you shouldn't be. Are you?"

"All the time."

"Pluto then brings the whole thing around you, intensifying the transformation, possibly in violent ways, which I very much suspect, because Mars is now coming up to Pluto at your midheaven and doubling the impact."

The astrologer looked back down at the wheel of figures he'd drawn, and traced his leathery, old finger around the wheel to its highest point. "Here is Pluto. It is bringing about the most profound depth of transformation imaginable, pushing you to the farthest reaches of the unknown, where this planet dwells. It may well involve influences emanating from the ancestral past, or from some departed friend—or enemy—for Pluto's moon is called Charon, the Boatman of the Dead."

His finger came around the wheel, to the horizon. "Here is Neptune, the illusion maker. As a film actor, you are an agent of Neptune. But with Neptune now on your ascendent, it has become hard for you to see things clearly. Everyone you meet confuses you. And, more importantly, you confuse yourself. You no longer know who you are. In fact, your identity has become like a dream."

The mobile turned slowly above the astrologer's chair, the planets tracking round the sun, defining time and its changes, giving the reference points for the seasons and those born to them, children of winter, children of summer, marked accordingly, with coolness or heat, inward turning or outward going.

"To have both Pluto and Neptune on your most important angles is a freakish thing. As I say, it is an occurrence that only comes about at great intervals, never more than once in a lifetime and most of the time not at all." His fingers returned to his silky beard, which he stroked thoughtfully as he studied the chart. "Neptune distorts reality. And the ultimate Plutonian type, of course, is Hitler."

*   *   *

Caspian sat in the back corner of a gin mill on LaCienaga, where movie stars were not expected, nor likely to be recognized. It was a favorite private haunt of his, and the only mistake he'd ever made was in once telling Myron Fish its location. Fish was just now walking through the door, and peering anxiously into its shadows. Caspian pressed deeper into his corner, but Fish spotted him and came hurriedly forward.

"David, what are you doing to us, you're due on the set in two hours."

"I'll be there, Myron."

"You've knocked the struts out from under me, David. We had a big interview set up, and the reporter is now elsewhere."

"He'll be back."

"When twenty million readers are involved, we like to get it on the first take." Fish sat down across from him, and sighed deeply. "The problem with living in a powerhouse is you get tired of your hair standing on end."

"You haven't got any hair, Myron."

"I'm too sensitive."

"Have a drink."

"David, I hope you're not getting schnockered."

"I'm fine."

"You shouldn't avoid the press, David. You're denying people a complete experience of you."

"I don't like interviews."

"Why? It isn't as if they're going to tie you to a pole while everyone stands around and laughs as they behead you." Fish signaled to the waitress, ordered a gin and tonic. "I've got a plane waiting for us. Two pilots in white uniforms."

"I've got one too."

"So now we have our own air force. Are you aware of the money you're costing us?"

"I had to see an astrologer."

"You shafted *Time* magazine to see an astrologer?"

"He's a very old astrologer."

"And our feature story will be running in the Horoscope Daily Bugle." The waitress brought Fish's drink, and he swilled half of it quickly down. "All right, so you saw your astrologer, it's over with, I found you, we'll go back and pick up the pieces."

"Now I have to see my analyst."

A few drops of Fish's drink trickled down his chin as he looked at Caspian dumbly. Caspian tapped Fish on the forehead. "Mental health time, Myron."

"David, what's happened to you? Astrologers, analysts."

Fish squinted toward him suspiciously. "Are you undergoing some kind of spiritual experience?"

"Neptune is on my ascendant."

"And DeBrusca is on my ass. David, *Time* was going to feature *his picture*. You can't buy that kind of p.r."

"I'm sorry, Myron. I'm carrying a lot of weight these days."

Fish snapped the rest of his drink back. "Where is this analyst at?"

"Gloaming Way."

"I'm coming with you."

Caspian finished his drink; they walked through the cool shadows toward the door. "And after your analyst, what then? Your palm reader? Someone who reads used Kleenex?"

They stepped out into the blazing light of the boulevard. Fish put on his dark glasses, pointed to a limo double-parked just ahead. "Does Carol know you're in town?"

"No, and I don't want her to."

"Confucius say—" Fish opened the back door of the limo. "—man sued five times for alimony keeps mouth shut."

Quatrelle sat across from him in the Winnebago. "You don't remember any of it?"

"I wasn't there. I wasn't acting. I was in Germany, at a munitions plant."

Quatrelle had drawn his magician's robe up over his knees; his powerfully muscular calves seemed strangely grafted onto his otherwise flabby form. He had an ice pack on top of his head, and a glass of iced tea in his hand. He sipped at it, eyes still quizzically regarding Caspian. "There was something in what you did yesterday, when the character finally speaks—your voice sounded different. A very odd quality, I can't quite describe it."

Caspian drank black coffee and stared out the window of the mobile home. "When I looked at the dailies, and heard that voice, I felt my bones had been replaced."

A knock sounded at the door, followed by the A.D.'s call. Quatrelle lowered his robe and removed the ice pack from his head. "Back to the burning wastes of Outer Fungo." He stepped out of the van and Caspian followed, into the piercing desert light. They walked together down a passageway formed by the caravan of trailers, and as they turned the corner, a production secretary, shielding her eyes from the glare, collided with Caspian; a handful of her expense chits went scattering in a flutter of white paper.

"Sorry," she said nervously, and knelt to gather up the chits, as Quatrelle eased Caspian away. "You look like you're being held together with Scotch tape."

"I—saw something."

"Her buns?"

"Something from the other side. A pamphlet that Felix tore up. A pamphlet of the Resistance."

"You know what resistance is? People won't spend more than $9.95 on a record album. That's resistance."

They continued through the corridor of vans, and emerged at the site of the day's shooting—an outcropping of desert rock, over which boom mikes hung like great-necked birds. Armas met them in the shadow of the rock. "Welcome back. We'll be ready here in a minute—" The director of cinematography was standing just beyond them, making a last check of the light through his contrast meter, holding it up like a smoked monocle. "We can do our master shot from here and then move to the end of the rock for David's closeup." Armas nodded and positioned the two actors.

"You've met in the dust, wanderer and magician, and there's a bond between you, the affinity of the outcast. The magician has emerged from stone, the computer guys have got a technique that will project Victor's image in the rock wall and bring it out, don't ask me how. David, you've seen it happen, and you know the man is powerful. You're cautious, but respectful, and a bond is forming."

"Tape marks are here—" The A.D. led Caspian to his position. The sheer rock wall towered above him, and the camera crew were a few feet beyond him, from where they would pull slowly back. "Look right, David, into the distance."

He stared into the shimmering tropical heat. *Gebrochene Blumen,* said the shadow.

"Gone? What do you mean, she's gone?" Felix passed a hand over his brow, cobwebs of alien thought covering his brain; he swayed, orienting himself. He was in a cold, stone block-house, standing before the resident doctor of the von Göttingen armaments factory. The doctor was looking up from his papers.

"I sent her away." He turned toward the window, through which the laborers could be seen, shuffling along in their skeletal march. "You told me to be sure she received good treatment. There's no good treatment here."

"Where is she now?"

"She is not shoveling coal, or hammering boilers."

Felix restrained his anger. And why, he asked himself, should she be so important to me, this child, this stranger?

"Where have you sent her, Doctor?"

"A colleague of mine, at the Danzig Institute, is conducting some innocuous experiments. I sent her to him. She'll be well fed, she's out of this poisonous atmosphere." The doctor paused. "My colleague is a ladies' man, that must be admitted, but considering the circumstances—"

Felix nodded. Considering the circumstances, being raped at the Danzig Institute was benevolent fate intervening. "And his experiments?"

"Diet, electrical therapy, a bit of psychology—" The doctor turned again toward his window, and the prisoner's compound. "She will live. I did what I could."

Felix opened the office door, signaled to Corporal Sagen, who went to their car and returned with a large crate. Sagen carried it into the office and set it before the doctor. The doctor looked at it questioningly. Felix opened it, revealing rows of medicines, ampules, syringes. The doctor's voice dropped to a whisper. "How did you—?"

"Use it discreetly."

The doctor ran his fingers tenderly over the bottles, then glanced up again at Felix. "All this, for that girl? Is she a member of your family?"

Felix stared blankly at the medicines he had brought, the question as great for himself as for the doctor.

He turned and left the hospital compound. Corporal Sagen was waiting stiffly at the wheel, his face pale, and Felix saw he'd been looking at those Jewish volunteers who'd just crept from their doghouses. "Drive."

They drove, for hours into the night, Colonel Mueller's name opening every checkpoint before them. Felix stared at the dark road, the trance of monotony overtaking him and playing with his mind—so that he saw dream figures, the contemplation of which suffused his being with an impossible happiness, for these figures were far from tortured Germany, far in time and space. They were from his tropic idyll, where all his bliss was stored.

If the secret of dreams could be learned, he reflected to himself, head still nodding toward the door as the car rolled along, if that secret of these blessed isles could be comprehended, a man's curse could be dissolved.

He felt the solace of the dream, silver tongues of the moon licking into his brain. And the sound of the car wheels on the pavement became the whirring wings of his dragonfly, doorkeeper of his dreaming.

I have one part of the secret. This earth is not as men believe.

"Mad thoughts, Corporal," he said, his head rolling straight again.

"Sir?"

"Doorways in the darkness, ones that occur when half asleep. Do you experience them?"

"If I drive too long, things jump out at me."

"Yes?"

"Monsters," said Sagen.

Felix straightened himself, and gazed out the windscreen at the bleak, darkened landscape. "Many of them on the loose these days."

Cannon fire sounded to the west, and the sky filled with flashing light. "For all this we thank our Leader," said Sagen, and increased acceleration.

"We are approaching Mecklenburg," said Felix, as their headlamps now illuminated rich agricultural lands. Two more hours would have them in Berlin. He searched the darkness for familiar landmarks, an inn he'd once gone to, somewhere near. There'd been a beautiful white gravel drive, the house was fir and cedar, with oak paneling. To spend an afternoon, with the humble wine and food of peacetime—such a day would seem a festival of the gods, now, when the best wines were bitter.

The monsters in the dark paraded through his mind, among them Lieutenant Colonel Emil Weiss. He felt the Gestapo Chief's web, spread across the countryside, woven into the people's lives, into the army, into industry; does not yet have enough to hang me. Waiting. Spinning.

Felix rubbed sleep from his eyes. "Through one of the doorways in our dreaming, Corporal, there lies the way to safety."

"Give me a concrete bunker," said Corporal Sagen. "Walls sixteen foot thick, the whole of it underground. That's the way to safety."

"Is it the only way?"

"I'd sleep quiet with several tons of earth over my head, sir, and so would you."

They passed the rest of the ride in silence, finally entering Berlin near midnight, and going straight to Bettinastrasse in Grunewald, where Colonel Mueller had acquired a mansion at ten percent of its value; its owners had vanished, *In Nebel auf-gelöst,* transformed into mist.

The edifice was dark as they entered its circular drive, and a guard came forward to identify them. Felix gave Sagen his leave, and proceeded alone into Mueller's study, where the colonel was sitting before the fire. "Sit down, dear boy, and join me in the last bottle of decent brandy left in Berlin." A second snifter was filled and Felix clicked glasses with his host. Mueller was in uniform, but had removed his black boots, his feet up on a low, gilt-edged footstool. He passed a tray of crackers and caviar to Felix, who took one and then, in his exhaustion, dropped it to the floor.

"Leave it," said Mueller. "It belongs to the underworld now, for by rights it has fallen to them. A practice in the ancient Roman household, I rather like the idea, don't you?"

Felix gazed at the spilt cracker, its tiny black beads upon the gleaming hardwood floor. "We need all the assistance we can get, I suppose."

"Yes, Germany itself belongs to the underworld now. We have sunk through a crack in the earth's crust, and will be swallowed up."

"I thought it was the Russians who are swallowing us."

"That is only our exterior portion. It is fate that eats us really. Down to the last vein."

"I find you cheerful before your fire."

"Tell me—did you find your little ladyfriend at von Göttingen's plant?"

"She was shipped to Danzig. To a doctor there."

"So many young people are moved about these days. There's a regular white-slave trade taking place among German officials returning from the East. They give women for presents. We're becoming quite like Hindustan."

Felix gazed into the fireplace. The dancing points of flame showed him their demonic aspect. "Gestapo Chief Weiss is following your career with interest."

Mueller sipped from his glass, held it admiringly to the light, set it down on the table beside him. "You must visit Marla. She has grown fearful."

"It might be better to retire her."

"A shipment of confiscated property is on its way from the Eastern Territories. A small fortune in gold and jewels." Mueller refilled his glass, returned it to his lips. "Part of it will go to the Reichsbank in Frankfurt, and part of it, with Marla's help. . . ."

"Who's involved?"

"Oh, the president of the Reichsbank. A man with—how shall I put it—refined tastes. I have a rather interesting file on his after-hours activity. In fact, I arranged for some of it myself." Mueller smiled, and rubbed his cheek lightly with his little finger, on which a field of diamonds sparkled in a ring. "He will meet with Marla, whose delicacy and tact will give the poor man confidence that he can trust in us never to betray him. In return we merely ask for a single piece of paper, showing that his bank received the complete shipment." Mueller poured more brandy into Felix's glass. "Half, of course, will be in your hands, traveling to an inn, which, conveniently enough, I now own. And there the treasure will rest."

"And Gestapo Chief Weiss?"

"He too will rest."

Felix stood, finishing his brandy. The monsters in the fire danced before him, flame fingers gesturing.

Mueller rose from his chair, stood before the fire with Felix. "My family will stop him on the last rung. His case will never reach the right ear." Mueller's hand came to Felix's shoulder. "It happens every day. An impenetrable curtain is lowered, from above, and ambitious Gestapo chiefs learn the limits of their power." The Colonel leaned forward, touched his fire with an iron poker. "We rule, my dear fellow, and we succeed. Count Wolf von Helldorf extracted a million marks from Jews in return for passports and visas. Göring got the coal, iron works, and palace of Louis Rothschild. I have gained a few small holdings of my own. Even the chauffeurs of the Gauleiters have made millions. And you yourself have prospered." The fire responded to the poker, the flames dancing higher, up into the darkness of the chimney. "Talk to Marla. Put her mind at ease. War is prosperity for those who are wise."

"Do you know von Göttingen has men living in dog-houses?"

"If they are living in toothpaste tubes and lengths of them squeezed out each day, it is no concern of mine, or yours." Colonel Mueller walked with him to the door. "See Marla, and return to me."

"How can I give Marla confidence, when I myself—"

Mueller took a sheaf of orders from his pocket, flipped them open. "That is the Führer's own signature. Gestapo Chief Weiss cannot harm you."

Felix stepped into the hall. It was bathed in the light of lamps held by centuries-old cherubim. Mueller stood in the glow, the medals on his chest softly shining. He'd never been near a shot fired in two world wars, yet held the Iron Cross. Returning Felix's gaze, he said, quietly, "A few hints on business, and the sanctity of good connections—our German army drives vehicles fueled by Standard Oil of New Jersey." Mueller smiled, turned, and withdrew into his study.

*   *   *

"Apple wine, do you remember? We drank it at that inn near Sachsenhausen." Marla held the glass out to him, from her bed. The lace of the hanging canopy cast a net of shadow on her arm; the table beside her held a nearly empty decanter and two glasses.

"I've drunk too much." Felix drew his trousers off the back of a boudoir chair, stepped clumsily into them.

Marla reached to the end table for a cigarette, her gown falling open at the neck and her breasts swinging forward with indolent grace. "You seem to have lost interest in me, my darling. Someone new? A little plum from the Nazi Schoolgirl's League? I know you've been traveling in the provinces." She lit her cigarette and stood, her form appearing in the long mirror beside the bed. She seemed to see a stranger, ran a hand through her hair. "I hate this paper moon I'm riding on. I'm through."

"It's not so easy as that." He tossed an envelope, stuffed with money, on the bed. "—with Mueller's regards. He's got a new assignment for you."

Marla turned toward her dressing table, opened her jewel box. Gems sparkled, on bracelets, rings, brooches. She ran her fingernail lightly upon their faceted faces. "Who is the gentleman?"

Felix buttoned his shirt, fixed his tie. "He could be worth a lot to you. There's no one quite like a bank president."

"You're the only hope I have," said Marla, snapping her jewel box shut. She turned toward him. "Only Felix the black marketeer can help someone vanish without a trace. You've fixed papers for others. Fix some for me. Because I'm getting afraid."

"So long as you're valuable to Mueller, you're in no danger."

"Emil Weiss has turned me white with fear. And Mueller will never protect me."

Felix took out his wallet, withdrew a key from it. "To my strongbox. Should anything happen to me, you will be in good shape."

"Any number of millionaires have been hung by the Gestapo."

"Not so many, believe me. And never the clever ones."

Marla held the key up, examining it closely, then turned it in an invisible lock. "Felix's heart. Out tumble his feelings. They clatter with the sound of coins."

"To match your own." He put his jacket on, and buttoned it slowly, carefully, stepping toward Marla's mirror. He gazed at himself there, in his uniform. "I've finally become a good actor, Marla."

"Oh, you always had something. A sort of unlikely presence. One looked at you and always asked oneself, how does this man dare to be an actor?" She stepped in behind him, and placed her arms around his neck. "I'm attracted to you, now that you have found a little Nazi schoolgirl."

He added a final touch to his tie, and looked at Marla's reflection in the mirror beside him. "Two dragonflies flying as one. Have you ever seen that? Such perfect poise, their bodies joined, their wings fanning together." He removed her arms from around his neck. "I must go. And you must entertain a banker."

"We'll all be taken by Weiss."

Felix adjusted the cap on his head, one hand sliding smoothly along the brim. "I'll get you papers to prove you were never anything but an insurance agent."

He turned to go, felt something cross in his brain, for a split second, a tiny misfiring he'd known before. *Petit mal,* he said to himself.

"David, Roma, very nice, we'll print that."

Caspian looked into Roma's face. She smiled and extended her hand to him. Beyond her were the camera crew, the set dressers, the makeup people, the techies. He felt it all slowly solidifying, his world, his film, his leading lady, with whom he'd just played another scene of which he had no recollection.

Roma slipped her arm through his. "A really high energy take," she said. "Armas loved it. You were lovely, of course, but did I come across? At all?"

You were perfect, Marla, said Felix.

Fay Roper's house in Beverly Hills was screened from outsiders by high cedar hedges. "A lovely piece of real estate," said Myron Fish, "and once it was mine."

He stood with Caspian on the patio. "Fay got the works, god bless her, with one of the most touching divorce court performances ever seen." Fish sipped his drink. "The judge was misty eyed. I was paralyzed."

Fish looked around his former house and grounds, and raised his glass to it all. "She'll be head of a studio someday." He turned back toward Caspian. "How're you feeling? Are you re-relaxing?"

"Totally."

"Julius wants you to relax for three whole days. That's why we're here."

"I'm relaxing."

"Then why do your eyes look like thin chicken soup?" Fish lowered his glass onto a patio table. From within his ex-wife's house came the sounds of a party in progress. "At least it's not my liquor she's giving away."

"Aren't you still paying her alimony?"

"Of course."

"Then it's your liquor she's giving away."

"How could that nice judge have done this to me? He looked like Cary Grant."

"You should have become his agent."

They walked together through the garden. Fish put his hand on Caspian's shoulder. "I'll tell you something about the ex-Mrs. Fish. One day our maid informs us she's getting married. For a wedding present Fay gave her the day off." Fish looked into Caspian's eyes. "A woman for whom the spirit of giving never dawned." He led the way up a flight of stone steps. Overhead, colored lanterns were strung through the trees. The pool was glowing with underwater spots. The guests talked in the soft, warm lantern light, as the music of a small combo came from the living room, bass and vibes playing discreet, quiet jazz.

Carol Caspian, in silver lamé pants and jacket, was coming toward them, a drink in her hand. Her jacket was sewn with little black crescent moon patches, and she wore a high black turban, from which her curls peeked out on her forehead. Fish took her hand in his. "You're the brightest thing at this party."

"Thank you, Myron, I thought maybe I looked like a Twinkie."

"Ravishing, my dear."

"Actually the shelf-life of a Twinkie is twenty-seven years." Carol tucked a curl back into her turban. "The packaging gives out first."

"Have you seen Fay?"

"She was talking to a dentist who looks like he's done time."

"I know the man," said Fish. "He takes full-page color ads. His office looks like a Turkish disco."

"But would you want his fingers in your mouth?" Carol turned to Caspian. "Enjoying yourself, darling?"

"He's relaxing," said Fish.

"I'm relaxing," said Caspian.

"*I've* been talking to Flametta Bonfili," said Carol. "She's had every possible kind of husband."

"She's doing a picture for Fay," said Fish. "They get along beautifully."

Carol peered in through the large, round glass window that joined the living room to the garden. "Well, I'm going back to Flametta." She kissed Caspian on the cheek. "I just wanted to see if strange women were hovering around David." She walked off, her lamé pants clinging to her trim hips.

"Not an ounce of fat," said Fish. "Where does she work out?"

"She *passed* out trying to follow the Jane Fonda video."

"To be blessed with thin genes. Mine are shaped like cheese blintzes." Fish tried to pull in his midsection, then gave up. "I've got to talk to some people here. Can I trust you to stay away from astrologers?"

"I'm fine, Myron. Stabilized by your company."

"I don't want you disappearing for three days."

"I'll be right here, breathing the air you used to own."

Caspian sat down on the stone steps to the garden. He saw Fay coming through a glittering bead door off the living room; the beads clicked softly as they fell behind her; she wore a fish-tailed black evening gown that trailed silently over the wooden deck; the top was sliced in a V to her navel, where a wide red sash was wound, long ends draped along her thighs. Her walk was the same sensual prowl she'd used in films twenty years ago, but tonight he detected a slight wobble.

"David, dear—" She sat down beside him on the steps. "—why all alone? Where's Carol?"

"Talking to Flametta Bonfili about husbands."

Fay glanced back over her shoulder. "The fire's lit in the

fireplace, I hope no one falls in." She shook out her pale, streaked hair, ran her hand slowly up through it, piling it on top of her head for a moment, then letting it fall again. "Do I look slightly snookered?"

"Just slightly."

"I thought I must. I *feel* slightly snookered." She leaned against his arm. "They're all used-car salesmen, David, with apes and elephants."

Caspian gazed down into the garden, to a grove of miniature palms, as Fay arranged the ends of her gown. "Apes and elephants," she said again, as if to herself.

"Who, Fay?"

"Everyone."

"I see."

"The producer can't be trusted, so we stick in an executive producer to oversee the producer. Only the executive producer doesn't know what he's doing either."

"A difficult picture?"

"A major fiasco, and it's all on my head. But do you know what I say?"

"What do you say?"

She turned her head toward him, her hair brushing his cheek. She gazed into his eyes, and he saw a woman from another era, the Berlin music hall star—Gerta Schaffers.

"I love the way you look at me," she said. Her hand moved tentatively toward his, then came gently onto it. "That day at lunch—remember?"

"Yes."

"David, my life's not all trade dollars and distribution fees. Do you understand that?"

Caspian looked off into the trees. Fay lifted his hand slowly and put it in her cleavage. "These were once very famous tits." With her other hand she cradled his neck and pulled his lips to hers. Her kiss was soft, knowing. Her mouth came away slowly. "There's a little bungalow at the bottom of the yard."

"Not tonight."

"When?"

"Fay—"

"You shouldn't send mating signals if you don't mean them. It's embarrassing for a woman, especially one my age." She pulled back, and tightened the sash at her waist with a sharp tug.

"Fay, you're a gorgeous woman. I looked, I'm sorry. For a moment—"

"Yes, it was enchanting. Let's leave it at that, shall we?" Fay got up, swept her fish tail around her, and glided off. She seemed suddenly very sober and he knew with absolute certainty that he would never make another picture at her studio.

"So that's just great," he said, standing up. He went down the stone steps and through the garden to the street, where his Porsche was parked. He climbed in, and peeled out, letting the surge of the engine carry his emotions.

"Go to a party and improve your business contacts."

He snapped on the radio, and headed down to Sunset. The boulevard wound smoothly through the stands of palm and other curtains of Beverly Hills foliage, a well-paved road down which actors had been driving for decades, thinking about their careers. He reflected on his own. Once he'd been so cold he couldn't get arrested, but now he was hot. Now he could afford to filter the asbestos out of his drinking water.

He headed into the Hollywood district, where the smooth ride turned into jerky stops and starts at the traffic lights. He swung over to the curb, parked, got out. He was in the shooting gallery of the soul; the garish lights of the Strip flashed and clashed, an uncorrected color print. The soundtrack was unadorned, music from record and video stores blasting into the street. Hookers, as beautiful as Flametta Bonfili, walked the pavement. Who hands out the breaks? he wondered. They're hustling at the Polo Lounge, and they're hustling on Sunset Boulevard, and one is legal.

"I knew an actor," he said out loud to himself as he walked.

"He had a three-legged dog named Tripod." He laughed, and walked along. The doorways were filled with people out working the night, selling smack, hot tape decks. On all sides was the tinkling laughter of the extras, and the star was Sunset itself.

"And me, I'm yours truly, Johnny Dollar." He laughed again, in the lights and sounds and tropical haze. He stepped into the doorway of a dimly lit bar, and glanced at his watch.

The time was correct, but the watch was not.

He stared down at the strange-looking timepiece—with a silver frame, and an eagle's wings scribed on it.

Felix looked up from the watch, and gazed along the wide expanse of Friedrichstrasse, its pavement glistening from the light rain that was falling in the darkness.

To his left was Behrenstrasse, the two streets meeting in a maze of store fronts, beer gardens, camera stores, tobacco shops. Some were lit, others had lights no longer. He kept his eyes fixed on the intersection. Precisely on time, the black Mercedes of Emil Weiss nosed into view. The Gestapo Chief's car crossed at Behrenstrasse, followed by his armed escort in a second black auto, its windshield wipers clicking back and forth.

He waited until they passed, then stepped to the corner. A delivery van pulled out of traffic and turned in at the curb. The lettering on its door identified it as a drapery cleaning service. He opened the door and jumped in beside The Weasel.

"You see him?" Felix pointed through the rain-streaked windshield, as The Weasel pulled back into traffic.

"He's in the sights," said The Weasel, moving the van quickly along Friedrichstrasse, a few car lengths behind the Gestapo escort.

"He's punctual."

The Weasel's black gloves held the wheel steady in the slow flow of traffic. "You'd better get ready."

Felix climbed into the back of the van. "It smells of cleaning fluid."

The Weasel spoke over his shoulder. "We guarantee no crooked pleats, no shrinkage, and no uneven hems."

Felix knelt and pulled a length of canvas away from an MG42, the big machine gun loaded, gleaming, neatly balanced on its two outspread legs. Beside it was a bag of hand grenades and a submachine gun; he passed the submachine gun to the front seat.

The Weasel stroked it tenderly. "It's a Kalashnikov. Russian. A much better weapon than the one our glorious German army uses."

"There's also a very fine bedspread back here," said Felix, shining his torch onto a richly brocaded fabric.

"I didn't have time to unload." The Weasel turned, and moved a car-length closer to the Gestapo caravan. Felix stood, and shined his torch on the sliding door panel. He moved the latch and the door slid gently open, onto the rainy avenue.

"You're letting in a draft," said The Weasel.

"Just testing."

"I've always been sensitive to drafts," said The Weasel. "I think it must be my blood."

Felix closed the door and moved to the rear exit of the van—double doors which opened out, a window in each of them.

"Forget those," said The Weasel. "We'll take him from the side. But don't open until the last possible second."

"Because of the draft, yes, I understand," said Felix, gazing out the back windows at the glistening street as it fell behind them.

"We'll have to be leading ahead of him; if his gas tank explodes it could catch us too."

Felix knelt beside the MG42. "Eighty rounds in thirty seconds. But I've only fired one of these a few times."

"At that range, a blind Pomeranian could hit him."

Felix crawled back toward the front seat, and knelt just behind The Weasel. The van moved slowly, and Felix's watch still more slowly; he was gazing at the tiny, ticking second hand. He glanced out the window and saw a familiar old poster plastered to a public wall. "If you save five marks a week," he read softly, "you can have your own Strength-Through-Joy Car."

"Nobody got so much as a wheel nut."

The van turned once more, and Felix watched as The Weasel drew directly in back of the Gestapo. "Not too much further," said The Weasel. "He's got reservations at the Artistes Club in the Skagerratplatz." The Weasel's hand moved the gear shift lever smoothly, the van speeded up, and Felix crept over to the sliding side panel, and gripped its handles.

"If I miss," he said quietly, "I'll blow the Artistes Club into next week."

"His escort always parks directly behind him. When you take him out, they'll be too numb to move. Machine gun fire is not those lads' specialty."

"I'm opening this door."

"Not yet," snapped The Weasel.

"You should have worn your long underwear."

The Weasel shifted the van sharply into second gear. "Open."

Felix opened the door. The Gestapo cars had both pulled in at the curb. He braced himself in the shadows of the van, his form hidden, and aimed the machine gun. He saw the face of Emil Weiss turning toward him, the Gestapo Chief's eyes opening wide in horror at the sight of the projecting muzzle; beyond him, he saw Weiss's ladyfriend for the evening, her face one from his own nights of love, long ago.

"It's Gerta!"

"Fire!" shouted The Weasel.

Bullets pierced the side of the van as the Gestapo escort pulled out around Weiss's car, firing from their windows. The Weasel gunned the van forward, and Felix staggered to the back doors. He kicked them open, braced himself, and hurled a grenade.

It bounced once, and rolled beneath the Gestapo escort car.

A second later the car erupted in a golden plume, doors and windows flying over the electric poles. Felix yanked the doors shut and crawled back through the careening van. Streets flew by the window, as The Weasel followed their escape route. "Why didn't you pop Weiss?"

"I couldn't with Gerta there."

"She means so much to you?"

"Apparently so."

The Weasel turned, on two wheels, crashed through a wooden barrier and took the van along a bombed street. The vehicle shook and bounced, the frame slamming violently on the pockmarked pavement. At the end of the block he brought the van to a stop at the entrance to a closed-off subway tunnel.

The Weasel leapt out, carrying the Kalashnikov, and Felix leapt out beside him. The Weasel pointed into the entrance and Felix climbed over the scattered bricks, and down the stairs. The Weasel took a grenade from his pocket, pulled the pin and tossed it in the back of the van. "Drapes returned, with no uneven corners."

He dove down the stairs beside Felix as the blast went off, burying the entrance in rubble and twisted metal. Led by the light of Felix's torch, they descended to the bottom of the stairs, and across the platform.

"Down we go." The Weasel slipped over the edge, onto the tracks; Felix followed, and they walked quickly, in the echoing darkness of the damp, empty tunnel. The torch played upon the glistening rails, the succession of ties, the stonework of the walls.

"I should have fired," said Felix.

"We sold Gerta French underwear, and hesitated to fire a machine gun at her." The Weasel pushed his little derby hat back on his head. "The lady is in our debt, so far as I understand such matters."

Their footsteps sounded in the hollow dome; the night's rain had seeped through its cracks, and was dripping into the tunnel. Felix played his light upon the gray body of a rat scurrying ahead of them; the animal ducked away to another track. He turned to The Weasel. "She couldn't see me. I was in shadow."

"We'll send her a rose, and a pair of little lemon panties. She'll know."

"But what do we do about Weiss?"

"When Death spares a man on a rainy night, his adversaries must pause too." The Weasel slung the Kalashnikov over his shoulder.

Felix played the torch beam upon the walls, then back onto the rails. The beam flickered, and went dead. "Give me a match, the bulb must be loose."

There was the sound of a match head striking in the darkness, and then a tiny flame danced to life in front of The Weasel's face. But they were not in a subway tunnel, and The Weasel was wearing dark glasses.

"It's not often a *pistola* like me gets to entertain a man like you, Mr. Caspian." Nino Carillo brought the match toward Caspian's cigarette. Behind him were the red clay walls of a Mexican beer joint. Nino adjusted his dark glasses, setting them delicately on his long, pointed nose. "So the drinks are on me."

The waiter set two glasses down. Caspian leaned a trembling arm on the table. "Nino, what is this place?"

"I told you, Club Serpentino. I own half of it. The half toward the ceiling." Nino laughed, and slapped both palms lightly on the table. "How's your hi-fi equipment? You got the latest? I got a system just come into my hands, I'll give you a hell of a buy on it." Nino laughed again, and raised the glass to his lips. "Only thing is, you don't get no warranty."

—————————————————————————"Whenever I'm depressed, I buy myself a toy." Ed Cresswell and Caspian walked toward the doorway of Nostalgia, and entered the shop, beneath a tinkling bell, into a land of fantasy. "One of my main suppliers," said Cresswell, as they walked down an aisle lined with velocipedes, wagons, doll carriages, scooters, and sandboats, all of them bearing the paint and lettering of long ago. Cresswell paused over an old mesh bag, filled with glass marbles. "Shooters," he said, holding up one of the ruby red alleys. "Must have more shooters." He handed the bag to Caspian, and moved on down the aisle.

"What are you depressed about?"

"About being a dirty old man in a toy store." Cresswell moved on down the aisle. "Look at this." He held out a gray, tin windup submarine. The original price tag, of fifty cents, and a label detailing its exploits, dangled from it. "Will dive underwater when wound." He handed it to Caspian. "This should make my bath time more exciting."

"Were your baths getting dull?"

"Ever since I lost my rubber duck." Cresswell paused at a display of little wooden windmills, carts, elevators, built from interlocking wooden sticks and wheels. He turned the cardboard blades of the windmill with one finger, slowly. "Life should be Tinkertoys."

"Maybe it is."

"No, something fundamental has changed." Cresswell walked on down the aisle. "Did you ever have a jumping rabbit—" He squeezed a rubber bulb, and a moth-eaten old rabbit, attached by a tube, jumped along its shelf. "—or a windup highway." He wound it up, and tiny metal cars and buses went along a metal track, through a tunnel, round and round. Cresswell leaned in over them, his nose directly above the little whizzing cars. "I was once the prince of fairyland."

"You still are."

"I'm just peeking in the keyhole now." The windup highway wound down, and stopped. "But I'm looking forward to senility, when all will be revealed."

They walked to the end of the aisle, where a little antique sulky hung on display from the ceiling. The seat was just big enough for a child, above two slender wheels, with two long shafts extending outward, to be pulled by a dog. "My dog will love this," said Cresswell. "I can pull him around all day."

A wooden Pinocchio puppet dangled over the next aisle, a green felt cap on his head, a tiny feather in it shadowing his long wooden nose. Beside him was a hand puppet, a decrepit old monkey in a shabby brown cloak. Cresswell picked the monkey up and put him on his hand. He made the monkey snap his head around, mouth opening and closing rapidly. *"Take your stop watch out of my dressing room or I'll shove it up your ass.*

"I like this monkey," said Cresswell. "He's got class.

"Hang in there, Ed. You're the best screenwriter in the business.

"He understands me." Cresswell handed the monkey to Caspian. "Put him in my pile."

"What about Pinocchio?"

"Dick-nose I don't need. My own conscience is enough."

They continued into the doll section, where a row of heads were lined up, to replace others that had been lost. There was curly hair, straight hair, moveable eyes, fixed eyes. "They're looking at you, Ed."

"Yes, dolls see right into the soul." Cresswell reached over and closed all the moveable lids. "If you don't mind—"

Caspian moved along down the aisle, to a large, Victorian dollhouse; each of its rooms held tiny pieces of furniture from the period, and its chandeliers, doors, and windows were perfect in their detail. Costumed dolls inhabited the rooms, from wine cellar to kitchen, and into the dining hall, where the family sat around a long table, tiny dishes before them.

Cresswell leaned in over the rooms with Caspian. "The maid is in the closet with the young son of the family, imprinting him for life."

Caspian fingered the tiny dishes. "Alicia would love this."

"And it only costs as much as a Korean automobile."

"I think she needs a little world she can arrange."

"Here's the guest room. Where her godfather the screenwriter stays when he's out of work."

"Let's do it before I come to my senses," said Caspian, and he and Cresswell carried the dollhouse to the front of the store.

The owner greeted them at the counter. "That piece is museum quality. I have a great theatre set from the same estate. A velvet curtain that opens and closes, scenery that lowers in and out, a moon that rises—"

"With a girl to swing on it?"

"A complete cast of costumed players comes with the theatre."

"I've seen the show." Caspian tore the check out and handed it to the owner.

"And now, Mr. Cresswell, a few items for you today?"

Cresswell held the puppet up, and worked the mouth. *"Don't sell me to this Chinese whoremaster, boss."*

". . . and the marbles, and the submarine. Will that be all then, gentlemen?"

". . . he runs a massage parlor for monkeys . . ."

The owner helped them out the door with the dollhouse, and over to Cresswell's car, a battered old Pontiac with a big back seat, into which they fit the house. Caspian and Cresswell climbed into the front and drove off down Santa Monica.

"You'll enjoy that dollhouse, Caspian." Cresswell sped along the boulevard, cutting madly through traffic. "And you'll find that the dolls move around when you're not looking." He shifted wildly, accelerated, and squeezed past the car in front of him. "Because they get horny just like everybody else in this world."

"Have you ever broken that gear shift off in your hand?"

"As a matter of fact, yes."

They struck a pothole, and the old Pontiac rattled to its frame, as Cresswell cursed and straightened the wheel; the traffic light ahead turned to red and he jammed on the brakes. Caspian looked out the window, and saw two men arguing on the street corner, one of them small and swarthy, in white suit and panama hat. "Looks like a deal is going down."

Caspian gazed at the man's small, impeccable form; his gestures were smooth, measured. He turned his head toward Caspian, and his silver-mirror sunglasses flashed in the sunlight.

"The rear of the building," said The Weasel, stepping into the car.

Felix pulled the car back into the moonlit street. "At times, I find myself in another land, talking to people I've never met before."

"Trust no one," said The Weasel.

Felix circled the great stone edifice of the Danzig Anatomic Institute. The gates were high, pointed shafts of iron, the walls thick stone with ivy growing round them. An army amphibian came toward them from the other end of the street, driven by the military police. The Weasel's hand went toward the machine pistol strapped beneath the dash.

The driver of the amphibian glanced toward them as they passed; three other military watchdogs rode with him. The Weasel removed the MPI with a soft click and laid it on his lap.

"They're passing," said Felix, eyes going to the rearview mirror.

The Weasel returned the machine pistol to its place beneath the dash, and Felix drove to the rear of the institute and parked, near the back service entrance.

They climbed out and The Weasel led the way through the darkened iron gate. The grounds were still, and the windows blacked out. Felix followed him along a pathway to the main building. The Weasel flattened himself against the wall, and turned to Felix, speaking softly. "How much is the girl's family paying us for this?"

"She has no family."

"We are here for purposes of charity?" A look of incredulity crossed The Weasel's face momentarily, followed by one of resignation. He adjusted the brim of his black derby, and crept toward the door. An SS man was on duty in the inner hallway, in a faintly lit little cubicle, where he was enjoying a cup of soup. The Weasel opened the door and stepped through. The SS man looked up.

"Order of the Bektashi Dervishes," said The Weasel, with a slight bow.

The SS man, puzzled, turned in his chair. The Weasel, in one swift step, had his pistol out and the muzzle laid against the guard's temple. "We want someone."

"You can have them." The guard's spoon was rattling in his cup, as he gazed slantwise at The Weasel's thinly smiling lips, and the glinting barrel of the pistol.

Felix stepped forward. "Inmate Number 2336787, Valentina Povanda. Where is she?"

"I just watch the halls."

"You'll watch them with a hole in your head." The Weasel released the safety on his pistol.

"I'll find her," whispered the SS man. He picked up the phone in his cubicle and dialed. Slowly, clearly, making sure The Weasel heard every word, he asked the whereabouts of Inmate Number 2336787. He nodded, and then carefully put the phone back in its cradle. "Come with me."

He led them down the empty corridor, and through the doorway at the other end. A strong smell of caustic soda and fat struck Felix's nostrils. There were barrels in the hall, and high stacks of boxes. A man in a white laboratory uniform was standing amidst them, a checkpad in his hand. The Weasel put his pistol deeper into the guard's ribs, and said softly, "Talk through the seat of your pants."

The guard gave a stiff wave to the laboratory chemist, and wished him good evening. "Lots of soap," he stammered idiotically, as The Weasel's pistol pressed against his kidney.

"Eighty kilograms," said the chemist. "It's not much for all our pains."

Felix looked past the chemist, through the open laboratory door, to where a vat was bubbling, the surface a slick, shining layer of grease. The guard jabbered a moment more, and then they were past the chemist and continuing down the hall.

"You did that well," said The Weasel. "I may find employment for you at my hunting lodge in Balderschwang."

"Don't blow me apart when this is done. I don't give a damn about these people here. I've got a steel plate in my head." The guard pointed to the long scar along his hairline. "Sometimes I forget things. Sometimes I forget whole days."

"And nights."

"Yes, that's right. Nights too. I've got shrapnel for brains."

He led them into the next wing. A human skeleton, joined by wire, stood in the hall, outside the doorway of a classroom. Its eye sockets cast the hollow gaze of death upon the three as they approached, and the guard led on, to a wide, marble staircase. They climbed with him, to a hallway marked with the names of various professors. He stopped before the door of Professor Wolfram Hessel. A soft light was coming through the glass. "In there."

The Weasel knocked softly.

There were scuffling footsteps and then a shadow approaching on the other side of the smoked glass. *"What is it?"* The voice was gruff, irritated.

"You've been awarded the Knight's Cross, Herr Professor," said The Weasel.

The door was opened, and the professor found himself gazing into the muzzle of The Weasel's automatic. He was a middle-aged man in tweeds, a gold watch chain across his vest and a pair of wire-rimmed glasses on his nose. Valentina Povanda was seated on his leather couch by the shaded window, in an institute gown of coarse white cloth. On the table beside her were two glasses and a bottle of wine.

The Weasel brought out the gray medallion of the Gestapo, and a folded piece of paper, which he snapped open in the professor's face. "This is Search Warrant V, issued against you in this matter."

"Matter? What matter?" The professor's ruddy countenance had drained of color.

The Weasel went to the young girl, and gave her his hand. "You must come with us." He gave her over to Felix, then turned back to the professor. "Put your affairs in order. You have until tomorrow to do so. We allow you this period of grace owing to your reputation." The Weasel paused, gazing at the numb and terrified scholar. "A pity you were not more discreet."

The professor sank down slowly into a chair. "I've—done nothing."

"I'm afraid that is not so, Herr Professor." The Weasel went to the table where the wine was sitting. He picked up the bottle and turned its label to the light. "Vintage Louis Roederer." He poured himself a glass, and sniffed it appreciatively. "A wine one can only obtain on the black market these days. But you, I suppose, have been saving it through the years, for just this moment."

"A trifle," said the professor, nervously removing his handkerchief from his pocket.

"And is it also a trifle to smuggle state prisoners out of the Reich?"

"Smuggle?" The professor's eyebrows rose in astonishment.

"You deny having assisted two black marketeers in the transport of children such as this one—" The Weasel pointed at the young girl. "—to Switzerland?"

"I deny it most emphatically!" The professor leapt from his chair, and The Weasel shoved him back down.

"At ten thousand marks the head? A pretty business. You have been seen at Langenstein Castle in the company of a Swedish businessman known to assist Polish Jews in escaping to enemy soil."

"I've never helped a Jew to escape! I've never helped a Jew in my life!"

The Weasel sipped his wine slowly, rolling it around on his tongue and then swallowing. He cocked his head back toward the professor, and his ferret eyes gleamed. "You were not overheard saying, *we'll rob everything there is to rob?* You deny having an illegal bank account? And dining lavishly and conspicuously at luxury restaurants far above your station?" He leaned in over Professor Hessel's chair, and said quietly, "You might have spent some of your profits more wisely."

The professor sagged, staring down at the floor, his expression that of someone who has wakened in a room he cannot recognize. His brow had broken into beads of sweat and his eyelid was twitching. The Weasel handed him a glass of the Louis Roederer. "The condemned man asked for the best."

The professor raised the glass, his trembling hand spilling half of it on his vest before it reached his lips. Then, slowly, as he drank, a light seemed to go off in his mind. He quickly rose from his chair, his hand going into his breast pocket. He brought out his wallet, and emptied it into The Weasel's hand. "A month's salary. It's all I have."

"A month's salary? You swine, you've been living like a god, and you offer me a month's salary?"

The professor wiped his brow with his handkerchief. "I have done nothing illegal. I'm a scientist. Far from helping our enemies in any way, I have mounted their very bones! Yes, ask the head of the institute himself. We use Jew bones for anatomical display. We get them by the carload."

The Weasel put the money into his pocket, and tossed the empty wallet on the desk. "You're a racketeer, Professor. You work with a crooked Party leader in Weimar. Your family has been enjoying fantastic privilege—" He twirled the chain of his Gestapo medallion in the professor's face. "—while my poor father slaves as a craftsman in a bombed-out cellar of Swavenkamp."

"I regret his circumstances," said the professor. "Deeply and sincerely." He turned in confusion, and his gaze fell upon a small framed engraving on his office wall. He walked over to it, removed it from the wall and handed it to The Weasel. "It's the most valuable thing I own. By Dürer, a sketch of his own mother."

The Weasel studied the etching carefully for a moment, then put it under his arm. "I should spend this night in prayer if I were you, Herr Professor. Pray that this humble servant of the Reich whom you see before you will lose interest in you. Pray that he mislays the warrant for your arrest."

"I shall pray for that, and for you, and your beloved father." The professor's eyes were moist. He hurried to open the door as The Weasel turned, and bowed as The Weasel passed through. Felix and the guard followed, the girl between them, and the professor did not lift his eyes to look at her, but remained bent over in supplication; they heard him close the door with the gentlest of clicks as they walked on down the hallway, The Weasel still swinging his Gestapo medallion.

"She is your daughter?" asked the guard.

"Yes," said The Weasel.

Their steps echoed in the empty stairwell. The guard pointed to a doorway at the bottom of the stairs. "You need not go back through the building. That door will take you to the court-yard."

He went ahead of them and opened it. The Weasel paused as they went through, and touched his pistol lightly on the guard's elbow. "When next you see the professor, gaze at him as if astonished that he is still among the living. I promise he will never speak of this night to you or to anyone."

The guard held the door for them. Felix followed The Weasel onto the dark grounds, the girl's hand in his. Valentina Povanda looked at him, her eyes darting from his face, to the stone buildings, and back again, but her grip on his hand was strong.

They went out through the gate, into the darkened street. Valentina turned, to look back at the institute. He followed her gaze, toward the professor's window high up in the stone build-ing. The professor's figure was faintly visible through the glass.

"We've found a family for you," said Felix, softly. "In the mountains."

She looked at him, uncomprehendingly. He put his arm around her and hurried her along to their car. No one moved on the street. The Weasel started the engine. Felix put her in the back seat. "We have a long journey, Valentina. The Weasel and I will sing to you."

Her gaze remained on the gloomy stone edifice of the in-stitute. He touched the dollhouse on the seat beside her. "We have something for you. See, Valentina? You'll be going to a house just like this, with nice big rooms. Here, you can move the furniture around."

She looked down into the dollhouse, out of which Felix brought a tiny bed. "This will be yours. In your own room."

Déjà vu, he said to himself. It has all happened before.

Caspian's head jerked backward, as if snapped by a string. Overhead were painted stars and moons, upon the ceiling of his daughter's room.

"Let's put it over here in the corner," said Ed Cresswell, holding the other end of the Victorian dollhouse in his arms.

Gaillard gazed at him across the low table, the soft morning light upon its smooth surface. "So why does Felix save the girl? What does she represent in you?"

"Innocence, I suppose. Something that deserves a chance to live."

"Yes, she's the part of you that is fresh and new. We've got to work to make it conscious, because this fragile creature may be your salvation. She could rescue you from the brutal patriarchal force in your personality, from the jackboots."

Caspian's fingers dug nervously into the puffy arm of the big easy chair. "Felix is still stealing my life. He still threatens my existence."

Gaillard's fingers came together in their habitual posture of prayer, raised to a point just under his nose. "Your ego is threatened. But not your existence. There's a difference."

"We've circled this before."

"Yes, we're circling. We'll touch the same point many times, until realization comes."

"And what's the realization supposed to be?"

"I certainly don't know." Gaillard's smile fell away, as he dropped into thought again. When he spoke, it was quietly, with no trace of combativeness in his voice. "I'm not sure either of us will ever understand what has happened to you. The soul is a mystery. We go to our graves unanswered."

Caspian nodded, but a sigh of quiet despair escaped him. "I'm acting out scenes in a movie I have no memory of. I'm turning in the performance of my life, so my agent tells me, only I'm not there to appreciate it."

Gaillard turned his head toward the window, where an insect's humming wings were beating excitedly in the arbor of leaves. "You're assailed by the archetypes. It's the most difficult thing that can happen to anyone. But if you can withstand it, you change your point of view, and the world will finally show you its benevolent face." Gaillard walked to the window, gazed into the leaves, where the humming wings still beat. "Right now you're looking at all the wrathful faces, and undergoing the collective male fantasy of taking action against them."

Caspian's eyes were fixed on Gaillard's form by the window, and he heard the bug as well, its familiar buzzing a kind of code for the elusive dimension beyond man. And then he realized that Gaillard was still speaking, but he couldn't hear him, could only see his lips moving, for the droning of the bug's wings had drowned him out. The drone grew louder; he tried to move, and couldn't, his brain paralyzed by the sound.

Now, he wanted to cry, *it's happening to me now!* But his lips were sewn like those of a dried and shrunken head. And like such trophies of horror, he felt himself severed from life, from all possibility of action, from everything except a frozen stare.

Time, for the severed head, loses shape, falls inward; the room too lost cohesion, the bright sunlit walls changing in texture and tone, becoming dark, becoming stone, as the window lost its tropic glow. And Gaillard, standing at the window, was himself changed, his hawklike features sharpening, the intelligence in his eyes turning to menacing power, and his clothes the uniform of a Gestapo chief, Emil Weiss. The room was furnished in the dark, heavy furniture of the State Police. Upon his desk a small lamp glowed, casting the only light. A door opened and another man, also in uniform, entered.

Caspian floated less substantial than the light from the feeble desk lamp—a thin wisp of thought, a vapor, a shadow that goes unseen in rooms like this, where a somber atmosphere prevails and ghosts, perhaps, may hover. A yellow folder was on the desk, and the name *Falkenhayn* was written on its tab. Caspian was able to read for a moment, with the shock and jerk of dreams, as the writing turned to shimmering liquid.

He drifted into the light of the desk lamp, and passed through, his wraithful form unbalanced, but intent upon staying. He merged with the smoke from Weiss's cigarette, then passed through it and turned slowly, facing the two men again. Weiss had picked up his cigarette and was gesturing lightly with it over the Falkenhayn folder. There was a squeaking sound, like a balloon being rubbed, and suddenly their voices popped clear.

". . . enough to hang him. But he's more valuable to us alive." A bit of gray ash fell upon the papers within the Falkenhayn folder. "Through him we get to Mueller. And Mueller is the trophy I want. I will see his head rolling into a basket, where it belongs." Weiss ground his cigarette out.

The other man drew the folder toward him, leafed through it quickly. "This looks tight enough. What about the woman?"

Weiss smiled, and turned toward the window. "Formerly employed at the Scala. She'll dance privately now. Her veils will fall."

Weiss closed the folder, put it away, brought out a second folder. "Bring in our prisoner."

The Gestapo aid left the room and returned with an army officer. The man was bruised, weak, knees threatening to buckle beneath him. He was shoved into a chair and the desk lamp shined in his face.

Caspian floated in the smoky light, his body drifting from side to side in an excited oscillation. The prisoner was someone he knew, from both sides of reality; on one side he was the officer at the brigadier's party, who'd invited him to go café crawling. On the other side, he was Ed Cresswell.

"You have been found guilty, and tomorrow you die with a rope around your neck. You may find yourself dangling there for as much as a half hour before death takes you. I can arrange for a cyanide capsule instead. Just give me one small piece of information concerning your Colonel Mueller—"

Caspian attempted to take Weiss's pistol from his holster but his hand passed through it. He floated toward the light, to try and somehow turn it off, to plunge the room in blackness and help his friend escape, but as he approached the light it grew brighter, like the tropic sun. He passed into it, unable to stop his flight, across the dimensions.

The sun came through a familiar window. Dr. Gaillard was at his desk, closing a folder. ". . . Jung talked about the wizard-like shadow in a man's psyche. A figure that makes us feel we're the victim of huge powers." He slipped the folder into his desk drawer.

Caspian felt the threads loosening from his lips. "The hour—is over?"

"Sorry, the clock just chimed. Didn't you hear it?"

*   *   *

He spoke into the telephone attached to the center arm of the rented Jaguar. "Myron, I'm going to be late to the set. I may not get there at all today. Stop screaming, Myron, they can shoot around me. Ed Cresswell's in trouble, and I've got to get to him." He cradled the phone in the receiver, swung onto

Coldwater Canyon Drive, and turned the Jaguar loose; by the time he reached Moonridge he'd be airborne. The car screeched through the quiet neighborhood; if he was stopped by a cop, he'd simply explain that he was following a clairvoyant vision.

He hit Mulholland Drive and swung left, toward Sherman Oaks. The Jaguar hummed along, and the weather was beautiful. In such beautiful weather, how could anyone have trouble? How could anyone run into any fate other than cold drinks and a suntan? How could the axe ever fall in L.A.?

He turned right on Sepulveda, and drove to the winding canyon road Ed lived on, high above the smog, with incredible views of golden pollution. The road was tiny and dangerous at any speed, and the worst driver on the hillside was Ed Cresswell. Should they meet now, there would be no time for explanations.

He slowed toward the top, crested, and went down the little dip to where Cresswell's house stood. He saw Cresswell's car, parked in the drive, and pulled in behind it. He got out, went to the front door and rang the bell, but got no answer, and the door was locked. He went to the back of the house, and shoved his elbow through a window. He climbed through, into the back hall; everything was spotless, perfectly arranged, the hallway lined with original Walt Disney art. At the end of the hall stood a life-size replica of the Tin Man.

He went through the hall, following the sound of Ed's electric trains. Ahead of him, over a doorway, was a sign saying Union Pacific Railway. He stepped beneath it, into the railroad room. A long freight was chugging along the huge oval of track. The gate crossings went up and down, and the man with the little electric lamp came out of his tiny house, waving the light as the train went by.

Caspian went quickly through the buzzing train room, into the living room, where Cresswell was unconscious in his chair, clad in a tuxedo, his tap shoes on, and an empty pill bottle still in his hand.

Caspian dialed Emergency, summoned an ambulance, then went back to Cresswell, yanking him out of the chair. Cresswell's head rolled, and Caspian slapped him sharply on the cheek. His jaw fell, and spittle ran from the corner of his mouth. Caspian shook him hard, but Cresswell's head just snapped around like a rag doll's.

"Come on, Ed . . ." He yanked Cresswell's head back, checked his mouth to see if he was choking. ". . . I've advanced you twenty-five thousand on that script you're writing." He spun him around, and hammered him between the shoulder blades. A mass of white mucus shot from Cresswell's mouth. Caspian hammered him again, and Cresswell's body hung limp in his arms.

He dragged him across the hall, into the kitchen, the metal cleats on Cresswell's tap shoes scraping noisily on the floor. Caspian propped him against the sink and put his head under the faucet.

"Wake up, Mr. Astaire, it's time for your big number."

Cresswell opened an eye, as water cascaded over his face, and he moved his arm, trying to come out from under the torrent. "Lemme die . . . goddamnit . . . can't you leave me . . ."

Caspian brought him away from the faucet, turned him around. "Come on, Ed, we're going to take a ride on the Reading Railroad."

Cresswell's other eye opened, bloodshot, beady. He stared through a groggy haze at Caspian. "You fucking heroes . . . always show up, don't you."

"That's our job, Ed."

"A man can't commit suicide . . . in the privacy of his own home anymore." Cresswell started to slide, down the front of the sink, his knees buckling. Caspian grabbed him, propped him up again.

"You can't die on me, pal. Not till you've finished writing our script."

"I had my tap shoes on. I was dancing with Garland . . . over the rainbow, at last."

Caspian got him under the arms and started him walking, out through the kitchen and back into the living room, Cresswell's tap shoes making a slurred sound on the hardwood floors, as his feet dragged along. "I should have cut my throat. But the sharpest thing I had . . . was a rye cracker."

"The ambulance is coming. They'll let you ring the siren all the way to the hospital."

Cresswell's eyes closed, and he was gone again. Caspian shook him hard, Cresswell's spindly body flapping about like a scarecrow's. His eyes opened slowly and he looked at Caspian. "I'm a loathsome human being . . . I'll show you. Now or never." He staggered in Caspian's arms, toward a large stuffed panda that set in the corner of the room. "Open the zipper . . . in back."

Caspian picked up the panda, opened the zipper. A magazine fell out.

"Read and lemme die."

Caspian opened the magazine, to pages of child pornography. "So you're a little kinky."

"I go out . . . with them." Cresswell's knees buckled and Caspian straightened him up again.

"Take it easy, Ed. You'll be ok. We'll get you what you need to be well."

"Guys like me, we're called . . . chicken hawks." Cresswell wretched, stomach heaving. "You can get anything you want . . . in L.A."

"Fine, Ed. We'll get you a chicken. You'll have a healthy relationship with a Rhode Island Red."

"Lemme die, will you . . ."

Caspian looked around him, at the house full of toys. The children must have had fun here, playing with Ed's trains and games and windup creatures.

"Why'dja come? You're supposed to be . . . making a movie."

"I had a vision."

"He had . . . a vision."

"The Gestapo nabbed you. They gave you a cyanide pill."

". . . weird, Caspian . . . you're weird . . . but you're here . . . I'm so glad you're here."

"When the ambulance arrives, there's no need to tell them everything."

"I'll tell them that from now on I'll only stick it . . . in soggy ice cream cones."

"Or your panda."

"No good, I took all his . . . stuffing out."

Carol Caspian sat in the bamboo swing, gliding gently back and forth on the patio and talking about a new client. "She owns Tours International, and she's as big as an excursion balloon, but she's sincere."

Carol's portfolio was open on the patio table, and Caspian was slowly turning through the latest ads.

"We did some of that in her house. There was so much marble around my teeth were chattering. The front porch pillars were shaped like champagne glasses."

"Handled in perfect taste."

"Wherever I go, I take plunger in hand. Tours International—offering you Palma de Mallorca, and all the paper pompoms you could ever want. See that rhumba line?" She pointed to a full-color ad. "Not one person under sixty. The glamour is breathtaking."

Caspian sat within the glow of a huge paper lantern suspended above the table, and let the familiar waterfall of Carol's voice play over him, as the musky scent of the heavy hanging trees came and went with the gentle night breeze.

"Day Number Two," said Carol, swinging toward him, "the Royal Palace of Rabat and an incredible dose of heartburn for lunch. Then we travel by private motorcoach—that's a secondhand municipal bus purchased from Yugoslavia in 1953, but we call them motorcoaches, to make you think of something large with a fully-equipped bar. The power of a colorful brochure is amazing, isn't it? It's an object in itself, if you see what I mean. Who have you been sleeping with, David?" Her bare toe glided up to his knee, touched it, glided away.

He gazed through the screen at the moonlit garden. Carol glided toward him again, and this time her toes didn't touch him. "You toad." Her voice was quiet; she had a deep wellspring of withering remarks in her, and he didn't want to do anything to release them. "Tell me, who is it? Roma?"

"I'm not sleeping with anyone, I'm losing my mind."

"That bitch, I'd like to panel her with contact paper." Carol pushed the swing angrily forward, and sent her foot through the screen. It tore easily, falling limply inward as she swung away. "So you got your pants sewed up. I hope you enjoyed it."

"I haven't enjoyed anything."

"I know all the signs, you louse."

"Call Gaillard. He'll tell you my situation. It has nothing to do with another woman."

"What a performance. You ought to be in pictures." She swung forward again, and kicked another hole in the screen.

He looked at the pair of gaping holes. "The mosquitoes are going to get in."

"Good." She came forward, sent both feet against the thin mesh, and made one large hole uniting the others. "You ought to be a tour guide on the Basic Guadalajara Vacation. You could sleep with all the blue-haired ladies in pantsuits. Why don't you grow a little mustache?"

"I've been going through a difficult—"

"—piece of tail. Yes, you poor darling. Suffering like that on Roma's hip."

"Carol, what are you trying to do to me? You know the pressure I'm under during a shoot."

"Roma relieves all the pressure of *your* shooting, I'm sure," said Carol, her feet swinging cleanly through the blown-out patch of screen.

Caspian stood and grabbed the ropes of her swing. She twisted toward him, aiming a kick at his knee. "How dare you interfere with my swinging."

"I want to save some of the porch, all right?" He brought the swing to a standstill, but knew better than to try and touch her. She was staring down at his rattlesnake boots, recently purchased in Nevada.

"Brothel creepers."

"I beg your pardon?"

"Brothel creepers, and that's what you are, a brothel creeper."

"Carol, there are things in my life you can't know about. Things I want to protect you from."

"Of all the crap you've ever handed me as an excuse for fucking other women, this takes the cake." She got off the swing and turned on him violently; the lace fringe of her white skirt caught in the jagged screen and tore. She looked down at it in anger. "Oscar de la Renta. Four hundred sixty-nine dollars and ninety cents, marked down."

"Well, if you'd stop chewing the scenery—"

She kicked over the bamboo coffee table, sending drinks and dishes flying. "I enjoy bizarre behavior." She picked up her portfolio and threw it through the hole in the screen, into the garden. "It makes me feel sexy."

He sat back down, exhausted; he should've been on the desert, but he wanted to spend one stabilizing evening with his dear wife. She was standing over him now, stamping her bare foot on the toe of his new boot. "Did you wear these for her?

Did you flash that cheesy smile of yours? Did you show her all your nice implants?"

"You're projecting—"

"Don't analyze *me,* you sleazebag. I've known for weeks and I wanted to spare us a scene, but when you come home looking like three cases of pussy—"

"Carol—"

"Don't call me Carol."

"What should I call you? Isn't Carol your name?"

She burst into a sob. "Oh, why do you have to hurt me?" She went limp, and flopped back down on the swing, her hands falling between her knees; her skirt was turned up at the hem; her lower lip was trembling and her mascara was running. "And with that porno queen, Roma French."

He knelt beside her. "I'm telling you the truth. I'm not having an affair with Roma, or anyone else."

"Get lost."

He stood, slowly, his own hands hanging limply at his sides. She was just getting a breather and would be after him again soon with deeper and more venomous invective. "Carol, I've been distant, I've been moody, I've probably been cold to you without thinking, but I'm one step away from a nervous breakdown. A twenty million dollar picture is riding on my shoulders and I haven't the faintest idea what I'm doing in it. I black out on the set, I don't remember even speaking my lines."

She looked up at him, streaks of mascara giving her the eyes of a sad circus clown. "Con is on so many levels."

"I'm not conning you. I'm in a dark space, darker than you could ever imagine. Going to bed or not going to bed is not what I'm worried about just now. I'm falling right out of the goddamn world."

"It's a living."

"Carol, do I look happy? I'm ready for a lunatic asylum."

She rose from the swing, and moved past him, out into

the yard. He followed her, into the silvery leafed plants of the moon garden. Hands folded in front of her, she was gazing down the shadowy gravel path, and he realized that she'd grown older, had lost some of her spark for the fight; she wanted peace. Gently, unobtrusively, he put his arm around her. She didn't pull away.

"You're not forgiven, I just can't deal with the situation."

"Neither can I."

They stood together in silence for a long while. Finally, with a weary sigh, she turned back toward the house. "All right, let's go take some Valium."

ight on the desert was cool, and the mood of the production changed with its falling. The circle of lighted vans and tents became a fabulous caravan camped in the sands. Caspian sat at a long table beneath an open canopy, where crew members had gathered, drinking coffee and talking beneath a string of bare light bulbs. Seated beside him was Myron Fish, eating pie off a paper plate. Fish looked at him suspiciously. "You saw your analyst again?"

"Yes, why?"

"How much is he soaking you?"

"He's reasonable."

"What's reasonable?"

"When you need help, anything's reasonable."

"I have a client, David, a very big rock and roller who shall go unnamed; his analyst charges him by the minute—four dollars a minute to be exact. The analyst drops in on him at his home, unannounced, while he's eating, entertaining, schtupping, or sleeping, so the doctor can see how he's interacting."

"At four dollars a minute?"

"Door to door. The moment the analyst steps into his limo to drop in unannounced the meter is running. He also travels with my rocker, to assist him with the mental stress of hotel life. Also at four dollars a minute. Do you know how my rocker pays for this? He gives the shrink points in his albums. The shrink has a year's contract. He's a very tough negotiator. You know something?"

"What?"

"I wish I were *his* agent." Fish finished his pie and pushed the plate away. A light bulb hung directly over him, his bald head reflecting its harsh light. "So—you fought with Carol."

"How did you know that?"

"When wives phone their husband's agent, it's for one reason only. So how do things stand? You've made up? Or do you need the name of the finest divorce lawyer in America? This is a man I should have had on retainer. I should have been paying him four dollars a minute to visit me at supper time, which is when most marriages go on the rocks. Studies have been made."

"By whom?"

"By me. My second wife actually pied me at the table. Lemon meringue, I'll never forget. The judge should have seen that. A professional witness would have been invaluable."

"Carol and I are doing fine, Myron. It was only a slight misunderstanding."

"Be prepared, David, that's all I'm saying. When I take someone out to lunch, I always call the restaurant to find out which credit cards they don't honor and those are the ones I bring. Simple footwork but you have to know it. Petite women do very well in divorce court."

The assistant director, walkie-talkie in hand, ducked in under the canopy. "Ready for you in five." Caspian nodded, and rose from his chair. Fish rose with him and they stepped out of the canopy into the darkness. "Don't let personal problems get in the way of the fine performance you're giving in this film."

"Myron, half the time I've been on camera, I wasn't even there."

"You've always been in the new wave of acting, David. We all recognize the ground you're breaking."

"I was in a slave labor camp in Nazi Germany."

"You use what works for you."

They walked along through the rows of vans, to the shooting site—a midnight piece of desert terrain, as forbidding as anything Caspian had ever seen, with a ragged mountain in the distance, outlined by the moon. The effect was that of an alien world of night at the far end of the universe. The crew stood in their circle of lights, props, mikes, as if at an oasis. Herman Armas was seated in his director's chair, a cup of black coffee in one hand and his viewfinder in another, squinting at the scene before him. Roma French sat beside him, attended by her entourage. Caspian sat down on the other side of her. She, the woman with whom he was supposed to be having a torrid affair, gave him an indifferent nod, for she was cold, tired, and suffering the effects of several long weeks of constant coking.

An amazon from Roma's planet walked by, clad in a brief costume which showed the rippling power of her extraordinary musculature. Fish, standing behind Caspian's chair, murmured, "She could crush my head like a grape."

The amazon took her place on the set, the gaffers gazing in fascination at the chiseled lines of her body. Fish continued quietly from behind Caspian. "And yet I feel I should represent her."

The A.D. motioned to Caspian, Roma, and the other actors in the scene. Caspian took his place and Roma stepped with her makeup man into outer darkness, to bend over a mirror in which her reflection was not the essential thing. A moment later she was beside Caspian beneath the lights, a look of supreme confidence in her eyes once more, and ready to act her socks off.

They tried several long takes on the shot, after which Roma's makeup man found it necessary to powder her forehead because of the shine, and powder as well the interior of her nose. Armas had meanwhile drawn Caspian aside. "That little twist of character you've been giving, David, it's not in this shot yet. That slightly sinister something, where your voice fogs up a little, know what I mean?"

"Yes, Herman, I know what you mean."

The clapboard sounded several more takes. Caspian drank lukewarm soup between each one, provided by whomever's hand extended from the darkness. It was past midnight, and the crews were working in a surreal daze, the mood of the shot improving as fatigue gained the edge. "We're getting there," said Armas. "One more and we can call it a day."

The mountain range was Roma's, the entrance to her court; her amazon guard was near. Caspian was her soldier of fortune from the stars. They were camped in the blue moonlight of her planet. Seated with them was Roma's prime minister, played by Ashley Summers, a star without benefit of talent; he was a ham of the old school, and as unconscious a performer as Caspian had ever known, but with a voice like velvet.

The amazons returned to their tape marks. Caspian, Roma, and Ashley Summers found their places in the foreground, and the camera crew signaled their readiness to Armas. Ashley Summers, beside Caspian, said, in his mellifluous bass voice, "That's Mars up there. One can see the stars so well on the desert. I'd rather be in bed."

Action resumed and Caspian took a step toward Roma—a step not completed, for Mars intervened, the planet suddenly rushing toward them, its brightness growing sharper, clearer, and then the larger planet, Pluto, appearing behind it—ominous, immense—as Roma and Ashley continued speaking their lines.

"Berlin, my dear lady, is built on soft alluvial sand, but here

in Frankfurt we are more firmly grounded. Something solid beneath the feet. The sort of ground to build a bank on, don't you agree, Lieutenant?"

The planets diminished suddenly, becoming two harmless globes on a rococo lamp, set upon a high arching wall.

"Forgive me," said Felix. "I was lost in thought for a moment. What did you say?"

"I said the soil of Frankfurt is charmed beneath the feet of Countess von Blaustein."

They stood together in the main room of the principal Frankfurt bank. Night had fallen, and the place was now emptied of employees; only a few lamps burned in the vast dome. Felix observed that Bank Manager Flick was in a nuptial mood; his deep, sonorous voice filled the empty cavern of the bank with a charmed echo, the echo of a man on whom Beauty has smiled. The necessity of dealing with the army might have made him uneasy, but Marla was from the inner circle of princes and barons; how could he doubt its nobility, or her sincerity?

"So, Lieutenant, our bank is to receive a shipment of confiscated property from the East." Herr Flick stood at a large mahogany desk, lit by a standing lamp shaped like an urn. Rich carpeting was beneath it, and Renaissance paintings hung upon the near wall. "And once we have received the shipment into our vault?"

"It is to be turned over to the municipal pawnshops for cash, this money then to go toward the financing of our war interests."

"Perfectly reasonable," said Herr Flick, his eyes returning to Marla's.

"The paperwork will be complicated," said Felix, "but we'll do our best to simplify it for you."

"Well, I certainly don't want more paper on my desk than I already have. There are much more important things in life." He turned again to Marla, who would vanish from his life like smoke from a cigarette once the municipal pawnbrokers received their goods. But for now, she touched his wrist, and said with an intimate smile, "That wine you wish me to taste?"

"Kitzinger Mainleite, the sunlight of Venus," said Herr Flick.

Felix removed his cap from under his arm. "Then we are perfectly clear on this business. Countess von Blaustein, can I have my driver take you to your hotel?"

She turned back to Flick. "You'll join me at nine?"

"With the deepest of pleasure." He bent over her hand, placed his lips and gray mustache lightly on it.

"Come round then," she said, gently withdrawing her fingers from his grasp. "We'll dine in my room."

Bank Manager Flick led them through the large echoing dome to the front door of the bank, and Felix and Marla walked down the granite stairs to the street, where Felix's car and driver waited. "You did well, Countess."

"It wasn't hard. His wife wears size fifty knickers."

They entered the car, and Felix signaled to the driver. Marla looked toward the street as the car moved on. As if to herself, she said, "Which were your happiest days?"

Felix removed a cigarette from the silver case she'd given him. "As a boy, when I was truly happy, I didn't quite know it. Something is always missing from happiness."

Her gaze remained on the dark street. A floppy felt hat was angled on her head, a bird's bright feather in its band. Her legs were crossed beneath her long, dark skirt. "In Leopold-strasse in Munich the lesbians still caress each other."

"Were those your happiest days?"

She ran a finger down through the misted glass. "Perhaps."

He smoked in silence, thinking of the shipment, and of those pawnbrokers he knew from the black market who would soon be receiving it. Arrangements could be made with them too; for a small commission he'd see they received the preferred merchandise from the Eastern territories, and small commissions add up. Take it wherever you can, for the Russians are going to take it all in the end.

Marla nodded toward the shadow of an old crone in the archway of a ruined building. "I could become a rubble woman." She adjusted her earrings, fingers touching the diamond chips, as the old woman was lost behind them in the darkness. "The entire country is a ruined emotion."

"But what were we before?" asked Felix.

"We were—for just a moment—happiness."

"Odd that I can't recall it." He lowered the window, tossed out his cigarette.

"You were happy in the theatre."

"I worked five minutes in 1935. A glorious end to a glorious career." He rolled the window back up, slid his arm across the back of the seat toward her. "But let's cheer up. With God and the Prussians all things are possible."

They rode in silence the rest of the way to her hotel. Felix stepped from the car with her into the street. She spoke abruptly. "I was followed here. Emil Weiss is watching your precious shipment too."

"It is an important state matter."

"Have you arranged my escape from this madhouse of a country?"

"Will you mind traveling part of the way in a packing crate?"

Marla looked up the street, to where a figure stood, withdrawn into a doorway, but still visible in his long leather coat. "How soon?"

"If you like, the day this shipment is finished and Bank Manager Flick has signed for it."

"I'll be ready."

"Well, then, gather up your jewels and banknotes." He placed a light kiss upon her cheek. "And Felix will ship you to Switzerland."

She let her eyes rest on his face. "You have always been a half-decent sort. And I've been cold as stone. But I couldn't help it, you know."

"As we say in the army, you worked for Germany all the same." He glanced toward the figure in shadow down the street. How close have they gotten to me . . .

He stepped back, put his hand to the door of the car. "Prepare," he said softly. "I'll ship you as handcut glassware, the best."

With a wink at her from beneath his hat brim, he slipped back into the car. As his car passed the Gestapo shadow in the doorway, he put his hand on his revolver. But the shadow remained where it was, only moving when Marla entered the hotel. He watched from the back window of his car, as the figure moved off.

The hotel was left behind, and the headlamps of the car caught the stone face of a gargoyle, grimacing from his little shelf on the side of a building. They watched over the city, demonic dream figures brought to life by headlamp and bombflash. And some of them were headless now, and so will we all be, reflected Felix, with limbs scattered to the rubble women.

The flickering of the stone face was like a bit of film, as the camera pans. He thought of his films, the few he'd been in, an unidentified figure in the background. But in this other film, the one we call life, I've become a player worth shadowing.

The car turned toward a military compound. Two guards, like dreaming toys, came to life, one of them stepping forward as the vehicle stopped. Following the identity check, his car was motioned through, the toy soldiers swiveling back to their dreamlike positions. The gate to the compound was lifted and the car rolled in, past gun sheds, ammunition piles, a deserted sports field. They reached the main building and parked. "Go in and tell them we've arrived."

The driver entered the building, closing the door gently

behind him, and then the only sound was that of a sentry, rifle clanking softly against his helmet as he marched in the darkness. The door to staff headquarters opened and Colonel Mueller's silhouette appeared, moving with a kind of dainty corpulence onto the stairs. Watching him Felix suddenly recalled the cabaret on Motzstrasse, heard the music again, saw the smoky stage in his mind, with a fat woman strutting arrogantly down it.

The driver opened the door for Mueller, who bent down and slipped into the seat beside Felix. "Close your mouth, dear boy, you look like a raw prawn."

"It was you," said Felix in a whisper, "on stage at the cabaret."

Mueller paused in adjusting himself into his seat. His eyes were little glittering beads. A faint smile crossed his lips. "And do you know who shared my dressing room, and later appeared onstage as Cleopatra? The man who is now head of the Gestapo's office for the Suppression of Homosexuality. So you see, dear boy—" Mueller settled himself, "—there's no telling where talent may lead you."

Mueller gave the driver instructions, then turned back to Felix. "You've seen our bank manager?"

"Marla has softened his brain."

"I must give her a suitable gift. Think of something, will you?"

"I'm arranging for some handcut crystal."

Mueller took out a long, gold-tipped cigarette. "So—you will be meeting the shipment, and performing the necessary tally of all items, rendering unto God and Caesar."

"Quite."

"You're a most efficient soldier, Felix. I will soon recommend you for promotion. You'll be wearing plaited silver threads on those sleeves. And when the war is over, and bigamy is legalized to increase the birthrate, as a high-ranking officer you will have your pick of excellent wives."

A rank of bayonets gleamed as a patrol marched into view, steel struck by the shafts of moonlight falling on the city. Mueller glanced at them. "Would they march if they knew a gentlemen's agreement existed between our industry and America's?"

"What is the agreement?"

"Oh, various targets are to be spared, because it would be bad for certain American companies." The column of men disappeared into the darkness. Mueller took out a scented handkerchief, patted his brow. "I've spent my war reflecting on its ironies."

The dashboard of the staff car glowed with soft light. A moth fluttered across the dash, attracted to the round little moons of glass. The driver brushed at it and it flew toward the back; its wings touched Felix on the cheek, and a memory suddenly surged, of a man within himself, a part of the spectrum always in waiting. A sudden heaviness fell over him, as the man within grew stronger. *He comes at the edge of sleep,* thought Felix, his head nodding.

"You didn't answer my question," said Quatrelle.

Caspian heard a faint click, and the door to the other world closed. He was riding in a limo, heading toward the airport with Victor Quatrelle. Which meant the desert shoot was done. And an entire evening had passed. "I was gone again."

Quatrelle's cheeks filled with air, which he released in a long, slow sigh. "Whatever it is you're smoking, I wish you'd let me have some."

"I don't smoke anymore. I don't drink. I don't even take vitamins. But I wasn't here today."

"You're here, you're available for interviews." Quatrelle opened the limo bar and poured himself a drink. "And if you disappear the *Hollywood Reporter* will find you."

Caspian sat in the screening room, as the recent footage flickered before him. The soul of his performance was Felix, the Berlin black marketeer—the Star Rover who'd fallen into an alien world and was determined to survive.

The picture was so far being stolen, however, by the Space Gnome, a gruff-voiced old midget who played the Star Rover's copilot. And now he was fatally wounded, in Caspian's arms, as the mercurial rain fell upon them in the desert.

"*I die . . . in a faroff world . . .*" He gestured weakly, his wrinkled face creased with a faint, bewildered smile, as the lights came up in the screening room. Myron Fish turned to Julius DeBrusca, who was seated beside him with a dead cigar in his teeth. "It's a fabulous use of people, Julius. I'm talking in terms of tears."

*   *   *

"I have such a stomachache," said Carol Caspian, "but look at this scrumptious ad. Terrific use of white space, a fabulous jar, a frank talk about skin care by a sincere dermatologist. Isn't he adorable looking? The lewd uncle who cares?"

Caspian sat beside her on the couch, eyes swollen from lack of sleep; the hourglass of the film had now been turned many times, and shooting at the studio had turned into a marathon. But he could be with Carol for a few hours each day, and though the air between them was still unsettled they'd resumed communication. Aside from giving his rattlesnake boots to their guard dog to chew on, she'd sought no further revenge. She drank Pepto Bismol and smoothed the ad with her hand. "I went into the meeting terrified my skin wasn't good enough for Dr. Dupré."

"And?"

"All morning long I felt a pimple coming through my chin. I kept trying to cover it with elegant gestures."

Alicia, playing nearby them on the floor, looked up from her electronic game. "Twenty invaders have just been plotzed." She laid the game down and crawled over to a jigsaw puzzle, whose pieces were scattered on the floor. "Can we work on this?"

"There's too much brown in it, honey," said Carol.

"It's a *field,* Mommy, with a lovely barn."

"It's just a lot of brown blotches, darling. Mommy will go blind if she tries to work on it with you. David, look at this ad—"

Caspian slid down onto the floor beside his daughter. "I used to do jigsaw puzzles all the time when I was a kid," he said, and began turning the pieces right side up. They were all brown, with no apparent difference between any of them. "Honey, where did you get this puzzle?"

"At the drugstore. I bought it myself. It's a field, can't you see?" His daughter held up the cover of the puzzle box, which showed a dark, blurred photograph, in brown.

Caspian looked at his wife. "They shouldn't be allowed to sell puzzles like this."

"Daddy," said his daughter, "it all fits together. I've done it once already."

"And what does it look like?"

"Like a *field*." Alicia began joining pieces, then looked up at her father, who was staring at the solid mass of brown. "Daddy's farblondjet again."

"He's been working very hard, darling," said Carol.

Caspian held up the cover of the box to his wife. "The photograph is out of focus. How can they expect anyone—"

"Daddy," said Alicia, "could I talk to you privately?"

He got up, and followed his daughter down the hallway to her room. They stepped inside and she closed the door. She put her ear to it for a moment, and then looked up at him. "You don't have to work on the puzzle."

"That's very kind of you, Alicia."

"Will you buy me an ant farm?"

"Yes, but we'll have to hide it from Mommy."

"I've got lots of hiding places."

"And if it breaks and the ants escape, you must never let Mommy know I bought it for you. We'll just pretend they wandered in here on their own, for something to eat. OK?"

"OK." Alicia nodded, and walked across the room to her Victorian dollhouse. She sat down in front of it, then turned back to her father. "I'll play by myself now. You can go back to Mommy if you want."

"Thanks, sweetheart." He bent over her, kissed her on the forehead. "Do you like your dollhouse?"

"Yes," said Alicia. "All the ladies are named Alicia. See? They're having tea on the porch."

"Very nice."

"Here's Ramona the maid, she's in one of the guest rooms, borrowing some jewelry. But she puts it back later."

"That's right, honey, and nobody mentions it to anyone because she's such a good maid."

Alicia turned back to the tea party on the porch. "Hello, Alicia, do you know Alicia? I'm *so* pleased to meet you, Alicia . . ."

Caspian backed quietly out of the room, and went down the hallway to the living room, where Carol was pouring herself another shot glass of Pepto Bismol. Caspian knelt and put the pieces of the brown puzzle back in their box. "She's playing with her dollhouse." He slid the box away under the couch, and sat down beside his wife. "How's she been while I've been gone?"

"She's been crying for days."

"What's the problem this time?"

"She saw one of those nature shows on TV, about all the trees in some jungle being cut down, and the baboons losing their habitat."

"It upset her?"

"She keeps asking me where the baboons are going to live."

"What did you tell her?"

Carol closed her portfolio. "I told her they were living in condos."

"That seems like a perfectly reasonable answer to give a growing child."

"All right, so I'm not the Mother of the Year. How am I supposed to know where the goddamn baboons are living? So long as they don't move into *this* neighborhood."

Caspian picked up his glass of cognac on ice, sipped it slowly. "It's not the baboons she's crying about. It's something to do with me."

"It's probably the both of us. I'm her role model and I've got no self-control. We had a caterer do lunch for the skin care people and just because there were five hundred sushi rolls left over, I had to eat them all." She put her portfolio into her briefcase and set it beside the couch. "I feel like a compressed air tank."

"If we get a flat tire—"

"—you can screw me onto the valve." She pressed her fists

into her stomach and bent over. "In college I used to get menstrual cramps like this. Hitting myself with a geography book sometimes helped."

"I advise a brisk walk." He gave her his hand and lifted her from the couch. She walked toward the patio door in a crouch. "I need a Bromo Seltzer."

"Bromides make you crazy, didn't you tell me that?"

"In a weak moment." She hobbled down the steps with him into the garden. "What a lovely evening for a bent-over walk in the yard."

"You'll feel better after some exercise."

"Why do you say that?" She continued along in her crouch, toward her herb garden. "I could make an infusion, if I knew where anything was."

"Or what it was for."

"I could be daring."

"You could be poisoned."

She straightened slightly on his arm. "We had an infusion at that little place in Paris. Near the Opera? I think it was thyme." She pointed to one of the herbs. "I think that's thyme."

"I wouldn't risk it."

"I might have an epiphany."

"Or you could be up all night on the toilet."

Her arm dropped limply down, she nodded, and they continued through the garden. "One's own backyard. One doesn't really appreciate it until one's eaten five hundred sushi rolls. But it's comforting, isn't it."

"Yes," he said, "very."

"And you're ok too," she said, putting her arm around his waist.

They walked on down to the edge of the little stream, and sat on its bank. "Do you remember when it flooded?" she said. "And we thought everything in the house would be ruined? And the first thing you carried out was a container of ice cream?"

He threw a stone into the stream. "I know what's important."

She put a hand up to his neck, and massaged it gently. "I do too," she said, quietly.

*   *   *

He entered the curtained doorway. The padded walls of the sound stage muffled his step as he navigated the long corridor. A hundred feet above him juicers treaded along their catwalks, setting the lights. Myron Fish stepped out of the shadows beside him, coffee cup in hand. "I've just put James Johnson Reilly into a picture whose theme is the asphyxiation of babies." Fish sipped his coffee, and matched his footsteps to Caspian's. "Last year J.J. suddenly grew artistic and spurned Hollywood. Only Hollywood didn't notice. So this year he's going to be seen running amok in a nursery with a bottle of chloroform." Fish stepped lightly over a thick cable and looked at Caspian. "You understand what I'm saying? There's a message in this for you."

"Save the hypnosis for your other clients, Myron, I'm indifferent to my career falling apart. I've got a much bigger problem."

"David, whatever problems you've got will be magnified enormously if you find yourself acting in a low-budget, Mexican dog-story film."

"You never quit, do you?"

"I can't afford to. I'm supporting five wives and an assortment of children." Fish tossed his coffee cup into a trash can. "Now tell me, what's the problem?"

"It's too complicated to explain, but the bottom line is that I'm going to have to take a few years off from filmmaking."

"Don't ever say such a thing, David. Not to the agent who's raised you like a son, only better."

They entered the next curtained doorway, onto the set. Roma stood with the assistant director at the entrance to a tunnel of light; its illusory depths had been created by laser beams shining into the empty spaces of the sound stage. Caspian stepped into the light. The A.D. was leading Roma to her tape marks, and a pair of technicians were turning on a smoke machine, sending clouds into the laser beams; the clouds increased the illusion of the electric tunnel's depths, the smoke undulating through the lights. Caspian found his tape marks near Roma.

"I love what you're both doing," said Armas. "Give me some more of it." He withdrew to his chair on the edge of the set, leaving his stars in the billowing smoke. Roma moistened her already shining lips, and the smoke machine sent out so many clouds the camera was unable to find her. "Stop the mother down," barked Armas.

Caspian stepped through the billowing smoke screen.

A large clock appeared on the face of a building, just visible through the fog. Felix crossed the misty station yard and entered the railway terminal. He glanced around, at the familiar waiting room of Pilsen, just over the Czech border, through which he'd brought black market goods many times in the old days.

"There are Weiss's men," said Corporal Sagen, nodding toward a pair of Gestapo agents standing by the doorway to the platform.

"I see only dead men," said Felix.

Sagen straightened himself, as in the distance, a train whistle sounded. "How is it to be arranged?"

"An accident en route." Felix turned and signaled the rest of his armed escort into the station. The Gestapo agents turned, and Felix strolled toward them at the doorway to the platform. "You're close to the front, gentlemen. You cannot be comfortable."

"Lieutenant Falkenhayn? We're to accompany you and your shipment to Frankfurt." The senior agent spoke, his breath bearing fumes of sauerkraut and bacon, his manner that of one who enjoys arresting people in the middle of their breakfast.

Felix clicked his heels, giving a little ceremonial bow. "It will be a pleasure to have you on the journey."

The whistle sounded more closely now and a faint rumble passed through the station floor. "This will be it," said the other agent, a sharp-nosed young man with the face of a handsome rodent. He opened the door to the platform and the group stepped through. Felix gazed up the tracks toward the approach of the steaming engine, and saw a soldier leaning from a window, a grizzled veteran of the Death's Head Division, returning for rest and recuperation. Felix separated himself a few paces from the group. The rat-faced agent moved with him. "Lieutenant—"

The agent's expression widened to profound surprise, as red flowers blossomed on his chest. Felix dove away from the machine gun fire, in behind a baggage cart. The brakes of the engine screamed and it halted a few yards up the tracks, as the bedraggled veterans of the Death's Head bailed out of it, firing as they landed, toward the muzzle blasts on the other side of the tracks. Felix turned, and saw the second Gestapo agent crawling toward him, eyes wide with terror, a man clearly not used to gunfire, except when firing his own pistol into the back of someone's head. He crouched in beside Felix, as pieces of the station blew away, the flying fragments of stone and cement as lethal as the shells.

"That's a twenty-millimeter cannon," said Felix. "The next one's going to blow this cart to kingdom come."

"Get me out." The agent's lips were quivering, the blood draining from his face, as the blasts of mortar and cannon shook the station yard. "I can help you. I know all about you."

"What do you know?" asked Felix, as the station roof flew off.

"Your activities—I'll have the file destroyed." The agent was babbling, eyes darting madly around, as huge fragments of the building flew through the air with hideous velocity. "I knew Gondolph, the counterfeiter."

"You arrested him." Felix released the safety on his machine pistol.

"Had I known he was your friend—"

"You would not have broken every bone in his body."

"I never harmed the man. And no harm shall come to you." A mortar blast lifted the platform, shaking it beneath them. The agent's eyes bulged. "We're going to be cut off—"

"We'll run for it," said Felix, pointing the muzzle of his Schmeisser toward the station door. "I can cover you. I'll give the word—"

"Yes," said the agent, going into a crouch.

Felix listened to the movement of the machine gun fire, then nodded. The agent ran like a maddened bear.

"Thank you, Ivan," said Felix, as the Gestapo agent danced madly for a moment and then fell, cut down in the arcing pattern of the Russian machine gun.

The Death's Head troops were fanning out around the station, launching flares, illuminating the station yard. Felix fired his Schmeisser, then cradled the machine pistol and rolled off the platform to the ground, joining the Death's Head veterans behind an overturned flatcar. The eyes that met his own were cold as the Russian snows—soldiers who'd survived Stalingrad, Kharkov, and the Panzer death ride.

Felix fired his Schmeisser from behind the flatcar wheel; after a ten round burst it jammed.

"Throw it away," said the soldier beside him. He pointed to an assault rifle, an MP 44 fitted out with a grenade cup; the man who'd held it was now staring into the night sky, a bullet hole through his forehead. A flare went up, Felix saw the Russian assault team in amongst the boxcars, and fired the grenade; the explosion blew the back of the boxcar off, and sent their shadows flying into the air. And he heard a song near his ear.

". . . *not every bullet finds the heart . . .*"

The soldier beside him was singing, as he and another veteran set up a machine gun.

". . . *the girls are smiling at us . . . the birds are chanting in the trees . . . the world is so beautiful . . .*"

The words were lost, then, in the rattle of the gun, as the two blasted away at the enemy. Felix stared at them for a moment, saw the soldier's lips still moving in song; his hands moved easily on his weapon, his head tucking in like a turtle's, instinctively, automatically, as if sensing the path of the bullets whizzing around him.

Along the entire station yard, the Death's Head soldiers were now advancing, firing, turning the attack, determined that nothing would interfere with their rest and recuperation. An anti-tank gun silenced the cannon, and mortar fire and grenades wiped out the machine guns. The firing from the other side of the station yard ceased, and Felix crept out from behind the flatcar.

"Partisans, that's all." A captain strode along the rails, a Luger in his hand. "Firing on us with our own weapons, no doubt." He waved his men back toward the train. "Let's move it, come on!"

Felix approached him, still carrying the grenade launcher. The captain looked at him. "Who the hell are you?"

Felix showed the captain the orders he carried, to provide the escort for the special freight attached to the troop transport.

"That boxcar full of old clothes?"

"And shoes in good repair, sir."

"There are already a half dozen men guarding that crap."

"We are to relieve them, sir."

The captain put his Luger into his holster with a sharp snapping move. "I want this train moving in five minutes."

Felix was joined by Corporal Sagen, and the rest of the escort. Sagen nodded to the two Gestapo agents, sprawled on the shell-pocked platform. "I see only dead men."

"They perished for the Fatherland." Felix led the way to the last car, where the original escort was regrouping, under a grizzled sergeant. Felix gave him the news that he and his men were to go on leave, joining the rest of the train. "The papers of transport, Sergeant, before you leave."

"Seems a lot of trouble for some Jew rags." The sergeant

scratched at the lice that were dining in his crotch, and handed over the papers.

"You may go, Sergeant."

"I have already gone." The sergeant turned to his men. "Move it." The train whistle was sounding. Felix climbed into the freight car with his squad. "Quickly." The stacked crates were sorted through, Felix reading out the numbers of the crates he wanted, four in all. The crates were tumbled out the door, onto the ground.

He handed a new set of transport papers to Sagen. "For Bank Manager Flick, Frankfurt."

The train whistle sounded once more, and the freight jerked forward. Felix leapt from the door, onto the dark ground. The freight car rolled past him, taking with it the sound of the wheels, which clicked on and away, down the tracks. He was left standing in the darkness, gazing across the station yard at the place from which the Czech partisan attack had come, but they had withdrawn now, back into the forest.

The train's dark body vanished then too, the last car snaking round the last bend in the yard. He turned toward the blasted stationhouse. From within its shattered depths, a lantern swung, back and forth at the window.

Felix waited, and presently the lantern came out, borne by a shadow, which descended from the platform and moved toward him. As it neared, the bewhiskered face of an elderly railroad man was illuminated in it. "Schaufel," said Felix, "are you in one piece?"

"I have plaster in my mustache," said the old man, peevishly, and set his lantern down on one of the crates. "Is this the stuff?"

"Yes, help me get it on that cart."

They lifted the crates up, the old railroader complaining of their weight. "What happened to your underwear business? The boxes were lighter."

"I'm handling other things now."

"Feels like ball bearings."

"Yes, Schaufel, ball bearings."

They pushed the baggage cart along the platform, to the side of the building, and out into the station parking lot, where Felix discovered his canvas-topped Kübelwagen with a piece of the station wall resting on it now, the steering wheel crushed beneath timber and stone.

"Out of luck there," said Schaufel, and then gazed at the shattered station roof. "Birds lived in the eaves . . ."

"Now they'll have to nest in your beard." Felix walked on through the parking lot, to the light lorry his men had come in, a six-cylinder diesel whose only damage was a few bullet holes through the chassis. Schaufel pushed the baggage cart up alongside it, and the crates from the Eastern Territories were loaded on, Felix removing their original seals and replacing them with the dark blue seals of the medical corps: vital medicines urgently needed, by Colonel Mueller's second battery, now assisting the citizens of Nuremberg. "Good," said Felix, climbing down from the back of the lorry and handing Schaufel an envelope.

Schaufel slipped the money into his overalls. "Listen," he said, bringing his watery eyes closer to Felix. He seemed unable to speak then, his face contorted with inexplicable emotion. "Listen," he repeated, his cheek twitching, "I've seen freight pass through here. Satan's own cargo." His eyes shot back toward the distant tracks, and he stroked his gray beard, drawing its strands out and tugging them nervously. "At times, I've been afraid to look. But I could hear." He turned back to Felix, blinked slowly. "I've heard the howling of the damned." He swung his lantern toward the tracks. "This is not a railroad. It's the river Styx."

Felix glanced toward the empty tracks, on which the new moon shone, the moon of thieves, his own moon, of those who work the crossroads by night. "You've done nothing wrong, Schaufel."

The old man looked back to the tracks. "I've waved my lantern. Do you understand? I've waved my good lantern, because that was my job. I helped that freight pass through."

Felix climbed up into the cab of the lorry. "Goodbye, Schaufel. I'll not be passing this way again."

"Nor will they." Schaufel turned, to where the tracks vanished to the East.

Felix started up the lorry. The border was close, and he must cross it. Little traffic would be met on the road. As for that traffic which would pass by rail, guided by Schaufel's fateful lantern, about that, reflected Felix, were I to lay myself down before it, would anything change?

He drove the short distance to the German border, each mile increasing his anxiousness, which turned to a numb sort of fear as the checkpoint appeared ahead—troops, wire fence, a lowered gate, and in his headlamps, the insignia of the Security Police. Bayonets and helmets reflected his lights as he slowed. The first face came clear, that of a cruel young god stepping forward, hand raised. I know you, reflected Felix, I've always known you.

"HALT!"

Felix turned the wheel, just slightly, so that the young god was forced to step back a pace. "Can't you drive, you lunatic!" shouted the youth, as he attempted to regain his balance.

"Control yourself," said Felix quietly, dangling his arm out the window, his transport papers fluttering idly in his hand.

The young field policeman ripped them from Felix's fingers. "You'd better explain yourself," he said, not even bothering to look at the papers.

Felix gazed down at the young man. "This truck is filled with medicine," he said softly, the dragonfly humming in his words, mindless, soulless, inhuman. He fixed the boy with his stare. "I've driven half the night, and have the other half to go. If one man dies because of your arrogance, you'll swing for it."

The young policeman ran his flashlight over the papers.

"Hurry," said Felix, extending his arm in a brusque movement.

"Pass," said the youth.

Felix put the lorry in gear and shot it through the checkpoint, with a thin trickle of sweat rolling down his armpit. In the rearview mirror, the figures of the Security Police blended into the darkness, and were swallowed. He drove, the moon of thieves on his shoulder. It led him across the night, traveling slowly, and brought him, some six hours later, to the Frankische Alps, soft rolling hills of chalkstone. He followed them, until he sighted the town of Weissenburg on the plain to the west, into which the sliver of the moon was sinking.

He drove down the hill into the town. The medieval walls surrounding the old center appeared in his headlights, and he could see the dark shadow of the low towers that lined the wall, and the higher tower of an old church. Uncertain of the way, he drove all along the walls, around the town, then finally found the market, where a nightwatchman pointed him toward the hills again, and the inn he sought.

He made his way back up the mountain road, to the carved wooden sign he was looking for, marked ARAUNERS KELLER. Mueller's staff car was parked near the entrance of the old building, and Felix brought the truck alongside it. A light shone in the lobby, and he saw a uniform pass by the window. A moment later, two of Mueller's men had stepped onto the porch of the inn, followed by Mueller himself, and the three of them descended the stairs, joining Felix in the courtyard as he lowered himself from the cab of his truck. The men looked weary from the late hour, but Mueller the night owl was far from sleep.

"No complications?"

"The roads are falling apart. A sea of mud."

"Ah, but you had this excellent vehicle—" Mueller gave the fender an affectionate pat. "—built by Mr. Henry Ford."

"The rest of the shipment is on its way to Frankfurt. This part—" Felix pointed in at the crates within the back of the lorry. "—can never be accounted for. We lifted it off the face of the earth."

Mueller ordered one of the men into the truck, and the other one jumped on the running board. They moved off with it, down a small drive. "Do you like my inn?" asked Mueller as he and Felix followed the truck, over the crunching gravel of the drive. He gestured toward the darkened windows. "You and I are the only guests."

The drive led to the hillside in back of the inn. Mueller's men were out of the truck now, and opening a pair of large wooden doors that had been fastened into the hillside. "These chalkstone hills are riddled with caves," said Mueller, "which have the ideal temperature for a beer cellar."

Felix watched as the cavernous interior of the hillside was revealed by a lantern held by one of the men; Mueller led Felix into the beer cellar, where a row of enormous wooden barrels stood. Chalkstone stalactites hung from the roof of the cave above the barrels. The moving lantern caused their shadows to dance first this way, then that, like rows of stiff-legged homunculi. "It is an excellent beer," said Mueller. "In fact, you may never have tasted better. So fresh, you see."

He opened one of the spigots and drew off two tankardsful. "To the health of our Führer, who is having his problems." The strong, malty flavor broke over Felix's tongue; the beer was thick and potent. The barrel from which it had come was tall and deep, its body ringed by large metal bands. The workmanship seemed as old as the village itself.

The two soldiers carried in the crates and Mueller ordered the nails removed from the lids, and when this was done, he gave the soldiers their leave. He listened to their retreating footsteps, then closed the doors to the cave. "Well," he said, hanging the lantern over one of the crates, "let us see what the East has given us." He lifted the lid. Diamonds, rubies, sapphires sparkled in the light of the lantern, the gems set in necklaces, bracelets, brooches, and rings.

"You're a wealthy man, Falkenhayn." Mueller dipped his hand into the jewels and dripped a handful of rings through his fingers. "We are both wealthy men."

Felix stood motionless, dazzled by the treasure of the Eastern countries, the legacy of many generations of its people. He lifted up a fistful of bracelets. "Gems are the eyes of the dead. Have you heard that?"

Mueller held up a gold stickpin, crowned by an enormous ruby. "The sun dwells in this. The sun of love, and life. The dead have forgotten such things." He moved to another of the crates. "Give me a hand, dear boy."

Felix took the edge of the lid and he and Mueller swung it free. The crate was filled with tiny gold nuggets. Mueller trickled a stream of them through his fingers. "Not worth the trouble you had to go through. However—" He tossed the handful back into the heap. "—we'll make something on it."

"Teeth," said Felix, staring numbly at the mound of gold.

"Fillings," said Mueller. "Gold is so much better than amalgams." Mueller opened his mouth and clacked his own teeth down several times, with a sharp sound. "All gold crowned. You're at the age too—you should have your own teeth capped with gold. Something to last you for the duration."

Felix turned to Mueller. "You've finally managed to disgust me."

"Because some Jews lost their molars along with their lives? My dear boy, don't play the saint with me."

"I'm not a grave robber."

"The world is a grave. We'll find our own way to it fast enough, so spare yourself sentimentality. Think like Krishna.

'There was no time when you nor I, nor these kings did not exist.' "

Mueller slid the lid closed on the crate of gold fillings, and opened another. "I can feel your offended sensibilities." He buried his arm to the elbow in bracelets, rings, and brooches, and lifted it, a sparkling shower running down his sleeve. "Cities are meant to be sacked. It has all been written by the divine hand itself." Mueller slid the crate's lid closed. "I feel myself exactly where fate wanted me. I'm innocent. I've grown as the sun has allowed me to." He smiled at Felix. "I have gone to Deputy Leader Hess's own homeopath."

"I want my share of this." Felix nodded toward the crates. "Now."

"And where will you put it? In a dog hole? At how many checkpoints will you be as lucky as you were tonight? You must wait with me, until the war is over. For a while bread will be worth more than diamonds but stability will return."

Mueller walked to the barrel at the end of the row. He picked up an iron pry bar, and inserted it between two of the metal bands that circled the middle of the barrel. The bands parted, and the barrel swung open into two hollow halves, its interior empty and dry. "A special modification. The carpenter took the secret of this barrel to his grave. An untimely death. Such a pity."

They loaded the crates, one by one, into the great barrel; the crates fit easily and well, snug against the curving walls. "Good," said Mueller, "and now we let our excellent porter age." He and Felix took hold of the two halves of the barrel and brought them together, the iron staves of the barrel meeting with a resounding clang.

"Safe from bombs, Gestapo, and invading armies." Mueller turned the spigot on the barrel. "The front of the barrel has a small reservoir, enough to make it seem like the others." The beer foamed into his waiting tankard. "And when that runs out, who has any interest in an empty barrel?" Mueller raised the tankard. "Should the Russians arrive, they'll drink themselves into a stupor and leave, cursing, perhaps, the one barrel which yielded so little."

He led the way back out of the cellar, and he and Felix brought the large doors closed upon the cave, which Mueller secured with a pair of padlocks. He turned to Felix with a smile. "How are your houses, by the way? Don't you have a place in Mecklenburg?"

"And in the village near Köpenick. They've both been destroyed."

"And everything you had there, lost. Trust me, dear boy. My hiding place is better."

"I'll not be cheated."

"I have no intention of cheating you." Mueller handed the key to the padlocks to Felix.

"Locks are easily changed."

"Then open them with a hand grenade." Mueller led the way back along the gravel drive, to the front yard of the deserted inn. Trees encircled the garden, and the moon had sunk behind them, its low, hanging form among the bare limbs. Mueller stopped, near a little goldfish pond whose surface was covered with boards. He stared down, as if into the water itself. "I have my little pleasures," he said, lighting a cigarette in the dark. He inhaled, curling the smoke on his tongue and then slowly releasing it. "To stand here, to breathe the night air with another human soul—that is what I know of the elusive wraith called peace."

"Then you have known as much as any man."

"Is that so? I'd like to believe that, that I have not missed something—something more exquisite?"

Felix lit his own cigarette, and gazed through the trees at the cold sliver of the moon. "Two of Weiss's men were liquidated at the station in Pilsen."

"The world is less troubled tonight."

"We were lucky. But Weiss is closing his trap on me."

"He'll never take you." Mueller strolled on, through the garden, a thin wisp of smoke trailing from his fingertips. "You're a member of the original Luminous Lodge. You were initiated by Baron von Sebattendorf himself. You have occult protection."

"The only reason I was there that night was because I thought it was a club for stage magicians."

Mueller brought his cigarette to his lips, emitted twin streams of smoke from his nostrils. "At one of the first Munich meetings, a medium produced an ectoplasmic form, which every one of us saw. *This,* she said, *is the new Messiah.* The form was Hitler's. His face became that of the most grotesque creature imaginable—a veritable demon. Sebattendorf himself ran from the room in terror."

"And this will save me from Weiss?"

"I will save you from Weiss." Mueller flicked his cigarette away, into the gravel. "But who, you must ask yourself, am I?"

Mueller turned to him and smiled; then, reaching into his pocket, he brought out a small emerald pin, in the shape of a dragon, which he placed in Felix's hand. "There are very few of these. Rasputin held one. Hitler certainly does." He folded Felix's fingers in upon the pin. "Did you know that there are one hundred Tibetans in SS uniform? Himmler has surrounded himself with lamas."

Mueller gazed into the moonlit branches of the trees surrounding the garden. "It is a peculiar mind, this planetary consciousness of ours. It is not human, you see. Actually, it's—a green dragon."

Mueller led the way out of the garden, into the roadway. They walked on it together, down the hill toward the village of Weissenburg. Its lamps were extinguished, its rooftops visible only as indistinct shadows below, over which plumes of smoke curled from hidden chimneys. Mueller's step was slow, steady; he seemed to savor the hour of the night, its smells, its emptiness. His high black boots creaked gently as he walked. "There are signs of spring," he said, pausing by a rock wall covered in the embroidery of a gnarled old vine. He reached out, to touch its leaves. "I feel new life."

Felix had stopped by a lamppost, to which a poster clung, faded, edges torn. He moved his eyes slowly over the gothic scroll.

PERISH JUDEA

"Hitler is a natural medium," said Mueller, standing beside him. "Those born in Braunau am Inn often are. He had the same wet nurse as the great psychic brothers Rudi and Willy Schneider. You came to the Lodge when it was fading . . ."

The black scroll seemed to dance before him; he heard a peculiar sound, of—clicking—like an insect's metallic song. He listened, transfixed, and then knew—it was the clicking of gold teeth in the mouths of the perished Jews. He put his hands to his ears, but he could not keep it out. "Mueller—"

"Yes, dear boy?"

The letters dripped black ink, the ink running down a white wall. Bright sunlight played upon the wall, a band of it falling over his shoulder. Caspian turned slowly, and saw Victor Quatrelle standing beside him, in Hawaiian shirt, floppy pants, sandals.

Caspian's body quivered, he heard a sharp crack like rifle fire, and he was fully back. Victor was shaking his head, as he ran his hand over the crude letters that'd been painted on a wall in Venice Beach.

PERISH JUDEA

He pulled his car into the circular driveway, parked, and stepped out into the cool night air of the canyon. A bat's delicate twittering swept past his ear, and faded off into the darkness. He crossed along the pathway toward the house, and up the front steps to the big wooden door.

"David, is that you?"

He walked through the kitchen and then descended the steps into the living room, where Carol sat reading on her eighteenth-century Italian sofa, which he suspected was a fake. He crossed and sat down beside her. She closed the book on her lap. "Long day of shooting?"

"Yes." He looked at the cover of her book, a handbook on dealing with stress. "Are you undergoing stress?"

"Why else do you think I sleep with my sunglasses on?"

"How's Alicia?"

"There's a note on the coffee table from her teacher. She

spent the day crying. Because *she* has stress." Carol opened the book again. "And all the rats in this book have stress." She looked up at him over the rim of her reading glasses. "Maybe we should buy a vibrating bed."

"I tried it once. I had to get off and wait until it stopped."

"Where was *this?*" she asked, raising her eyebrow.

"It happened in a motel, years ago, in another country."

"What country?"

"I think it was Gambia."

She smiled, and took off her glasses. "Why are you looking so sexy tonight? What have you been up to?"

He touched the hem of her white kimono where it crossed her knee. "Do you remember when we bought this?"

"The Havana Cigar Convention?"

"Macao. You'd lost three thousand dollars at the gambling tables."

"I had a system." She pulled the kimono up along her thighs and examined them critically. "I ate too much again." She stretched her perfectly shaped legs out. "Do you think I look like a donkey?"

He slipped down on the floor beside her, and ran his hand slowly along her calf. She leaned off to the side a little, eyeing him curiously. "Well, well . . ."

He drew her down to the floor, onto the big plush cushions spread out there. Her kimono fell open; she held her arms out to him. "Come here, you load of old rubbish."

*   *   *

He rose in the darkened living room, Carol beside him, asleep beneath an afghan cover. He went up the stairs to the kitchen, where he ate quietly, gazing at the greenhouse flowers. Upon their petals were dark lines—the honey guides—created by the flower to draw the insect deeper into the pollen cup. And some of the flowers, with the same dark guide lines, hid a cup of water in which to capture the insect.

And then the petals close, thought Caspian. And then we drown.

He went down the hallway to Alicia's room. Her nightlight was burning—a lamp in the shape of a high-button shoe, with door and windows lit by a small bulb inside. Every time he looked at the bright, little latticed windows, glowing with yellow light, he thought of it as one of the coziest pads in town.

Alicia's closed eyelids were still puffy from crying, from the sorrow in her life which he couldn't understand and was helpless to remove. He arranged her blanket over her, straightened the stuffed toys in her bed, and left her in the care of the Old Woman in the Shoe who, perhaps, was the best kind of help for her malady. He walked down the hall and stepped out the side door, onto the deck. The big, gnarled oak trees formed a canopy over his head, curtaining the stars. The owl was hooting close by in the trees, its hollow, spectral sound the quintessence of night.

He felt the pull of the hills—had a sudden image in his mind, of exactly where he must be, for there one of his questions would be answered.

He stepped from the deck and walked through the garden. The cat lifted up her head from the herbs where she was stalking, her pointed ears silhouetted in the moonlight. He stepped through the gate, and walked along the road; a breeze bearing the scent of primrose blew over him, its tantalizing sweetness luring night moths, like himself.

He followed the road deeper into the canyon. Crickets serenaded from the underbrush, their message passing from spot to spot, as if announcing him. The road turned and the landscape opened out, the moon appearing at the tip of a distant volcanic spire. He entered the underbrush and saw the dried riverbed snaking on ahead of him, foliage hanging down on either side, and the moon penetrating the cracked, hard surface.

He tracked along the riverbed, the crickets still attending

him from the grassy edges of the bank. Fluttering somewhere above him, a nighthawk made its little sputtering cry, and passed on. The dried bed entered the flat, arid plain. He climbed up the bank and stepped onto the plain, as the moon broke free of the canyon tops, its points downturned. To his right a shadow moved, and a bayonet glinted in front of him.

"Password."

"Valkyrie." The word came from his lips as if made of mercury, liquid and smooth.

A column of trucks was approaching in the darkness. He was under a foreign moon.

I've crossed over. I'm here, with all my marbles.

The trucks drew to a halt, and uniformed men descended.

He saw a network of railroad tracks running toward the moonlit horizon, and the convoy of trucks was drawing up beside the rails. The tailgates of the trucks were lowered and human cargo came down in a tumble—men, women, children, clutching each other, struggling with their parcels. Military voices herded them toward a line of cattle cars waiting on the rails, as the cold moon looked indifferently down. He moved closer to the shuffling herd, until he could see the face of each citizen, and each one wore the same expression of nightmare.

An SS sergeant stepped up to him. "Yes, sir, may I assist?"

"I'm waiting for my train."

"Very good, sir. But as you can see, this is a civilian transport."

"Yes, so I've noticed." The exchange passed in mercurial tones, as if his tongue were speaking a sequence already fixed, which he followed, slightly behind each inevitable word.

The sergeant returned to the ragged civilian column. Caspian stepped in behind him. The citizens staggered past, a sea of unknown faces, confused and stumbling victims of terror. The cold night air had penetrated his overcoat, and he buried his hands deeper into the pockets. A woman fell, was yanked to her feet, her child twisting with her in a mute scream. The woman's coat fell open, revealing only a short slip beneath, hastily put on in arrest, over her tiny form. Her hair was a mass of curls; her mouth was turned down in misery, as she lifted her sobbing daughter. Her eyes met Caspian's—and they were eyes he'd gazed into year in and year out; the uncertainty in his body turned to fury, as his wife and daughter staggered past.

He charged the line and pulled them out of it.

"You cannot change their course," said a voice behind him. He whirled about, pistol drawn.

A face made of bone gazed back at him. Upon Death's black overcoat, the gray shoulder straps of an SS general were sewn. Death smiled, gold teeth flashing; he nudged Carol and Alicia back into the herd shuffling toward the cattle cars.

A cry rose in Caspian's throat—the scream of a train whistle emerged. Its screeching wail increased in intensity, peaked, and then slowly diminished, becoming the sound of crickets.

He was standing in the dried riverbed, gaping at the spear points of a moonlit cactus. Death's paralyzing grip loosened upon him, became a shroud, softer and more yielding, and it slipped from his shoulders.

He moved back along the riverbed, and through the underbrush, to the road. A car passed, and he watched its moving headlight beams searching the turn, and then vanishing. He walked slowly along the road, through the canyon walls. The lights of his house appeared.

He entered by the back door and walked down the hallway to his daughter's room. She was asleep, among her favorite fuzzy animals, the light of the Old Woman in the Shoe upon her troubled face.

Gaillard set his pipe down on the table between them, beside a pouch of aromatic tobacco, whose fragrance came into the air now and then, for Gaillard often picked it up, tapping it, or opening it absentmindedly as they talked. "You've had an interesting week."

"I landed on the other side with complete awareness. I was there, on top."

"Not captive to Felix's thoughts?"

"No longer just an observer, or like somebody watching through a keyhole. I was the entity. And yet, everything seemed to happen just a pulse beat ahead, with me following."

"Were you free to act as you pleased?"

"Only to a point, and then events took over." Caspian leaned forward. "So it seems to me that I've fallen into a time that's already fixed. A film that's already been made. I can star in it, but I can't change how it turns out."

"Then Felix's life is something that's been lived, presumably to its conclusion."

Caspian nodded. "But my life, here, today, now—it's still open-ended. Anything could happen. I'm going somewhere, but that destination can't be seen or predicted. The difference is— I'm alive, and Felix is dead. But the film of his life is still running, somewhere."

"Felix wouldn't see it that way, of course."

"No, he'd see it just as I see my life—a film in production."

"And how did you feel about the constraint you experienced there?"

"I was helpless to save my wife and daughter. What do you think?"

"The image says you're losing them. Your feeling for them is slipping away, and you're powerless to intervene. It's bad business to let feelings die, you know. Men, especially, dry up very easily."

"Well, then, show me the light."

"This process is torturously slow. There aren't any great conversions. We're like ants with grains of sand."

"Tell me again—I'm completely sane."

"You're not claiming to be the heir to the French throne, if that's what you mean." Gaillard struck a match and brought it to his pipe. "Look, I can tell at a glance if someone is psychotic. It can be seen in the exaggerated gaze of a child of eighteen months. You don't have that look."

"You're not just trying to bolster me up, to hold together somebody you know is fragmenting, and who can't take the truth?"

"What do you want me to do—have you committed? We're working our way through a fantasy system you've constructed. I believe we'll get to the end of it."

Caspian sat in the thin cloud of pipe tobacco. "The American Indians say that Death is confused by smoke. He'll accept it as a substitute for the human soul."

"Very nice," said Gaillard, and puffed a thick cloud of it into the air over their heads. "Here's some for both of us."

* * *

Caspian entered the dark interior of the sound stage, and made his way along through spotlight stands, stacks of flats, reels of cable, and on by a canteen on wheels, where some of the crew were taking their complimentary snack of powdered soup and cheese crackers, and a cardboard cup of brackish L.A. coffee. Their conversation, muffled by walls covered in padding and baffles, was still audible:

". . . this blind short order cook, he did it all by feel."

"Yeah, well, I wouldn't want his thumb in my yoke."

Caspian came out near the *Star Rover* set, where Julius DeBrusca sat with his entourage, watching how his money was being spent. His voice, a deep baritone, rumbled in the air. ". . . there'll always be a dumb blonde."

Caspian walked on, to where Victor Quatrelle was sitting, in the dark robes of the space wizard, script in hand. Caspian sat down beside him. "I want to find someone who works magic. A warlock, a real practitioner."

"Give me a day or so," said Quatrelle. "There are some weirdos at my health club."

* * *

"Yes, there was a Luminous Lodge," said the gentleman across from Caspian in an office on the University of Southern California campus—a bookworm's retreat, piled on all sides with volumes on religion, anthropology, and magic. "The Lodge's full name was Thule Gesellschaft. It's great adept was a man called Eckart. He is supposed to have initiated Hitler in Vienna."

Caspian sat on the other side of the professor's desk, a tower of old books beside his chair. "Did they have any real power?"

"They were the foundation of the Nazi Party. If that isn't power, I don't know what is. Just think of those frigging rallys they had—a hundred thousand shining helmets, a hundred thousand gleaming bayonets. We in America look on it as political, but Hitler himself said, 'You make a mistake if you see what we do as merely political.' It was magic, and it worked."

"But could they do things like—dematerialize?"

Professor Sobol swiveled in his old oak chair and put his feet up on the desk. "There was a guy named Haushofer. A student of Gurdjieff's in Tibet in 1903. He was supposed to be able to make a seed sprout and grow to maturity in a few seconds. He taught Hitler about the power centers in the body, and Hitler knew plenty about that, it's in the volumes of his table talk. He said he had the 'eye of the Cyclops.' " Sobol rocked back in his chair, fingers folded in his lap. "Well, he had *something*, didn't he? Admiral Donitz wouldn't go into the same room with him if he could help it, because he lost his will. Here's a crusty old navy guy who's faced hurricanes and Christ knows what else at sea, and he won't go into the Chancellery because Adolf throws a spell on him."

"But Hitler was destroyed."

"So he blew it. He isn't the first black magician to go up in a puff of smoke."

Caspian swiveled in his own chair, slowly, back and forth, between two pillars of books with frayed binding and yellowing pages. "Do you know anything about a green dragon?"

"A Japanese secret society. With Tibetan overtones. The SS had a Doctor Scheffer in Tibet, hanging out at the monasteries and working with the lamas. There was supposed to be a Tibetan sorceror in Berlin called 'the man with the green gloves.' " Professor Sobol pivoted his chair toward the window. "The popular notion is that shamans and sorcerors fight each other with flying dog bones and crap like that. But the MX missile is also an occult object."

"I'm looking for someone who practices real magic."

Sobol's chair creaked as he leaned back again, foot against his desk drawer. "Not my pigeon. Sorry."

Caspian stood. "Do you think that Nazi magic could pull someone's soul from their body?"

"They pulled the soul of an entire people from its body. Germany was the nation of Goethe and Bach. What happened to it? I'm only a secondhand historian but my view is they got zapped. Has somebody been zapping you?"

*   *   *

". . . ABC in a death wish picked it up," said Myron Fish. "They should have bought a dairy farm instead."

"You never know what's going to bomb," said Julius DeBrusca, "but sometimes you know."

DeBrusca's secretary sat beside him, writing in his notebook, and Caspian sat across from them at a makeshift dining table that'd been erected on an unused corner of the set. "I'm delighted with what you've given me in this picture, David," said DeBrusca, turning toward his star. "*It* will not bomb, that I can tell you for certain. We'll be mounting an ad campaign like the world has never seen. Galaxies will tremble."

Myron Fish lifted his cup of powdered soup. "I've been named in a paternity suit."

"It happened to me," said DeBrusca. "She was as crass an individual as you could possibly conceive. Her father was a slumlord, she ran a hotdog stand, and she claimed I'd popped her between the ketchup and pickle."

An A.D. stepped in behind Caspian. "Ready for you."

DeBrusca raised the tip of his cigar, in a sort of blessing to his star, and returned to counseling Fish on the intricacies of paternity suits. Caspian followed the A.D. along the back lot street, beneath the great black tarpaulins that had transformed it into a gigantic cavern.

Waiting in the street beneath a circle of lights were the

black-uniformed guards who would be capturing him—interplanetary guns for hire.

"David, you know what you're going to do." Herman Armas gave Caspian a confident nod. "You'll leave these actors littered around you." He gestured toward the black-uniformed extras, and walked on past them, to his position near the camera. "Ok, everyone, let's get serious."

Caspian took his place, against a sleek metallic wall, and the cameras rolled. Black figures grappled with him.

"You're under arrest for crimes against the State."

He struggled, according to the script, and they held him, also according to the script, but their grip felt like handfuls of fog.

Felix woke, startled. He sat up in his bed, the voice still ringing in his head—*under arrest for crimes against the State.*

Not today. Today I cease to be a member of the State.

He got up from bed, moved sleepily around the room; it was small, shabby. His uniform hung over a chair. He left it there, dressing instead in a threadbare suit of civilian clothes. He went to the window, and looked at the street. It was empty, except for piles of rubble; the opposite side of the block had been bombed to ruins.

He went to a small dressing table, on which sat a battered theatrical makeup box. He opened it and took out a jar of liquid rubber. Applying it to one half of his face, from the forehead down across the cheek and chin, he created a surface that was shriveled and pockmarked. One eye was covered by it, the lid like an overfried egg. When the thick film of skinlike rubber had dried, he coated it with a purplish dye. The effect was that of a burn victim, one who had been roasted by a flame thrower.

In his jacket were discharge papers, an old pay book, and a citation for valor in action with a light infantry battalion at Monte Casino. Nested with the rest of it were his other identity papers—labor and housing registration, ration stamps, civilian ID card, and a permit for travel.

He felt the rubber crevices of his face, and when both dye and rubber were dry, he drew a black hood over his head, through which he gazed out of small, oval slits. He carefully fit his old fedora on over the hood, and angled the brim far down on his forehead.

Then, taking up a cane, he limped to the mirror. His Walther was strapped unobtrusively beneath his jacket. A derringer was holstered inside his sock.

He turned toward the uniform on the chair. "Farewell, Lieutenant Falkenhayn. You served the Fatherland."

He tapped his way down the stairs slowly, and entered the twilit street. American fire bombing had given the sky a reddish tinge. The wind blew over the ruins, lifting swirls of building plaster into the air and sending it whirling down the block. But it was springtime nonetheless, and the trees, covered in dust, were blooming.

He made his way slowly along the street. The rubble scuffed his shoes, and the spring wind whirled red brick dust around him. He could smell peach and apple blossoms, mixed with the sulphurous scent of bombs.

He turned the corner and saw a body, swinging from a lamppost, strung up by the SS the night before. They were rampaging now, hanging deserters, and a good many others into the bargain.

He stopped beneath the lamppost and looked up at the body—that of a boy of sixteen. The boy's cap was still on, tilted rakishly over his brow, above a broken neck. He swung in the breezes of spring.

Felix moved on, leaning on his cane, tapping with each step. The setting sun had increased the flaming hue of the sky. An elevated section of the U-Bahn hung in twisted pieces against the red clouds. He walked beneath it, its jagged shadows falling around him like a cage. He walked on, block after block, as the darkness fell. The moon rose, fire-bomb red. Sulphurous clouds rolled past it, turning it yellow, and orange, then back to red again. In the rubble of a tiny garden, violets were peeking out.

From behind, he heard the low auxiliary gear of the Kübelwagen. It rattled along over the broken street, and pulled in beside him at the curb. Four SS got out. The leader's shoulders were broad, his head attached without benefit of neck; the red moon glinted on his coal-shovel helmet, as he strode toward Felix. "What the hell is that covering your head?"

"It is to spare my wife," said Felix, softly.

"Spare her? I'll spare her the sight of you for good." The SS officer stepped up to Felix, wrenched the cane from Felix's hand and snapped it over his knee. "There's nothing wrong with you, you shitbag. I've dealt with your kind before, hiding behind wounds you never got, in battles you never saw." He turned, snapped to one of the others. "Bring the rope, we'll make quick work of this one."

He put both fists on his hips and gazed at Felix's calm, steady form. "This is the avenue of the dead, didn't you know? You should have stayed in bed this night."

"Yes, I should have. But the air is good for my lungs."

"Well, breathe deeply, it'll be the last you'll get for awhile." He pointed toward the next lamppost. "That one's for you."

"How many men have you hung, Captain?" asked Felix, his lips almost whispering through the mouth of the hood.

The SS captain smiled. "Enough to fill a phone book."

The other SS had brought the rope. The captain reached out to Felix. "Masks are only for firing squads. And so, my hero—" He grabbed the hood, and tore it from Felix's head. It fell from his hand limply, as he gaped at the shriveled mass of burned flesh that covered Felix's face, one eye sealed, the whole of it a monstrous purple hue. "Mother of Christ, forgive me."

"And now," said Felix, "may I know from whom I have received this insult to my honor?"

The SS captain stepped away. "No one, no one at all." He bent, picked up the hood, tossed it back to Felix. Then he turned and, with his men, climbed back into the Kübelwagen. Its motor came on with a roar, and the tires squealed as it shot away down the street.

Felix resumed his slow march. The spring moon continued to rise. The sound of the front was near, and the flak towers were awaiting more bombers. Still, the city continued its life; in the midst of the destruction a trolley came along. He boarded it, and rode through the ruins, to the old theatre district. He rang the trolley bell, and swung down, onto the street, outside the Burckhardt Auditorium.

He crossed, and entered the side alley of the theatre. The stage door, as promised, was open. Stacked inside it were the cans of petrol he and The Weasel had been storing over the past weeks. His footsteps were soundless in the hall, and one hand was in his jacket, on his Walther. Gerta Schaffers had said it would be safe, that no one ever bothered the theatre. Nonetheless . . .

He went quietly through its back corridor. He paused in the wings, by the hanging folds of the curtain. The theatre was still, and empty. No rehearsal, no play today, with the Allied tanks coming nearer every hour.

He stepped past the curtain, onto the stage. Its somber spaces were dark, devoid of scenery. But his step echoed in the high open space, as he crossed to center.

" 'Life's but a walking shadow; a poor player, that struts and frets his hour upon the stage, and then is heard no more . . .' "

His voice was soft, but carried along the curving walls of the theatre, and from the darkness at the back, he heard a slow, solemn clapping. The Weasel stood from his seat and walked down the aisle to the stage. "Good, you get the part." He studied the burn scar on Felix's face. "That's a nice piece of work. I should have you build me a new nose."

Felix went down the steps and met him below the apron of the stage. "Are we ready?"

"A hamlet in north Westphalia," said The Weasel. "No

bombing there at all. The innkeeper is a friend, and the chief of police is Freddy Sossong. We sold him the best champagne he ever drank."

"What are we driving?"

"I found an Austro-Daimler, a most incredible machine. We'll be taking a kid I know—Willi Sievers—not many brains but I owe him one and he'll make the Daimler fly." He looked at his watch. "He'll be along in a minute." The Weasel reached in his pocket and drew out a leather portfolio. "Gondolph's last work." He held up the Defense of Berlin order, which commanded everyone to cooperate with its holder—Wehrmacht, SS, Gestapo, and Nazi Party.

"It should be an interesting run." Felix took out a cigarette, lit it.

"Nothing's ever guaranteed, but we've come this far. It would be pleasant if we made it to the end." The Weasel took one of Felix's cigarettes. "How's Gerta these days?"

"Very happy. She goes to the Luftwaffe Club now. She says she'll be leaving Berlin in a Fokker-Wulf Condor."

"With her legs in the air."

Felix turned toward the stage, and gazed up into the fly space overhead, where bars and sandbags hung. "And if we meet the Russians?"

The Weasel took another set of papers from his pocket, and three cloth stars. "We're Jews on the run."

Felix nodded, stretched his arms out along the edge of the apron. "I've grown tired. I think I shall have a yard and raise some flowers."

"I had a packet of seeds once." The Weasel exhaled a stream of smoke above the stage. "I cherished them but they failed to grow."

"They were afraid of you, Weasel. They decided to stay in their nice warm shell."

"I sometimes imagine what they would have been like, if they'd grown there in my window box."

"You'd be a different man today."

"I think you're right. I was quite lonely after that."

Felix looked at his watch. "Where is this driver of ours?"

"He's absolutely dependable." The Weasel looked at Felix, his narrow little eyes brightly mocking. "Unless he's holed up with some piece of strudel." He laid a hand on Felix's shoulder. "You've gotten jumpy in your old age, Falkenhayn."

Felix ground out his cigarette on the floor. "We were talking about flowers."

The Weasel removed his bowler hat, ran two fingers along the brim, then studied the plush white lining. "Has Marla gotten word to you?"

"She's in a villa at Lugano. She says it's always springtime there."

"As in my heart." The Weasel put his bowler back on, angling the brim down toward his cold little eyes. "You remember Fat Fritz? He was arrested inside a dead cow."

"A gourmet's hiding place."

"They shot him and ate the cow." The Weasel straightened the starched, white cuff that inched out of his jacket. "All of the old gang have been nabbed. The path of the dead is well trod." He smiled. "When it's our turn the road will be smoothed down."

Felix paced below the stage. They would work their way across Germany, slowly. They'd helped others to do the same. He ran his hand along the surface of the apron. "Dust. Entertainment is hard to find these days."

"There's a belly dancer on Morhingerstrasse. For one egg she'll give you private lessons." The Weasel straightened his other cuff. He cocked his head to one side. "Here comes Willi."

They stepped into the aisle. The front and side doors of the theatre opened simultaneously. Black leather coats glistened, and amidst them, Gerta's feathered hat.

Felix raced along the base of the stage, bullets whining

into the apron above his head. The Weasel was just behind him, firing his automatic, and two of the Gestapo spun violently backward in the aisle. Felix dove on stage and crawled into the wings. The Weasel slid in after him, wrapped in the folds of the curtain, from which he struggled free. "She sold us, the bitch." He looked at Felix, and Felix saw his friend's whole life in his eyes—a single dream, a packet of flowers, and the path of death well trod.

The Weasel edged forward along the curtain. "I'll shoot the feathers off her." He leapt out, firing, and was cut down by machine pistols. He fell forward, his arm off the edge of the stage, the pistol dangling from his finger.

Both wings of the stage filled with Gestapo. Felix threw his pistol down, and stepped out onto the stage with his hands in the air. Gerta was coming down the aisle with Emil Weiss, the bird of paradise feathers lightly bobbing on her hat. At the base of the stage, she looked up at Felix, her eyes moistly shining. "You move so well on stage. I *am* sorry now, darling."

The Gestapo closed in on him. "You're under arrest for crimes against the State."

Words from a dream, thought Felix.

"Good, David, that last take was fine. We won't need you again until tomorrow."

*   *   *

He walked with Carol along Rodeo Drive. Her low, sharp heels clicked rhythmically on the pavement; her arm was through his, and her wrist was covered in gold bangles that jingled against his sleeve. "I found that if I break my tranquilizers into little pieces and nibble on them, I'm much more tranquil."

"A long awaited medical breakthrough."

"When the client is a man who can't tie his own shoelaces, I find myself starting to sound like a mynah bird." She tightened her grip on his arm. "David, what I'm really trying to say is, now that shooting is almost over, you should think about medicating yourself for awhile. Because you look like Howdy Doody on the night he stuck his wooden pecker in the wall socket."

"If tranquilizers were the answer, Gaillard would have given them to me."

"I heard wonderful things from the coffee cart man about Elavil. Wouldn't you like your mood enhanced?"

"How has it affected the coffee cart man?"

"I don't know, maybe his doughnut floats. How deeply can I delve in the two minutes I buy coffee from him? He seems much more cheerful."

They turned onto Carmelita Avenue. He tightened his arm against hers. "What time is our reservation for?"

"One-fifteen. We'll start with the marinated mussels and work our way into the schnitzel Holstein."

He started to answer, but felt a sharp pain in his groin. He buckled forward, had to stop. "Wait . . . a moment . . ."

"David, what is it?"

"Like . . . I'd . . . just been . . . kicked in the balls."

"Oh Jesus, is this the beginning of a terrible sexual disease?"

"Give me . . . a second." He straightened, as the pain began to subside. He ran a hand across his suddenly perspiring brow. Carol's hand came to his chest, stroking him. "What could suddenly be giving you a pain in the balls? Besides me, I mean."

"It has something to do with Felix."

"David, are we in a play by Samuel Beckett?"

"I think the Gestapo are torturing him."

"David, we're on the way to the Bistro, with soft lighting and evocative Parisian decor. There *aren't* any Gestapo in Beverly Hills. I'm *not* panicking. *You're* going to take Elavil as soon as I can talk to the coffee cart man."

"It's ok, Carol. It's all happening on the other side."

"Oh my God, he's talking like a nut cake, my own husband." She straightened her gold bangles compulsively, then looked up and down the street. "Should I call Gaillard?"

"I'm fine. Let's go to the Bistro."

*   *   *

Myron Fish sat across from them, a plate of cannelloni in front of him, and a Belle Epoque maiden painted on the pillar behind him. He was talking to Carol, his manner unperturbed. "I've heard the story from him, sure. How I sell furnaces to Hitler. I was upset at first, but I don't let it bother me now. Why? Because he's just turned in the best acting job of his life. He's hotter than he's ever been, he can get his price anywhere in town. That's the bottom line of mental health."

"You're a comfort, Myron," said Carol, before her untouched dish of schnitzel Holstein.

"I'm a realist. Look at him—" Fish pointed a fork at Caspian. "He's here, he's eating, he's lucid. Aren't you?"

"Perfectly."

"I had a client once who *was* crazy. He'd come to my office dressed as a postman." Fish looked at Carol, fork still pointed at Caspian. "Does he leave the house dressed as a postman?"

"No."

"So he's obviously not crazy. He's difficult. I'd go so far as to say he's warped. But not crazy."

"David, do you swear to me you're not crazy? Do you swear I'm not going to end up like Mrs. Nijinsky? Swear it over my schnitzel."

"I swear it."

"All right, I'm going to eat now, because my blood sugar is falling, but I'm still dreadfully concerned. When we finish you're to go straight home and spend the day potchkeeing in the garden."

"Fine," said Caspian.

"See? He's agreeable." Fish gestured again with his fork. "He'll go home and potchkee in the garden. He'll see if the artichokes are growing. Maybe he'll even talk to the artichokes about Mussolini. These are just artistic eccentricities. Nothing that a wife or agent should be concerned about."

Fish sat in Caspian's dressing room, coffee in one hand, a sandwich in the other. He held the sandwich up to the light. "I wonder where Julius gets these, they taste like blister packs." He bit into the sandwich and turned to face Caspian. "You're looking better, are you feeling better?"

"Much better." Caspian lay on a dressing room couch, feet up, a newspaper in his hands.

"I'm giving your new contract to Laventhol and Horwath's investigative accounting service. They'll go through it with radar and a finely tuned screw-job detector. A single word in that contract could cost you millions."

"Whatever you say, Myron."

"You're into big dollars now, my son. We're talking major profit participation. A man would be judged mentally deranged not to have Laventhol and Horwath monitoring finances. Of course their fees are not low."

"Of course."

"But we're going with them. I just wanted you to know. In case anything should happen to me."

Caspian laid down his newspaper, and looked at Fish. "What's going to happen to you, Myron?"

"You know I'm fighting a paternity suit."

"They give capital punishment for that nowadays?"

"The strain, the pressure. This, from a girl I took to my bosom, who entered my home, fed my dog, shared my innermost thoughts. I was going to manage her career for her, David. I was going to open the magic door for her."

"Perhaps you waited too long?"

"These things take time. I was carefully seeding the field."

"Apparently you also seeded the girl."

Fish mournfully chewed his sandwich. "My accountant has advised a vasectomy."

"He does it right in his office, does he?"

"A man in my position, whose professional work brings him into contact with strings of upwardly mobile young actresses—" Fish let the sandwich slip from his hand. "How could she do this to me? How could she stoop so low? You know what it means, don't you? It means I'm going to have to buy the little poozle off. Because litigation would kill me. I talk tough, David, but inside I'm tender."

"I know this, Myron."

"I've been in divorce court five times. Do you know what that does to you? When I look in a young girl's eyes for the first time I seem to see her lawyer looking back at me."

A knock came on the dressing room door. *"Ready for you, Mr. Caspian."*

Caspian stood, folded his newspaper. His space helmet was on a chair by the door. He put it under his arm and stepped outside, leaving Fish staring morosely at his sandwich. He walked down the long hall, and out into the bright sun; a minibus was waiting to take him to the set. It was a short ride, through the studio complex, out to where the giant tarpaulin was hung, over the back lot street. He climbed out and entered the darkened area, where the camera, light, and sound crews were setting up.

He stepped onto the set. The A.D. was waiting at the chalk mark, and Herman Armas and the cinematographer were close by, conferring on a shot they'd already done twelve times.

"The waterfall of repetition," said the A.D. wearily.

"Patience, my lad." Caspian toed in at the mark.

The A.D. lifted his megaphone. *"Let's have some quiet."*

Armas and the cinematographer took their positions by the camera, and Caspian closed his eyes, awaiting the cue.

"Here we go—quiet please."

"Rolling."

"Speed."

"Action."

Caspian stepped forward, walking along the wet street, wet so the image would glisten; the metallic walls of the alien, underground city were glistening as well. He had to make his way to the far end of the street, where a laser image awaited him—the ship of the Star Rover, in preparation for leaping through the frame of time-space, with its solitary pilot on board.

He walked slowly toward the image, which glowed with laser intensity. The wave of vertigo hit him just as he neared the ship; he maintained himself upright but at the cost of feeling his stomach rise to his throat. It, and every other organ seemed to be inverting itself. A second later, he could not tell if he was on his feet or his head; the street itself was spinning crazily.

The burning lasers were converging, into a single blazing sun, blindingly bright. His skull throbbed with pain, the blazing light burning into his sockets; then the contour of the light revealed itself more clearly—a circular orb, a sun without corona, and then—a light bulb, no more than that. He shielded his eyes from the glare, and tried to orient himself.

To his right was a concrete floor, to his left a stone wall. A stench of urine filled his nostrils. Encrusted blood was on his lips. He passed through these sensations, and kept sinking, down past the pain, down toward oblivion, the hiding place he knew was there. David Caspian was fading, into the tiny observation post in Felix Falkenhayn's mind, from which Caspian could witness events as one witnesses dreams, where fantastic torments may take place and yet leave the ego unscathed. It is Felix's dilemma, he thought, as he descended still deeper. I'm only a fragment from the other dimension, I have nothing to fear, I need only wait until this passes . . . need only wait. . . .

He descended, to the level he sought, out of harm's way, and Felix rose from his cot, vaguely puzzled by the strange sensation he'd had, of a tiny entity roaming around within him. But it had vanished now, taking its foreign thoughts with it.

He staggered to the heavy wooden door of his cell, his pounding head seeking the cool iron of the frame. He rubbed his brow slowly back and forth, but the pain was deeper than cold could penetrate; it was everywhere in his head, and deep in his gums, where his teeth were rattling loose.

He thought of Marla in Lugano, where it is always spring. He imagined her seated at a table beside the lake, sipping a cool drink beneath a tropic palm. And thinking of the friend who directed her escape? She's thinking of investments. She'll be dining with a banker from Zurich.

I must get my own money, and buy out of 27 Lindenstrasse. Any of its rubber stamp officials will be overjoyed at the prospect of getting rich. They'll shuffle a few papers, bury someone else in my name, and release me into the streets.

He pulled back from the door. Footsteps were echoing along the hallway. He listened, waited, watched the bolt being drawn, and now the door swung slowly open. Sergeant Ritt, smiling, stepped in, his great bulk filling the doorway. "So, how is the Lieutenant today? Enjoying yourself?"

Felix stared back through swollen eyelids; the sergeant stepped forward. "Get dressed."

Felix pulled on the gray prison-issue shirt and trousers, taking care to stay out of Ritt's reach, but the sergeant did not seem inclined to kick him just yet. He conducted Felix into the hall, and propelled him forward with a shove in the back. Felix stumbled ahead of him, and Ritt came just behind, conversing quietly. "I'm surprised that a clever lad like you has wound up here. I mean, you knew they were after you, didn't you? And you decided to stay in for one more hand, right? One more turn of the card? Stupid bastard . . ." Ritt's voice rumbled in the hollow passageway.

". . . but you've got a fortune tucked away somewhere, don't you?" Ritt's voice continued beside his ear. "And a lot of good it's doing you. Now I, I don't have a coin to call my own. But I'm free and you're not. So who's the rich man, Lieutenant?" Ritt shoved him again, up a flight of stairs.

The upper hallway was flooded with sunlight, coming from a nearby window.

If I can hold out, just long enough to do business with this Ritt. He's given the hint. "We must talk," said Felix, softly.

"Later," said Ritt. "If you last that long." He led Felix to a smoked glass door, opened it, and Felix stepped through. Frankfurt Gestapo Chief Oswald Poche was gazing at him from his desk. "I've been looking forward to another chat with you, Lieutenant."

Poche lit a cigarette, and stood, beside a window looking out onto the day. Through it I'd fly, thought Felix, to—where? To Ravensburg, to Mannheim, to Westphalia where a burning wheel is rolled downhill at the summer solstice. And within the wheel, he saw a man, pinned there, in flames.

Poche exhaled a stream of cigarette smoke toward the window, then turned to Felix. "I can have you executed or I can set you free. No one will countermand my order." Poche came around his desk, and leaned against the edge of it, arms folded, his mild blue eyes meeting Felix's.

"You have worked with a number of enlisted men." Poche inhaled, blew a column of smoke toward the ceiling. "I have their names, of course. But there is no evidence against them, for you were very skillful in masking what they did. However, they committed crimes, in my jurisdiction, connected with a shipment from the Eastern Territories, which was received here in Frankfurt. Provide me with an affidavit concerning their crimes against the State, and you will go free."

Felix gazed back at Poche through swollen eyelids. He wondered, vaguely, how much more pain was ahead of him. "I am unaware of any criminal activity amongst those who served under me."

"I see." Poche smiled. "And Mueller?"

"Colonel Mueller is an irreproachable leader."

"You expect that he will help you now, I suppose."

"I assume he will be a witness in my defense."

"You assume that he will buy your freedom. Isn't that it?" Poche stubbed out his cigarette. "But I wonder about that, Lieutenant. Why should a decorated officer of such high rank and social standing jeopardize his reputation by saying one word in your behalf?"

"I cannot predict what Colonel Mueller's actions will be."

Poche pushed away from his desk, and walked to the door. He nodded to Ritt. "Bring him along."

Felix walked beside Ritt, down the hallway of the building no citizen ever wished to visit, called by all the House of Tears, where an execution could be staged for the price of a few cigarettes. Decorated soldiers had died here for having said that perhaps the Führer had made some mistakes as a commander; old women had perished here for mumbling aloud that their country had forgotten them.

Gestapo Chief Poche led him to the other wing of the

building, to a windowless hall lined with closed padlocked doors. He had Ritt open one, and beckoned Felix in.

Mueller hung naked on the wall, his arms twisted up behind him, his fat, pink stomach a mass of dark bruises. His breasts were flabby like a woman's; his legs, Felix saw, were shaved smooth. Mueller lifted his head weakly, his puffed cheeks trembling, his eyes small watery slits. "Dear boy . . ."

Felix swayed, and Ritt propped him up.

"His arms," said Poche softly, "are twisted out of their sockets. A rather uncomfortable way to die."

Poche turned, gestured to Ritt, and the sergeant led Felix out, toward one of the other doors. He opened it and shoved Felix in. Upon the wall were empty chains from which to suspend a man; on a table lay a variety of devices, cold, glinting in the harsh light, as if their cruel, mechanical souls were eager to be at work. "We'll have an expert along in a few minutes," said Poche. "It's wonderful to watch him work. An artist."

Ritt ordered him to strip, and handcuffed him to a chair. He and Poche left him, then, closing the door with a gentle click, whose soft sound went through him like a snakebite. His body was shaking, so violently that the handcuffs rattled on his wrists. He understood—from the beginning of time there had been no other destination but this room, this chair. No success, no plan, no scheme could have changed that. Precisely this.

The door opened again, and a small, jovial looking man entered. He carried a doctor's satchel, wore a carnation in his lapel. He smiled at Felix. "It's quite warm today," he said, patting his brow with a handkerchief.

He opened the bag and took out a number of scalpels and steel prods, which he laid neatly on the table beside his other implements. "We really should have a fan in this room, the air is much too close. Still—" He smiled again at Felix, in a kindly way. "—there is a war on, and we all must bear with the shortages. Now, let me see . . ."

He studied his instruments for a moment, then picked up

a slender scalpel. "May I just test this a moment?" He laid it lightly on Felix's cheek, and Felix felt a trickle of blood run down his face. "Excellent blade. One would think it'd be dull after so much use." He held it up to the light, nodding in satisfaction, then looked back at Felix. "I don't know what I'd do without them."

"You'd manage," said Felix, tasting the blood on his tongue.

"Would I? Yes, I suppose I would. One improvises." He gave a small, elegant flourish in the air with the scalpel. "I always like to start with the genitals. It can save time, you see. We don't actually sever any of the main arteries, so you need have no fear of dying. We'll have a whole afternoon together."

The man's hand was small, freckled, delicate. He lowered the scalpel, and Felix strained upward against the handcuffs. His chains did not break, but he felt himself rising, so that he was now looking down at his tormentor from another angle, slightly above the chair. In the next moment, he found himself floating at the ceiling, near the harsh light of the bulb.

And David Caspian was rising too, out of his cellular retreat, up into the full consciousness of this body he found himself in. He filled it out, entered every nerve and fiber with his awareness. He was handcuffed in a chair, with a madman bending over him.

His head snapped back, and he saw there was another in the room, a ghostly presence outlined against the ceiling, a floating figure.

Auf Wiedersehen, said Felix.

"No!" cried Caspian. "Come back! You can't leave!"

He strained against the handcuffs, as Felix faded into the ceiling.

*   *   *

Felix stood on the artificial street, beneath the great black tarpaulin, and oriented himself with slow, robotlike moves of his head. He moved an arm, a leg, and felt the peculiar rhythm of David Caspian's body—a confident stride, carefully choreographed gestures—an actor's trained vehicle. The streams of neural energy ran from brain to fingertips, and he observed it all, and then slowly blended with it.

He walked, cautiously, in a dark area of the set where he would not be noticed. Language patterns were forming, and the kaleidoscope of memory—bits and pieces brightly tumbling around the inexplicable core of personality.

He was in an unlit corridor between mock theatrical buildings. Timber was piled there, and empty light stands. He stepped carefully around them, walking the length of the corridor, and emerging into another wide, unlit street of facades. He listened to the sound of hammers, machinery, distant voices, all of it echoing through the closed labyrinth of the lot. It fell into place, new sensation assimilated; beneath it, there remained the faint residue of the House of Tears, but he felt those memories fading, with a droning sound, of insect wings.

"David, there you are, I was just about to page you." A young man was coming up the corridor, holding a walkie-talkie. "Everything ok?"

"Yes," said Felix, "everything is fine."

He followed the man back along the corridor, and his step became more solid, more controlled. There was a heavy atmospheric pressure still working on him, and he fought against a quiver inside, the quiver of a soul straining to return to its source. The emanation around him was alien, and there would always be, perhaps, these pressures of a time outside his own; but he would grow used to that, as to all things in this land of eternal summer.

The assistant director led him to the street of the interior, where the camera crew was waiting, with Herman Armas.

"David, sorry, I have to get it one more time."

"Perfectly all right."

Armas looked at him in silence for a moment. "Yes, that's the quality, that fine edge. You've got it back now." Armas gave his A.D. a signal. A bell rang and silence fell on the set.

"Ready."

"Picture up—here we go—quiet please."

"Rolling."

"Speed."

"Settle down—and *action.*"

*　　*　　*

Caspian stood slumped in the inner courtyard of the prison, gazing out at the gray dawn above the walls. A pair of soldiers, still sleepy, were positioned in the center of the courtyard, beside a chopping block. A third soldier, beside Caspian, gave him a gentle nudge with the butt of his rifle. "One quick blow," said the soldier quietly. "Nobody feels a thing. I've seen it before. You'll be gone before you know it."

Caspian looked for the flaw in the texture of the morning, for the fluid instability of a dream, which he could take advantage of. *I should be able to fly, over the prison wall.* The atmosphere of the prison yard, though tremulous and somehow metallic, did not yield. It held him, as did the prison. His footsteps, as he staggered forward, were corporeal and solid, and the pain which accompanied his body was real. When that pain had grown unbearable, he'd confessed, that this part of time wasn't his, that he was a man from another era, that Felix's crimes were nothing to do with him. The torture artist said he'd never heard such original screams from anyone.

Caspian brushed his hand across his face, as if trying to wipe away the scene before him; his fingers touched his split, swollen lip, as he muttered to himself, "It's a mistake. I don't belong here."

"Steady, friend."

The soldier braced him at the elbow, and Caspian straightened, with the torn ligaments of his battered legs and torso pulling painfully, but it felt good to walk upright. He could see more of the sky, and feel more of the day; by afternoon it would be mild. Now, a faint mist was rising from the damp prison wall, but the sun would burn it off. And men would circle the prison yard, taking exercise, and countless moments would yield their gifts, of what men hoped for, and what they feared. The sun would cross high above the prison wall.

He could see his own faint shadow on the ground, marching with him. The alien, metallic air was heavy with a dark pressure, as if a layer of future time were weighing on top of it, time already filled, with birth and event, and the enormity of change. "I'm in the wrong world."

"That's certain," said the soldier, his boot heels thudding in the earth beside Caspian.

Caspian's body was trembling, and a faint film of tears had formed across his eyes. From beyond the prison walls, a flight of blackbirds were singing, their song like a bubbling fountain. "That's a good sound to go out on," said the soldier. "You just listen to them, with all your heart. And next thing you know, you'll be with them and I'll still be standing here, with a rifle cutting into my arm. Understand?"

The birds wheeled into the air, circled, settled back down beyond the wall, their excited song of spring still sounding. The scent of hyacinths came to Caspian, mingled with the sulphurous smell of gun powder, and the charred ruins of the city. Upon the prison wall, an ivy vine was coming to life again, green leaves covering the gray stems of the previous year.

Double *dicho:* A man may cease to be, yet still exist. A man may still exist, yet cease to be.

"Yes," he said, "it's a lovely morning. There never was a lovelier."

"Never," said the soldier.

Caspian lowered his eyes back to the ground again, where his shadow walked, its outline faint but its presence somehow comforting, for it walked with detachment, was an invulnerable sort of clown. Caspian straightened once more, assuming out of habit the proper demeanor, that which the part demanded. One had to remember the camera; the best actor never forgets, no matter where he is.

He chose his step carefully, and chose his thoughts carefully too. He knew now that other wanderers had been lost through the crack in time; he could feel their puzzled souls echoing out of other eras, the despairing few who'd gone the same way as he. Had they chosen to do it, to enter that cobwebbed doorway lit by spectral lamps? Had he? Or had the hinges of time simply slipped, a mechanical stress, an accident that'd occurred as he was passing by?

"Nothing can happen to us that has not already happened," he said, in a voice that seemed to echo with the other wanderers who had gone before him, and whose faint whisperings were his counsel. He looked at the soldier. "This day is already in the past. We're all already dead."

"That's the spirit," said the soldier, and together they finished the walk across the courtyard to the block, where the executioner joined them, bearing a bright, medieval axe.

*   *   *

"Perhaps he was defeated by the Luminous Lodge," said Felix, seated across from Doctor Gaillard. "There were peculiar powers concentrated in the Third Reich. In any case, he is gone. And I am here."

"I see," said Doctor Gaillard. His gaze had narrowed as he stared at his patient, seated across from him.

"As it was his practice to tell you everything, so shall I, as I conform to the pattern of his life in most details. Naturally, I expect that what I say to you will remain, as before, a matter of the strictest confidence." Felix straightened the immaculate crease in his trousers. "I have difficulty enough in keeping up appearances. And I've not yet fully adjusted to the pressures of the dimension."

Completely mad, observed Doctor Gaillard.

"And if not the Luminous Lodge, well, something worked against him, which I doubt you or I shall ever understand," said Felix.

Utterly and completely mad, thought Gaillard, gazing into

Caspian's eyes. He saw that the complex which had taken hold was diabolically clever; dislodging it would be extremely difficult, perhaps impossible. But we must try. Yes, for certain we must try.